Trouble Grande

A Cassidy Adventure Novel

by
Kelly Rysten

CCB Publishing
British Columbia, Canada

Trouble Grande: A Cassidy Adventure Novel

Copyright ©2018 by Kelly Rysten
ISBN-13   978-1-77143-366-2
First Edition

Library and Archives Canada Cataloguing in Publication
Rysten, Kelly, 1960-, author
Trouble grande : a Cassidy adventure novel / by Kelly Rysten. -- First edition.
Issued in print and electronic formats.
ISBN 978-1-77143-366-2 (softcover).--ISBN 978-1-77143-367-9 (PDF)
Additional cataloguing data available from Library and Archives Canada

Cover artwork credit: by Kelly Rysten: www.kellyrysten.com

Author photo on back cover by Erica Stephens Photography:
https://www.facebook.com/ericastephensphoto

Publisher: CCB Publishing
               British Columbia, Canada
               www.ccbpublishing.com

Dedicated to the memory of my father
Henry Daniel Saastamoinen
who always believed in me and encouraged me
to share Cassidy with others.

Other books by Kelly Rysten

Kelly Rysten is the author of the Cassidy Callahan Adventure Novels. Cassidy Callahan is a young woman who grew up on a quarter horse ranch. Given free run of the local hills she developed an eye for tracking, and with the help of Detective Rusty Michaels, she joined the local search and rescue team to track lost hikers. Unfortunately she is also a terrible trouble magnet, and her job brings her into contact with more trouble than the police can keep her out of. One adventure follows another as Cassidy tracks her way from one mishap to the next.
The books are:

Triple Trouble
Published 2009 – ISBN 978-1-926585-41-3

Car Trouble
Published 2010 – ISBN 978-1-926918-03-7

A Cache of Trouble
Published 2011 – ISBN 978-1-926918-87-7

A Double Dose of Trouble
Published 2012 – ISBN 978-1-77143-025-8

A Shot of Trouble
Published 2013 – ISBN 978-1-77143-107-1

Looking for Trouble
Published 2015 – ISBN 978-1-77143-249-8

Trouble in Hollywood
Published 2016 – ISBN 978-1-77143-294-8

A Little Trouble
Published 2017 – ISBN 978-1-77143-337-2

Kelly is also the author of an action adventure romance novel that incorporates the hobby of geocaching. College student Gwendolyn Brody agrees to enter a geocaching contest to help her friend Tony win a trip to the Caribbean. Follow their hilarious cross country trip as they accidentally grow ever closer to each other.

Geogirl
Published 2014 – ISBN 978-1-77143-150-7

Chapter 1

Lights twinkled over the mantel and wound around the banisters. Silk poinsettias marched up the stairs. The fireplace was crowded with stockings. Dad, Mom, Martha, Steve, Zack, Randy, James, Jesse, Patrick, Wyatt, me, Rusty, and Katie. Old Frank's stocking, with a big, felt gold star and patches at toe and heel, still hung in his honor though it remained empty. A ten foot tall Christmas tree filled one corner of the ranch house living room. There were no decorations on the bottom two feet of the Christmas tree. They had been removed. At first they were pulled off one at a time and batted across the room where they shattered underneath the sofa when they hit the wall. That was great fun, hearing the balls shatter. Shortly thereafter the bottom two feet had been stripped of all ornamentation. It was Katie's first Christmas.

My mom and Martha went all out to make Christmas special for the kids.

My nephews, Patrick and Wyatt didn't know anything but ranch Christmases. To them Christmas was a weeklong party culminating on Christmas morning. It was Martha making candy. It was Grandma sewing matching shirts for the two boys. This year Grandma had a new challenge. She sat at her sewing machine, brow furrowed in concentration. She was making ruffles. She hadn't done ruffles since my sister was school age. She'd sewn for me, too, but never ruffles. For me she sewed leggings made of the lightest leather so it would move with me and be silent when I tried to stalk deer, and colorful western shirts that I could wear in barrel racing competitions. So ruffles were a new challenge.

"Grandma? Can we give Katie the pockets early? I want to play with the pockets with her," Patrick said.

Katie had a pocket fetish. She could not leave a pocket alone. Every pocket she found had to be emptied. So my mother had made her a quilt made up of pockets. Buttoned pockets, Velcro pockets, zippered pockets. Each pocket held an irresistible challenge for Katie.

"No. It's a Christmas gift. You can wait."

"But Grandma, can I hide stuff in the pockets? I've been saving stuff to go in them."

"It already has things in the pockets. Rattles and teething rings and little hair barrettes."

"Can I put *my toys* for her in the pockets?"

"It depends on what they are. Babies can't have things they might swallow. There are lots of things Katie can't have."

"I saved Dad's old cell phone when it died. I got a calculator at the Ninety-Nine Cent Store and took the batteries out. I found a toothbrush holder that has a hinge so it's all one piece."

"What's a baby going to do with a dead cell phone, a dead calculator and a toothbrush holder?"

"She pushes buttons, she tries to eat it. It doesn't matter what she does to it, she just thinks it's a big people thing so she likes it. She always goes for big people things if she has a choice."

"What's she going to do with a toothbrush holder?"

"Try and open it. She loves opening things, that's why you made the pocket quilt for her. It won't take her long to figure out the zippers and buttons and Velcro. I have a toothbrush holder and a travel soap holder and a washed out shampoo bottle. She will like opening and closing them. It's good for her to try and figure stuff out. She's a thinker like Aunt Cassidy."

"If I look them over and they seem safe, you can put them in the pockets, but she can't have it early."

"Rats, I like watching Katie think. She's funny when she thinks."

"Why don't you give her one of the toys early and she can be working on that one until Christmas," Mom suggested.

The toy Patrick chose to give to Katie early was a clear plastic bottle. He'd done his homework. The cap was too big to swallow, but the neck was narrow enough that she couldn't reach in. He rolled up a patch and put it in the bottle where it promptly unrolled and stayed in the bottom, tempting Katie to try to get it out. And boy did she! She tried diligently to pull the patches off the officers' uniforms back home. The lid was one challenge, but even with the lid off she couldn't get the patch out. She held the bottle this way and that reaching in with tiny fingers. She shook it and watched the patch move around but it never came out. That little homemade toy kept her busy for close to an hour. To make matters worse, when she gave up, Pat pulled out the patch with tweezers, showed her it really did come out and then put it back in again.

"Patrick, you're mean to your cousin," Jesse said.

"She's not complaining," he pointed out.

"Da!" Katie called out holding the bottle out to Rusty. Rusty dropped his keys into the bottle so Katie could get something out. She shook out the keys, handed them back and went after the patch.

"See, I told you she was like Aunt Cassidy," Patrick said.

"We need to take Katie to the mall," Mom announced. "All the grandkids have to have one picture taken on Santa's lap."

Jesse looked worriedly at Wyatt. "You aren't going to cry this year, are you? You know Santa's friendly."

"He might be friendly, but he's weird. Why would anybody wear a fuzzy red suit and a floppy red hat?"

"It's tradition," Jesse pointed out.

"Then how old is Santa? That tradition is older'n Grandpa. Some traditions just don't make no sense."

"How would you know he was Santa if he didn't wear the red suit?"

"Santa still looks like Santa even if he doesn't wear the suit. Everybody knows Santa has long white hair and a big white beard. He could wear slacks and a dress shirt just like the other workers at the mall."

"Somehow I don't think people would line up to have their picture taken with Santa if he looked like everybody else at the mall. You just have to accept him as he is, red suit and all."

"I want to ask him why he doesn't leave tracks," Patrick said.

This was going to be an interesting trip to the mall.

There must have been a hundred kids in line when we got there. There was no way Katie was going to make it though this long line without losing patience. I stood there with Jesse and we crept forward one kid at a time. Katie noticed the girl ahead of us in line. She had a shiny red and green hair clip. Her hair was in little ringlets, carefully styled for a picture of her on Santa's lap. One grab from Katie, the clip was gone and the girl's hair fell flat.

"Ashley, what have you done to your hair?" the mother wailed.

"I didn't do it! That baby took it!" Ashley said.

"Well, you can't see Santa like that!" and off they went to restyle Ashley's hair.

A few minutes later Katie noticed the mom in front of us. She had a big purse and Katie lunged for the cell phone poking out the top. She caught the lip of the coffee cup the woman was holding and the whole cup of coffee poured into her purse.

The woman gasped. Patrick's mouth fell open as he gawked at the drippy purse. Off ran the woman with her three kids. We stepped over the coffee and took our new spot four people closer.

"Katie you sure are lucky you're a baby!" Patrick said. "Once you get to be two they get real mad when you do things like that."

The next group was onto us.

"Don't even get close!" the mom said.

"She just likes people," Patrick said in Katie's defense.

And cleaning them out of anything she thinks is interesting, I thought. Katie was patient with this group. She watched them. The woman didn't have any pockets. Her purse was on the floor. The boys took over where Katie left off.

"Santa is not magic," said Wyatt.

"Yes, he is, how come he doesn't leave footprints if he isn't magic?" Patrick countered.

The little boy ahead of us in line said, "Santa isn't magic because magic is evil. Santa isn't evil. He does good things for kids."

"Then why don't his footprints show up? I put sand around the chimney and I checked for tracks and there weren't any," Patrick said.

Rusty was having a blast. Kids being kids, that's what he enjoyed.

"Maybe Santa is smarter than that and found a different way in," the kid said.

Hmm, that was possible, too.

"How does he get his reindeer to fly if he isn't magic?" Wyatt asked, unknowingly siding with his brother.

"They're just flying reindeer," the boy countered.

"So Santa's not magic? Just his reindeer?" Pat asked.

"The reindeer can't be magic either because magic is evil. Who ever heard of an evil reindeer?"

"Then how do they fly?" Wyatt asked.

"I don't know! But they are not evil and Santa's not evil either! Mom! That boy says Santa's evil! I don't want to see Santa if he's evil!"

The mom looked irritated.

"You begged and pleaded to be able to see Santa and now, after spending an hour in line you don't want to see him?"

"No, I want an ice cream."

Off they went with a huff and we stepped ahead another four people. As they were making their way through the crowd the kid said, "Santa wouldn't have brought me a Corvette, anyway."

"Uncle Rusty?"

"What is it Pat?"

"Can you buy a car if you don't have a driver's license?"

"You can buy one, you just can't drive it."

"What if Santa gives you a car?"

"You still can't drive it unless you get a driver's license."

"Can Santa give somebody a driver's license?"

"No, you have to get it the same way everybody else does."

"Rats."

The line inched forward, snaking around the planters and the stage set up for taking pictures of Santa.

"No Katie! No cell phones," Patrick said as he retrieved a phone from Katie's clutches. Jesse held the phone up.

"Did somebody lose a cell phone?" she called out.

A woman nearby claimed it. Two minutes later Katie had it again. This time the woman looked at me suspiciously when I gave it back, so I handed Katie to Rusty and he put her on his shoulders. She grabbed hold of his hair and bobbed up and down like she was riding a horse. She reached down over his shoulder hoping to get to a pocket.

"Can I ride up there, Uncle Rusty?" Wyatt asked.

"After you talk to Santa."

Patrick crossed his arms over his chest, clearly unhappy with his little brother. "You're six years old, Wyatt! You can walk for yourself."

"But I like to be the tallest every once in a while instead of the smallest."

"If you act big, people will treat you like you're big," Patrick said wisely.

"No matter how they treat me, I still have to look at their butts when I walk," Wyatt replied matter-of-factly.

Patrick couldn't argue with that. "I don't look at people's butts. I look at their feet. People do interesting things with their feet. Even if there are no tracks the feet act like they are making tracks. I learn a lot by watching people's feet."

Rusty got tired of Katie reaching for his pockets so he put his car keys in his shirt pocket and held her where she could get to it. She deftly plucked the keys from his pocket and chewed on them victoriously.

"Hiiiiii," a little girl said to Patrick. "Why are you, like, all western?"

"I'm not," Patrick replied.

"Yes you are. You look like a cowboy."

"My dad works on a ranch. This is just normal."

The little girl looked Rusty over.

"He doesn't look like a cowboy. He looks like Brad Pitt on steroids."

"That's not my dad. That's my uncle."

Considering what happened last time Patrick was approached by a girl at the mall I thought he could use some help so I elbowed Rusty and pointed down. Rusty flashed his movie star smile.

"Hi," he said.

"Hiiii," said the little girl, tugging on her mom's shirt.

"What are you going to ask Santa Claus for?" Rusty asked.

"A horse," the little girl replied. "Think he could cut a deal with your dad?" she asked Patrick.

"I think animals bigger than puppies are out of Santa's control," Rusty told her.

"So are babies," Patrick told her. "I asked him for a baby cousin. It didn't work."

"Sure it did, it just worked a little late," Rusty told him.

"Nah, I think baby cousins are up to you and Aunt Cassidy. I don't think Santa had anything to do with it. At least, I hope not, now that I know more about how it happens."

"Lindsey, turn around," her mom told her. "Come on, put on a big smile for Santa."

Patrick looked at Wyatt. "Are you ready?" he asked.

"Yeah, I'm ready, but I still don't see why we gotta do it."

"How are you going to get what you want if you don't tell Santa what that is? Plus we gotta be a good example for Katie. Don't cry or she'll be scared of him, too."

Wyatt looked up at Katie, "I don't think she's scared of *anything*."

"Well, don't give her any reason to be."

"Patrick...Pat it's your turn," Jesse said.

Pat walked confidently up to the old man on the stage.

"Ho, ho, ho," said Santa Claus. Patrick wasn't fooled for a second but he wanted to be a good example to Katie. "What would you like for Christmas?"

Pat sat on his lap and smiled for the camera, right on cue, "Nothing, I just have a couple of questions. How come your footprints don't show up?"

"Well, now, what makes you think they don't?" Santa asked.

"I spread sand around the chimney and on Christmas morning I checked for tracks and there weren't any, not even a scrape, no secondary sign...nothing. How did you do that?"

"Secondary sign?"

"Yeah, like whiskers, or red fuzz stuck in the chimney on your way down."

"Maybe," Santa confided in him, "it's magic."

"I heard that magic is evil."

"Christmas spirit is not evil. How can you explain the feel goody feeling you get when you wake up on Christmas morning? How do you explain the way people suddenly want to do good things at Christmas? There's good kinds of magic, too."

"How do the reindeer fly? I studied all about birds and how they have hollow bones and they hardly weigh anything so it's easy for them to use their wings to fly. But reindeer don't have wings. They're big. I don't see how they could possibly fly."

"I see you're quite a thinker. Can I tell you a secret about reindeer? They adapt."

"All animals adapt to the environment around them."

"Ah, so you know."

"I still don't know how they fly."

"ADAPT: Advanced Disgravitational Altitude Parallelism Tactics."

"Ummm," said Pat.

"What that means is that they have evolved this ability to defy gravity as long as it's within certain parameters, like altitude. You know what parallel lines are? Like the yellow lines on a road? They keep going and going and never meet?"

"Yeah, they do, when a double double area comes up they do meet."

"Well parallel lines never meet. So imagine this invisible line around the earth, *parallel* to the surface of the earth. Disgravitational tactics work in this certain area between the surface of the earth and oh, about three thousand feet up."

"That doesn't make sense. Gravity affects things more the closer to the earth they are. So if reindeer could fly, seems like they would do it easier *over* three thousand feet, not under."

"But we aren't talking about gravity. We're talking about disgravity. Disgravity only applies to reindeers. That's why I chose them to pull my sleigh. They're the only animal with ADAPT. Are you sure there's nothing you want for Christmas? Usually kids give me a long list."

"I never know what I want for Christmas, because I just like to explore. Long as I have space to explore, I'm happy. My brother is another story, though. Good luck."

My mom joined the group. "What did I miss?"

"We now know how reindeer fly," I told her. "They adapt."

"Well, we all knew that," she said.

"No we didn't, it's not what you think."

Wyatt approached Santa nervously. He looked to Katie and put on a brave front.

"Did Patrick ask for anything for Christmas?" Mom asked.

"No, just like usual," Jesse answered.

"Rats, I always hope he'll want something buyable."

"Ho, ho, ho," said Santa Claus. "Come up here, my boy. What can Santa bring you for Christmas?"

"I want a set of space Legos, a remote control dune buggy, some jumps for it, action figures…"

I could see mom and Jesse mentally going: space Legos, check. Remote control car, check.

"Can I ask you a question?" Wyatt asked Santa.

"Sure, if you make it quick. There's lots of kids waiting for their turn."

"Why do you wear the red suit and why do you ride in a sleigh?"

"Tradition. Christmas is a tradition itself so I stick to tradition."

"Does the sleigh have ADAPT?"

"Hmmm, I never thought about that. I suppose not, since the reindeer evolved that way. I think this merits a scientific study! I wonder if ADAPT is something that can be applied to things that are close to the reindeer. Or is it the sleigh? Maybe I could hook up a Mazarati to the reindeer and fly in that!"

"I think a 1953 Buick would be more your speed."

"No, a Studebaker! I always wanted a Studebaker!"

"Yeah, that would work, too, as long as it was red and white. But the suit would have to go. You can't wear a fuzzy red suit in a Studebaker."

"You want to hear a secret?"

"I guess."

"I like Hawaiian shirts."

"You do?"

"Sure, at the North Pole when I'm in my nice, toasty, warm house I like wearing Hawaiian shirts. I pick them up in my travels."

"I better let the next kid have a turn. She should be easier. She can't even talk yet."

"Ho, ho, ho, Merry Christmas!" Santa boomed.

Rusty carried Katie up onto the platform. He lifted her high in the air. "Okay, princess, you smile real big for Daddy."

Katie loved to fly. She grinned broadly and drooled onto Rusty's forehead. Rusty lowered her down to Santa Claus's arms and wiped the drool off with his sleeve. As soon as she got close she whipped Santa's glasses off.

Wyatt leaned toward Patrick, "Guess I should have warned him about that," he said.

"Ho, ho, ho," Santa boomed. "Let me see here, who have we got this time?"

He wrestled his glasses away from Katie. Katie was looking for pockets. She found one and quickly pulled out a flask. The lid flew off when she shook it covering her and Santa Claus with eau de Jack Daniels. Santa blushed. Rusty went to his rescue and glared at him disapprovingly.

"What? A job like this...you'd have one too!" Santa said.

Rusty found the lid and put it back on tightly then backed off.

"Katie! Big smile! You want it? Big smile! Santa!...come on Santa, big smile!" Flash! We all crossed our fingers on that one. Rusty gave Santa his flask back. I doubted Santa had another drink until he found a pair of pliers.

"And what does the little lady want for Christmas?" Santa asked.

"She just got it. A pocket with something interesting inside."

The next kid walked up saying, "I thought Santa Claus was supposed to drink hot chocolate."

"This is a special flavor of hot chocolate," Santa replied.

"Now wasn't that fun?" Mom said as we left the scene of the crime.

"It wasn't as bad as last year. At least Santa isn't as weird as he used to be. He likes Studebakers and Hawaiian shirts," Wyatt informed us.

"I don't know," Patrick said. "That ADAPT stuff sounded like a bunch of phooey."

"We'll know for sure if we find Studebaker tracks on the roof," Wyatt said.

"Santa can't park a Studebaker on the roof. The peak is too sharp," Patrick observed.

"Hey, yeah, I better go ask him about that," Wyatt said turning around.

"Oh no you don't," chimed in all the adults.

"Why does Katie look like an old man in a peep show?" Dad asked, eyeing the pictures lined up on the wall of all three grandkids.

"She wants a flask of whiskey," I explained.

"Only your kid..." he said.

Chapter 2

"Why can't Katie have Christmas candy?" Wyatt asked.

"Too much sugar will make her stomach ache. She can have a tiny bit. Put a little fudge on your finger and let her lick it off."

"No!" he said quickly. "I tried that once and I thought I was going to lose my hand."

"Aunt Cassidy?" Pat said, disillusioned. "Disgravity isn't in the dictionary."

"There are lots of *dis* words in the dictionary. You can add *dis* to almost any word and it changes the meaning of it."

"I think Santa was being *dis*honest playing a trick on a kid."

"I think they just don't have all the *dis* words in the dictionary because they would take over. Or maybe Merriam Webster hadn't *dis*covered that one yet."

Later Patrick came to me much more cheerful.

"I looked it up on the Internet. To get a word into the dictionary it has to appear in print and people have to use it when they talk. So maybe, if we get people to use the word enough, *disgravity* will get added."

"I don't think that's a good idea. For one thing, Santa told you ADAPT was a secret. If you tell everybody that reindeer have ADAPT the scientists will think they can use ADAPT for space studies. They will go up north and kill reindeer and find out what makes them fly and then they will get wiped out. You could be responsible for reindeer becoming extinct. I think saving the reindeer is more important than adding a word to the dictionary."

"They wouldn't let reindeer become extinct if they were useful. I might be able to *save* the reindeer."

"I don't know. Lots of useful animals nearly got wiped out from people hunting and trapping them to make use of them. I think, before you do that, you should go talk to the deer about it."

"Okay. I can do that," he said simply.

The next day Patrick mysteriously vanished. Nobody seemed concerned. I was, because I knew he valued his time with Katie. I knew it would take a lot to displace his time at the ranch house.

"Don't worry," my mom said. "If Snoopy is gone, or if Elan is gone too, they are off in the hills doing Indian games together."

"Indian games?"

"Elan comes up with challenges and Patrick sticks with them until he learns whatever lesson the challenge was meant to teach him."

I walked down to the paddock where Patrick's little black and white horse lived and Snoopy was gone. Patrick wasn't playing Indian games, though. Later in the day he appeared somewhat thoughtful. He didn't run for the playroom like I expected him to. He came to me quietly.

"I can't do it," he said simply.

"You can't do what?" I asked.

"The reindeer deserve to be left in peace," he stated.

"What made you decide that?"

"I went to the deer flats. I sat in the trees watching the deer and I asked them about the reindeer. They didn't answer me. Elan said to wait and an answer would come on the wind. So I sat there and watched them and I thought about people coming to the deer flats to take a deer and I couldn't stand it. I don't like to see even one deer be hurt. So to think of people coming after the reindeer seemed just as bad... So I can't do it."

"I think you made a wise choice. I don't think it matters if disgravity ever makes it into the dictionary. It can be a secret between you and Santa."

"Do you think Santa's reindeer are happy?"

"Santa's a very wise man. I don't think he would take them and make them do something they didn't want to. Besides, can you imagine taking a mule deer and making it pull a sleigh? There's no way you could do it unless they wanted to. I think the reindeer do it by choice, because Santa Claus is nice to them and they understand each other."

"I hope Santa doesn't make them pull a Studebaker. I think that would be humiliating for a reindeer."

"He has stuck to tradition all these years. I don't think Wyatt convinced him to change."

He sat there, cross-legged on the floor, thinking, then he rose and climbed the stairs.

Katie laughed and bounced in the saddle as I rode Shasta sedately around the corral. She tried to eat the saddle horn and patted the pommel in time to the horse's movements. Rusty stood at the fence nervously. He knew I could stay seated on just about any horse. He just wasn't sure I could keep Katie seated at the same time. There was no need to worry. We were just walking in a circle talking.

"Wave to Dada! Katie! Wave to Dada! Hi Dada! Look! Another horsy. Can you say horse? What does a horse say? Neeeiiiigh. Neigh."

I was afraid to trot. She'd knock her chin on the horn and that would be the end of the ride. Mom took pictures of Katie's first horse ride. When Shasta got bored walking around in a circle I handed Katie over to Rusty and let

Shasta run. I missed the long rides Shasta and I used to take when we were both young. I would ride out the back of the ranch and look for tracks to follow and deer to stalk. There were lazy summer rides with no plan, just a horse and his girl. In those days there were no neighbors nearby. There were deer, coyotes, foxes, and rabbits out there in the hills, miles of oak forest to explore, track, hike and ride. We knew the land ten miles from the ranch in any direction, knew where to find a fox den, meadows of deer, secret game trails. I would ride out to a favorite observation spot and crawl around in the brush. I'd sit by a game trail for hours waiting for something to wander by. I'd lay outside burrows with nuts in my hand hoping a critter would get curious enough to take food out of my hand. Those were good days. Days when the worst trouble to happen to me was getting stuffed in my locker by the school bully or getting charged by an angry mother fox when I disturbed her den.

Okay, back to the present. I couldn't say the present was worse than my past. My past was just more peaceful. My present was definitely more interesting. It was broader. It felt richer.

Christmas morning was a riot of sights, sounds, smells and tastes. First was Katie's wake up cry. I hurried to change Katie, feed her, and bathe her. It was still dark out so we had a little time before everybody else got up.

Next I heard Martha's footsteps in the kitchen. Pretty soon the aroma of cinnamon rolls would come floating up the stairs. We met in the kitchen. She was rolling out dough and I was looking for mashed carrots. Katie loved mashed carrots. She hated peas, well, at least baby food peas. She would pick up frozen peas one at a time and gum them to death. Mashed carrots had to come before the bath. No use doing it the other way around unless I wanted an orange baby for her first Christmas pictures.

I found the carrots, pulled a bib over Katie's head and was spooning mush into her face when we heard scraping and then footsteps on top of the house.

"Santa Claus is running late," Martha observed.

"That's not Santa Claus," I replied. "I bet that's Patrick checking for Studebaker tracks on the roof."

"Patrick! Now how would an eight year old get up on the roof? He isn't even big enough to haul a ladder out!"

Sigh. "I know how he did it. He'll be fine."

"How did he do it?"

"The same way I did it when I was his age."

"You need to show Steve so he can fix it."

"Too late now. Patrick's proven he will find a way up and he's proven he knows his way around up there. Let him be."

"But an eight year old could get seriously hurt up there."

"So could anyone else. Patrick is fine. When he comes in don't even ask him about it. Don't punish him. He's just a kid satisfying his curiosity. A kid needs to satisfy his curiosity every once in a while."

I stuck a spoonful of carrots in Katie's mouth and she sneezed, spraying orange mush all over the table and us. I got up to find a damp rag.

There was a soft thump behind the dining room window and then we heard Patrick's soft footfalls on the back porch. He tried the back door and Martha let him in. She gave me a look that said she really wanted to scold him for getting on the roof and I gave her a look that said to just wait.

Patrick looked over the cinnamon roll dough, drew lines through the carrot mess on the highchair tray and rinsed off his hand at the sink.

"Santa didn't get himself a Studebaker," he said. "Leastways, he didn't make the reindeer pull it."

"That's a good thing," Martha said. "Santa needs to stick to tradition. How did you find this out?"

"I looked for tracks. If Santa had tried to land a Studebaker on our roof it would have made a big mess. It could have wrecked the roof."

"Maybe he learned on the first roof that it didn't work," Martha said.

"Hey, yeah, we probably aren't the first house on his list," Pat said. "Well, it don't matter. Did Santa come last night?"

"Of course he came last night! He can't not come!"

"Next time I see Santa I need to ask him why he delivers my presents to your house. All my friends say Santa delivers the presents to their house."

"I think Santa just has a feel for these things. Plus, he knows if the presents were at your house you'd be tempted to peek," Martha said. "Is Wyatt up, too?"

"Nah, he never wakes up till the sun comes up."

"What are you doing up so early?"

"I always get up early. I like to see the ranch when it's still covered in dew. There are little trails through the dew where the critters walked. It's like reading the newspaper. You know how dad always reads the newspaper before he comes to breakfast? I read the yard and the paddocks. The rabbits like Snoopy's paddock the best."

"Go turn on the Christmas tree lights," Martha told him.

"Oh, wow! Santa *did* come!" Pat exclaimed in awe.

"Remember, Katie's presents are in there, too. They aren't just yours and Wyatt's this year."

"I know. I couldn't think of anything I wanted anyway."

"I'm going to cut the cinnamon rolls. Why don't you roll them up for me and put them in the pan?"

"How come cookies taste better raw but cinnamon rolls taste better cooked?"

"To teach you patience."

"That doesn't explain the cookie dough."

"That's to teach you temperance."

"Can I lick the glaze bowl?"

"Are you sure you want that much sugar? Your mom won't like that."

"I won't tell her, if you won't tell her."

"She'll know."

"How would she know?"

"Believe me, moms just know these things."

"Can I have some coffee then? It's not so sweet."

"Choose your poison," Martha said. "I know you can't have both."

"Then I choose the glaze bowl," Patrick said.

"He tricked you," I told Martha. "He knew good and well he couldn't have both so he used that to get what he wanted."

"To get the glaze bowl you have to work for it," Martha told him. "When the rolls come out of the oven you have to get as much glaze as you possibly can on those rolls. *Then* you can have the glaze bowl."

I took Katie upstairs and gave her a bath. When I came down the first pan of rolls was on the table covered with fresh glaze. The scent of cinnamon filled the house. Patrick was scraping glaze off the table.

"I spilled a little bit," he said with a wink.

"Humph," said Martha.

By the time my mom and dad came downstairs the kitchen smelled like cinnamon rolls and berry cobbler. We started hearing more noises upstairs. There was a tromping on the front porch. Ranch hands gathering at their usual breakfast time.

Zack had gone to visit his family. Steve always stayed at the ranch. We didn't ask about his family. Elan's family didn't celebrate Christmas. Randy lived full time at the ranch. He was practically adopted. And James spent Christmas with us because he was family.

Christmas was a complicated affair where the employee/family lines became blurred. Dad considered the hands employees. They got a bonus check. Mom thought of the hands almost like family and at the very least they were folks who needed a Christmas just like anybody else. So, checkbook in hand she did her best to try to make their Christmas like other people's. The gifts were small and thoughtful but there wasn't much a ranch hand needed when their belongings all fit into the bunkhouse or car. New wallets, belt buckles, their gifts were never very original. They were really there for the show. When I was a kid it was the contrast between my sister and I. The girlie girl vs. the tomboy. Jesse would ooh and awe over all the frilly dresses and play make-up and hairstyling tools. They were pleased to see her enthusiasm. On the other hand they were always looking over my shoulder to see what I got. They wanted to teach me how to use my first bb gun and they were responsible for teaching me how to use a hunting knife without cutting my thumb off. I thought I got the better deal out of it even though I got far fewer gifts I could really use. The way I saw it, I had the ranch hands. They gave me as much in their many lessons as they ever gave me in gifts.

Now the show had changed from the Jesse/Cassidy show to a three ring circus. Patrick was much like me. He quietly accepted his gifts, obediently thanked those who gave them to him and quietly put them to use (or passed them down to Wyatt if they were toys). Wyatt, on the other hand, was a boy version of Jesse.

"Oh cool! I asked Santa for a remote control dune buggy and here it is!" Rip! Tear! Struggle with the twist ties and tape. More ripping and tearing. "Anybody got batteries?" Pretty soon wrapping paper was flying as the dune buggy zipped around the living room. Wyatt would get so absorbed in his play that he'd forget he still had a dozen more gifts to unwrap.

"Wyatt, why don't you see if you can find some jumps under the tree somewhere?" Jesse asked prodding him toward maybe sometime that morning getting all his gifts unwrapped.

"Can I try the car?" Randy asked.

Katie had more fun with the paper than she did opening presents. Mom insisted on helping her with it. Patrick opened his gifts one at a time keeping an eye on Katie. He was waiting for one certain package. When someone discovered it under the tree he crawled through the mound of paper to help Katie with it.

"Lookie, Katie! Open it! Come on! Just rip it!" He sat patiently while mom helped Katie with the wrappings. He was itching to help because he'd been waiting weeks for Katie to get this gift. It was *the pockets*! "Lookie Katie! Grandma made it for you! Here, spread it out. See?" He threw the quilt out on the floor and flopped down on top of it. "Look! It's pockets! Katie look!" He opened one pocket and showed her that there were things inside. Katie crawled around on top of it patting the lumps and bumps hidden within. She grabbed the quilt and pulled it to her. "No, no, Katie!" Pat said.

"It's okay, Pat. Let her investigate it anyway she wants to. It's her toy," Mom said. "It's going to take some time for her to figure it out. You can't expect her to open them right away. She's never had to do buttons and zippers before."

Patrick had to put his patience into overdrive as Katie set the quilt aside and went for the paper again.

"Kaaatie," Patrick called. "I found a cell phone!"

A cell phone? She knew what a cell phone was. That was one of those things people usually took away from her! It was almost as good as a TV remote! She crawled over.

"Lookie!" Pat, pat, "There's a cell phone in here!"

The pocket was held closed with a large button and a loose button hole but Katie didn't need to undo the button. She just stuck her hand in and pulled the cell phone out.

"Hey!" Patrick said.

"Da!" she called holding up the cell phone. She stuck the phone in her mouth, checked the buttons, waved it around. It was the end of Katie's gift unwrapping for a long time. She took the phone and crawled over to Rusty. "Da! Dada!"

Rusty took the phone, put it up to his ear. "Hello?" a short pause, "It's for you," he said handing it back to Katie. She put it up to her ear but nothing happened so she put it back in her mouth.

Martha brushed a mound of wrapping paper off the coffee table and filled the top of the table with cinnamon rolls, cobbler, plates and silverware, coffee, sugar and cream. Katie went for the coffee.

"No, no, Katie! Hot! Ouch!" said Patrick running through the paper to catch his wayward cousin. I got a cinnamon roll and held out my hands for Katie. Patrick dragged her over.

I fed her little bits of the rolls as we unwrapped more gifts. I think only Patrick's limited interests kept my mom in check. She wanted to keep things even but nobody could think of what to buy Patrick. When I saw the mound of gifts growing I counted my lucky stars Patrick took after me. If he'd been like Wyatt we would have had to rent a moving truck to get home.

The dune buggy zoomed by and it looked like a big kid toy so Katie slid off my lap and headed in the direction the dune buggy went. She'd never catch it. It lurched over a jump and came to a crash and a rolling stop. A light bulb went on in Wyatt's head and he ran off to the kitchen. He came back with a trash bag and started stuffing it with wrapping paper.

"Wyatt, that's so thoughtful of you to help clean up," my mom said.

He looked a little guilty. "I'm not cleaning up. I'm making a place for my car to land where it won't break."

When the bag made a loose pillow he tied the ends and placed a jump on either side of it. Off went the dune buggy, up the jump and over the trash pillow.

"Guess it takes some figuring," he said.

Kids playing. A baby crawling for the nearest forbidden object. Piles of wrapping paper. Twinkling lights on the tree, even though it was now broad daylight. Guys standing around arguing in friendly tones about who was going to do what ranch chores. Everybody knew who was good at what. They knew how to get them over with in record time but it was easier arguing about it. Coffee and spices. My dad sitting back in the big easy chair thinking this was what he worked so hard for. All the ranch running smoothly. All his family together, happy and healthy. Mom crawling around with the kids, camera in hand. Jesse trying a new top up to her for James approval. This was a ranch Christmas.

"And Christmas was like this the whole time you were growing up?" asked Rusty.

"Yeah, except Jesse and I were the only kids. There were fewer people," I answered.

"It was right boring," Dad put in, which surprised me because he was the one who hadn't wanted kids in the first place. "Until we let Cassidy loose and she had to be extricated, chased down, or hog tied. Then Christmas was normal."

"Oh, boy!" Patrick said. "Okay, Grandpa, start with the extricated one. What does extricate mean?"

I glared at him. He knew better than to tell Patrick stories from my childhood. Patrick was the one who would run out and try the same things just to one-up me. He chocked it up to adventuring. The more adventures he could get into the more like me he thought he was. So I wasn't very happy with Dad.

"You'll see. This was a Christmas when Satan was still young. We didn't know what a terror he was going be. At the time he looked like a very promising racehorse. Oh, we knew he could have a temper but we thought we could train it out of him or direct that bad attitude into speed on a track. And so here was Cassidy, coaxing Satan to take a saddle for the first time. Just like any young un, he didn't like the feel of something on his back. She spent hours out there talking him back to a calm, trying the blanket. It was at Christmas that she finally got a saddle on him. There he stood, tall and black and perty as all get out. Cass was proud as the dickens. She stood there grinning ear to ear. She looks at Old Frank. Old Frank's grinning at her, too. 'I ain't stopping you,' Old Frank said, 'you earned this ride. I say go for it.' So it didn't take Cassidy but half a second to be in the saddle and it didn't take but three for her to be out of it. Satan turned into the devil hisself. He had the durndest sidewinding buck you ever saw and before you could say 'Bob's your uncle' she was in the dirt again and Satan was mad as a cat on fire. He charged Cass and she lit out and jumped into a barrel. That crazy horse done attacked the barrel! He kicked it sending it flying across the corral and into a fence post. Then he reared up and brought his front hooves down on the barrel and we thought Cassidy was done for. Steve roped Satan and pulled him off and he's a buckin' and snorting and running circles on the end of the rope until he decided Steve was his next target. We just dragged him to the next corral and turned him loose to calm down and we all come a runnin' back to the barrel and we all peeked inside wondering what we were going to find. And there was Cass, all arms and legs and scrunched into that barrel so tight she couldn't move! The barrel was only half as big as it was to start. She was like one of them contortion artists trying to get her out. First we thought we'd have to cut her out. 'You okay, Cass?' we called in. She couldn't hear a thing, what with all the racket of having a horse attack her barrel and all. It took another half hour to get all her arms and legs back in their right positions. Once she was put back together, it was a tight squeeze to stand up, and Steve pulled her out."

"I bet you never rode Satan again!" Patrick said.

"Oh, no, I got up on him many times," I replied. "I knew he'd make a fine horse if he'd just come around. He just got meaner and meaner the more we tried."

"So what does extricate mean?" Pat asked.

"It means to take something out of something else."

"In fact I think it was that same Christmas that Satan lit out into the hills with Cass on his back." Dad went on, "We'd got him calmed down and we decided maybe if we put two ropes on him and just let him feel someone on his back…Well, it were a bad idea. Cass talked to him and petted him and worked her way into the saddle. Took him two seconds and a snort to figure out he was stuck and form a plan of attack. He lunged forward yanking me and Steve off our feet. Old Frank's in the saddle on a workhorse so he gets out another rope and Satan isn't going to be caught so he lits out dragging us both. We see the fence coming up and let go. Satan didn't miss a beat jumping that fence. He takes off into the hills, Cass in the saddle."

"That was one of the best rides I can remember. That horse could run!" I added. "Only problem was, when he tuckered out he was still mad. As long as I stayed in the saddle he fought me. He wasn't trained yet so I had two choices, ride him out until someone found us, or let him loose and start walking. I rode him out for a while but I knew I could be out there all night. That horse was so stubborn. I finally turned him loose, and ran for the nearest climbable tree. When he was making his own way back I started back by a different route."

"When that devil horse appeared with no rider we didn't know where Cass was. Old Frank put him back in the barn and Steve went out to search the hills. Cass could have tracked herself down but there were so many tracks going out the back of the ranch he didn't know which were which so all he could do was go out looking. Well, them hills cover a lot of ground. He came back after dark, no Cassidy. He was fit to be tied until we told him Cass had made her own way back."

"Bet that was the last time you rode that horse!" Pat said again.

"Well, no, actually that ride convinced me he really could run. So, for a few days, I doubled my efforts."

"You put two bull headed young uns together and you could start a war," Dad said. "Cass was determined Satan would race and Satan was determined to be as mean as could be. He tried everything in the book and Cass tried everything in her book, too. Finally they just decided to hate each other."

"I don't hate Satan, but I don't know why you keep him either," I said.

"Two reasons," Dad said. "I don't want him to kill someone and he's the best advertising I got. Lots of folks have tried to buy him. I don't tell them what a SOB he is. I tell them he's not for sale, but I got some other horses that are. Can't be rode, can't be showed, can't be bred, but he's a dandy horse to look at."

"After working Satan for a few weeks I was ready to take on the bronc riding event at the rodeo!" I said, "If they would have let me compete I would have entered, but women weren't allowed to enter that one. I had to settle for barrel racing."

"Woman, hell, you was just a kid," Dad said.

"Don't you ever try to ride Satan," I told Patrick.

"I wouldn't worry about that," Steve said. "Pat has his own tales of woe when it comes to that horse," Steve said.

The morning wound down and the hands returned to their chores, the adults started bagging up the wrapping paper that Wyatt had left behind. Wyatt retrieved the bags of paper and dragged them up to the playroom. He cleared a big area, tossed the bags of wrapping paper into the middle of the room, flattened them as best he could and threw a blanket over the top of it all. His dune buggy was now going off road. As I watched my nephews play with their Christmas presents I wondered what kind of a kid Katie would grow into. Would she be like Patrick? Quick and earthbound. Or like Wyatt? Quiet, creative and extravagant. Somehow I thought she'd be somewhere in the middle.

Rusty appeared in the doorway. He was downcast, hands in pockets.

"Hey, come sit with me," I said patting the floor next to me.

"Come down stairs. We have something we need to talk about."

Chapter 3

Uh oh, I didn't like the sound of this, but I followed Rusty downstairs to the living room. He sat on the big, leather couch facing the fireplace. The fire, usually warm and friendly, crackled and sparked mirroring the tension in the room. I sat beside him and his arm came around me. He took a deep breath.

"I checked the messages at the house," he said simply. "You ought to hear them."

"Is it bad news? What happened?"

"If it was shocking news, I'd just tell you what it was. I think you need to hear the messages first."

"Okay." I held Katie a little closer.

He called our house and punched the code in to get our messages. He handed me the phone. When Katie tried to grab the phone he took her to his lap.

"Message one: *beep* Hello? Cassidy? This is detective Whitman in San Diego. I'd appreciate a call back at your earliest convenience. My number is…"

"Message two: *beep* Hello, Cassidy? Michaels? I need to speak to Cassidy as soon as possible. My number is…"

"Message three: *beep* Michaels, where the hell are you two? This is Slick. I know damn well you don't want to talk to me but this is important. Call me. Now."

"Did you call him?" I asked.

"Message four: *beep* All right, don't call me, but I've tried Border Patrol. The guys have reached a dead end. I don't know what's up but I need a new pair of eyes. The trail's fading every time you ignore me. Call me."

"What kind of a case has he got?" I asked.

"Where's Patrick?" Rusty asked.

"I don't know, but Wyatt's upstairs. He could be anywhere."

Rusty got up and looked around, climbed the stairs and walked down the hall. Patrick was nowhere to be seen so he came back downstairs and sat on the couch again.

"Chase hasn't been heard from in several days. He was on patrol and vanished. Problem was it wasn't an official patrol. He just went out in the Bug. They found the bug. They didn't find Chase. Like the message said, they followed the trail for a little ways and then they hit a dead end."

"Several days? Chase's trail is hard to read when it's fresh. If he was hiding his tracks there's no use even looking."

"That's what I told Slick."

"But…"

"I knew that was coming. You know this could be a mess. He could be sitting in the desert with a broken leg. Or it could be he ran into trouble. It's easy for Chase to do that down there. Some Mexican family with a grudge. It could be anything. Just knowing Chase it could be anything. Throw in his work with Border Patrol and the police and it throws a whole new light on it. We don't even know what country he's in."

"I can't ignore it. I can't turn my back on him. You know I have to try."

"No."

"Rusty! I can't leave Chase out there, whether he's dead or alive. I need to do what I can. If you were going to say *no* then why even tell me about it?"

"Because you'd have learned about it eventually and I wanted to be up front about it. But I won't have you tracking Chase into the desert. It's too dangerous. It would be like sending you out after Kelly all over again."

"And I found Kelly. And I made it back. I have to try. I have to. If I don't, I couldn't live with myself."

"Babe, if I'd known what you were up against when you looked for Kelly I wouldn't have let you go. If you'd saved Kelly but I'd lost you I couldn't have lived with myself. This could be much worse. This isn't the woods of California. This is a whole bunch of nothingness. There's no hiding out there. There's no cover."

"I better bring a shovel, then."

"Cass… no."

"Slick wouldn't have called me unless he was out of options. He's tried his trackers down there. He's tried an air search."

"What makes you think you can do more?"

"I don't know if I can. But I can go down there, put myself in Chase's moccasins and see what I come up with. He'd do the same for me."

"It's his life. He'd do it because it's what he does."

"And?"

"And what?"

"So, what is it I do?"

"Cassidy… there's a huge difference between you hiking off into the woods looking for a lost hiker and following Chase into one of his border disputes. He isn't exactly popular down there, on either side of the border."

"It's only tracking. Nobody can fault me for walking through the desert."

"BORSTAR's out there. They'll take care of it."

"If they were taking care of it, Slick wouldn't have called."

"They've worked with Chase for years."

"Then they know there's no use trying to guess what he might have been up to. You can't speculate when it comes to Chase. You have to take what few facts he chooses to leave and work with those. If they have searched and done flyovers of the area, then we're down to seeing the invisible… or something happened to take him out of the area. Will BORSTAR work with me?"

"If you came with Slick's approval, wore your uniform and know what you're talking about, maybe. Maybe they'll tell Slick to take his little Skipper tracker home. Slick is a little less popular than Chase no matter what side of the law you're on."

"What about your dad? Would they accept me by his recommendation?"

"I told you, you're not going."

"Well, I can't just sit here when I could be doing something."

"Can I do it, too?" Chimed in Patrick.

"How long have you been there?" I snapped a little too harshly.

"I just got here," he said defensively.

I sighed with relief. Patrick idolized Chase. There would be no peace if he knew Chase was missing. I didn't want to tell Patrick unless I absolutely had to. Rusty had other ideas.

"Pat, when was the last time you talked to Chase?"

"A couple of days before you got here," he answered.

"You're sure?" Rusty asked.

"Yeah, it had to be because he asked what we were doing for Christmas and I told you were coming. Oh, and he said to tell you 'hi.' I forgot."

"Did he say what *his* plans were?"

"He didn't know yet. It depended on what Elan was doing. He said he might go home to Arizona but since his family wasn't there anymore he was wondering if there was any point to it. Then he asked to talk to Elan."

Rusty and I looked at each other.

"Run and get Elan for me," Rusty said. "If he's doing chores tell him it will only take a minute and it's very important."

"Yes sir!" Patrick said. I got the feeling he knew he was on a borderline Cassidy adventure. If he just had patience he might just get drawn in. I meant to see that didn't happen.

When they came in the door, heads together, jabbering away, pondering this turn of events, they reminded me of old time country cousins despite the fact that one of them was a Navajo and the other a sandy haired, freckle faced white boy. I was glad to see the bond and mutual respect the two had for each other. When they saw Rusty and me standing there tensely they stopped.

Rusty looked to me and said, "There's no use sending him out. He'll find a way to hear."

I nodded for him to proceed knowing he'd do so carefully.

"Thanks for coming, Elan. We need to know what Chase's plans were for the past week. Patrick said he was thinking about going to Arizona. Do you know what he decided to do?"

"He asked if I was going home for the holidays but I didn't see much point to it. There are other Indian traditions I would go home for but we don't celebrate Christmas. This time of year is not so important to go home. He understood that because he practices many of our same traditions. He decided to stay in California. He was going to be at your parent's house in the afternoon on Christmas day."

"What about before then?"

"He said he had some tracking he could do."

"That doesn't sound like he was just wandering out in the hills to find animal tracks. What was the purpose of this tracking?"

"He didn't say. You know Demothi," Elan said, using Chase's Indian name. "One sentence speaks volumes."

"So you agree, this wasn't idle animal tracking?"

Elan looked thoughtful, "Yes, I agree. He had a purpose in mind."

"Did he say where?"

"Otay."

"Are you sure?"

"Okay, what?" Patrick asked.

"Not okay, O*tay*. I think it's a wilderness area," Elan said.

"It is and it's not far from Chase's house. Do you know why he was going there?" Rusty asked.

"He said he was looking for something. He aimed to find it before Christmas."

"Well, he didn't do it," Rusty mused. "He was looking for some*thing*, not somebody? And it involved tracking?"

"That's the impression I got."

"And it was more business than pleasure."

"I'm not sure there is a difference to Demothi," Elan said.

"Did he leave you with any other facts? You're talking about a ten square mile area," Rusty said.

"He said his car should blend in at the gun club."

Rusty took note of all these things and it all seemed to make sense to him.

"Thanks, Elan, you can go back to whatever you were doing."

"I think it can wait," Elan answered. "I think you worry for nothing. Demothi knows how to make his way. If he can do it in Arizona he can do it in this Otay place."

"What happened to Chase?" Pat asked.

"We don't know. Detective Whitman has been looking for him. They found his car and a trail but they lost the trail."

"Maybe, Demothi wishes not to be found," Elan said. "If he doesn't want to be found, he won't be found."

"That's what we hope," I said.

"I've got some phone calls to make," Rusty said. "I think I can get more answers now."

For the next few hours Rusty nervously paced the house. I guess some of the people he needed to talk to were unavailable. At dinner Rusty, Elan, Patrick and I were a quiet lot. Everybody else was talking ranch talk and complimenting Martha on the Christmas dinner. Though I enjoyed the family time and the camaraderie, my thoughts kept straying waaay to the south, to a barren patch of desert, an empty Baja Bug, and an invisible trail of footprints into the wilderness. I could picture Chase's tracks, or lack thereof. He'd be hiding his tracks if he was looking for something he shouldn't find.

Rusty's cell phone rang and he excused himself from the table. Patrick almost jumped out of his seat even though he didn't know exactly what kind of fix Chase might be in. He and Elan exchanged glances and I quietly put more tiny bites on Katie's highchair tray. Katie picked up a tiny bite and held it up.

"Ma! Bye!"

"Yes! Bite!" my mom praised her. "Yummy bite!"

I couldn't share her excitement. My tracking senses were piqued I needed to be down there. Even if I couldn't see the tracks, I had to look. If Rusty even nodded I'd be packing my bags.

"Cassidy," Mom said. "You've got that look."

"I'm sorry, Mom, I've got a search pending. I can't help but worry."

"Not at Christmas! You can't leave in the middle of your once a year visit!"

"I don't know if Rusty will give in. So far he'll hog-tie me before he'll let me go down there. Maybe he'll find out more. I hope so. I need to give it a try. He knows I have to give it a try."

"Well, I hope it can wait a few days," Mom said.

"Mom! When someone has been missing for several days in a remote desert area, you can't be slow. You never know how much water they had, or if they are injured. Too many things can go wrong."

"Chase?" Patrick asked.

I glared at my mom.

"Yeah, it's Chase," I admitted.

"Don't worry, Aunt Cassidy, Chase is wily, just like you. He'll be fine."

"I wish I could have as much faith in him as you, Pat. I know he's not lost, which tends to point to other things, like an injury or trouble of some kind. Even Chase needs food and water. He can get along without shelter. I guess it's trouble I'm worried about more than anything."

"That's because you're too used to trouble yourself," said Jesse.

"But that's just it," I said. "Chase usually knows how to avoid trouble. If it's trouble, it's real bad trouble. If it's an injury, it's a bad injury."

Rusty came back and sat down, looking even more dejected. It scared me. I didn't know if he found out something that would send me packing or he found out some bad news about Chase. I didn't want to ask at the dinner table but the silence was stretched so taught I thought it was going to break.

"Elan was right," he said at last. "They didn't find his car at the gun club but they found it on the side of the road near the gun club. The place where his car is parked is a spot where the border of the wilderness area is only about a tenth of a mile from the road. They know he parked there purposely and went in on foot."

"How far did they track him?" I asked.

"Less than a mile."

"Who did you talk to?"

"Alfredo Montez. We always called him Monty. Good guy, very knowledgeable. He doesn't know what to think of this. He hadn't heard anything that would send Chase into the Otay."

"When they searched his Bug what conclusions did they make?"

"No sign of foul play. It looks like Chase parked, he walked into the wilderness area and he didn't come out."

"What's the terrain like there?"

"Dry, rocky, rotten tracking."

"What makes it rotten tracking?"

"The soil is hard, it has little rocks in it. It's not sandy like at home. There's lots of small shrubs, brush, no cover."

"At least it's winter. Did you talk to Slick?"

"No, but talking to Monty is better."

"What agency is Monty with?"

"I wish I didn't know."

I smiled and he knew he was sunk.

"So," I said, "will he work with me?"

"He didn't think you could do more than the guys down there have done."

"Most guys wouldn't. Will he work with me?"

Rusty dug into his dinner wishing the topic would go away.

"I'll call him," I said.

"You don't have his number."

"I can find it easy enough."

Mom and Martha looked disappointed.

"At least eat a good dinner before you go," Martha said.

This triggered a flood of dinner conversation.

"You're not going after that beach bum, are you?" said Dad.

"Can I go too?" asked Patrick.

"No," I told Patrick, then to Dad, "Chase is not a beach bum. He just dresses like one when it doesn't matter. He's a tracker. They need him down there. He's very useful to have around. Plus, if they don't have him they might start calling me down there. I don't want to be called that far afield. I'm having enough trouble being able to go on calls close my house."

"Are you going to leave Katie?" Mom asked.

"No, Rusty's parents live in San Diego. They'd love to keep Katie if Rusty needs to work. Do you think your Dad can fix me up with some gear?" I asked.

"No, he was never into camping and backpacking. We'll have to stop by the house."

"We don't have time for that."

"Then do what Chase would do," Elan said.

"What's that?" I asked.

"Borrow it from Chase."

"I couldn't do that! I'd have to break into his house!"

"You can't do that?" Elan asked.

I pictured Chase's old mobile home. Yeah, I probably could get into it if need be. If the cat wasn't standing guard. And he probably had gear stowed somewhere, even if he brought his search pack along. I thought I could scrounge enough to get by. Searching Chase's house would tell me something about the purpose of his trip, too. My mind went into trip planning as the conversation flowed around me at the table.

Chapter 4

All the flights were booked over the holidays and there was no way to fly to San Diego. Shoot.

"Dad? I need a flight to San Diego. Didn't you say you had a doctor friend who flies? Think I could hire him?"

He scratched his head, thinking. "You need someone who understands the urgency of the situation."

"Who would that be?"

He picked up the phone and punched in a number off the top of his head.

"Hank, this is Wayne Gordon. I got a situation... I got a daughter who's a tracker. She needs to be on a search ASAP on the Mexican border... I know... I know. It's Christmas here, too. Some folks don't get lost at handy times. I'd be willing to pay her way."

"Dad, I can..."

"He wants to talk to you," he said handing me the phone.

"Hello?"

"What's going on?"

"It's like Dad said. A retired officer has disappeared into the Otay wilderness. I'd like to go find him."

"Retired officer?"

"He worked for the San Diego Police Force for many years. Recently he has been working with the Border Patrol and Search and Rescue."

"Was he armed?"

"Probably."

"And he has extensive experience in the outdoors."

"Yes."

"And you think you can find him?"

"I don't know. If there was a situation that seemed more hopeless I haven't run across it. But I have to try. I'll drive down if I have to. But if I could find a flight it would be much quicker. Time is short in the desert."

"You can find your way from San Diego?"

"Yes, sir. That's what I was hoping. I have contacts in San Diego."

"And your dad is okay with this?"

"It doesn't matter. I'm going whether he approves or not. The sooner I get there the sooner he can be found. If, he can be found."

"You have your doubts?"

"Nobody can be certain of anything when it comes to Chase. He's a...

unique individual. I don't know about the trackers down there, but I've tracked Chase before. He doesn't make it easy, but I've learned a thing or two about tracking him. I can put myself in his shoes. If he wants to be found, I can find him. If he was being discreet for some reason, then it's doubtful I can."

"Have your dad draw you a map. Be ready first thing in the morning."

"Yes, sir! Thank you."

I dove into my bedroom closet to see what camping gear had been left behind when I left home for the Marines. I came out victorious. I found a bivouac sack and a stove. That was two things I didn't have to worry about finding at Chase's house. Clothes were a problem. I needed a uniform, or camouflage. If Chase met with trouble, I wanted to be able to move over the land invisibly. There wasn't a military surplus store in the country open on Christmas day. Chase sure had lousy timing.

Elan appeared at the door. "Do you know what you're in for?" he asked.

"Yes, and no. I've tracked Chase before. The desert is going to be dry and rough. The tracking is going to be next to impossible. My gear is questionable. My experience will see me through. Does Dad have a camp shovel anywhere around here?"

"If it's a tool it's around here somewhere." He stood there wondering if he should pursue what was on his mind. He was in Rusty's camp. I knew the guys didn't expect Chase to be found. To be honest, I didn't either. Chase was either out there, or lynched. If he was out there, he was fine. If he was lynched, there was nothing I could do about it except get out in one piece. At least trouble left more tracks than Chase did. I'd have some warning.

Rusty joined Elan at the door.

"You can't just run off like this," Rusty said. "This is a complex situation. There are political ramifications you aren't even thinking of."

"I know, I'm trying not to."

"Cass, you can't ignore them."

"I can if I stay in the Otay. If Chase left the wilderness area it becomes a Border Patrol case. I know that."

"What am I supposed to do in the mean time? You can't just run off at the drop of a hat."

I rounded on him. That phrase just hit a nerve with me. "What would I have done if friends hadn't dropped what they were doing and come? Strict? Kelly? Fifty people outside a mine digging, just in case there was something left to find? Chase has dropped everything and come to track a scene for you. Or have you forgotten? Two men? A yellow van? Chase tracked that scene for you. He came because he cared. Not because he was ordered to. And what are you supposed to do? You know you can stay here. Mom will help with Katie.

Or you can come to San Diego and your mom will help with Katie. You aren't without options on this one."

He sighed and stared at his feet for a few seconds. "It's been a month. One trouble free month. I thought we could make it two."

"We will, either I can track him or I can't. It depends on how careful he was after he left his car."

"I'll call Mom and Dad," he said.

"I agree with Rusty," Elan said as Rusty went to find a quiet spot to talk to his parents. "Demothi knew his risks. He would never ask you to walk into danger for him."

"He didn't ask."

"Give him a few more days. Perhaps his mission in not complete."

"His mission? What do you know of his mission?"

"I'm not convinced Demothi is missing. I think he is not found."

"Slick Whitman wouldn't call me unless he had to. He has as little to do with us as possible. If Slick was willing to endure the wrath of Rusty he means business."

We followed Dad's directions to Hank Lawrence's house. A big field stretched out for four acres on either side of the house and a corrugated Quonset hut housed two small airplanes. The landing strip was a flat dirt road down the middle of the field. Hank just about backed out when he saw me.

"You're taking off into the desert to look for a border patrol agent/police officer/outdoorsman/tracker?"

"Yup."

"I hate to tell you this, but you don't have a chance. Your dad is willing to let you venture out there? What does this guy say about it?" he said indicating Rusty.

"He's used to this. It's my job."

"Where's your gear?"

"I'm going to have to pick up most of it in San Diego. Unless you want to stop briefly in Joshua Hills."

"The deal was San Diego. I want to get there and back today."

"Okay, I'll just have to make do with the gear I can scrounge."

"I'm not sure I'm doing your dad a favor. Anything happens to you out there and I'm going to catch hell."

"No you won't. Dad's used to things happening to me." I turned to Rusty, "I'll do my best to get outfitted with a radio. I doubt there's a cell tower within fifty miles. If I have to back out, I'll meet you at your parent's house."

"What would it take to make you back out?"

"If I get to where border patrol gave up and I don't get anywhere that day, there's almost no use continuing. It's less than a mile from his car. The circle-until-I-pick-up-a-trail method doesn't work with Chase. He doesn't leave enough of a trail to catch it on a random pass. I'm going to be taking it slow because I need to pull everything I can out of the trail."

"Don't leave the wilderness area, particularly to the south. If you're heading south and you hit a paved road or a little river you've gone too far. Turn right around. You don't want to end up in Mexico. Just mark the last sign and go turn it over to BORSTAR again. You'll have done everything you can do. Dad will meet you at Gillespie Field. He can put you in touch with Monty. Monty can take you to where Chase's car was parked."

"Was?"

"They weren't going to leave it out there."

"Why? That site held information I need. It was a landmark for Chase if he came back out! How would he get home with his car towed away?"

I boarded the little plane with very mixed emotions. I knew I couldn't expect the authorities down there to preserve the site for me. They didn't even know I was available to try looking for Chase. This was their investigation. They could do what they wanted with it. But they were sure making it rough for me to try and pick up where they left off.

It was hard to leave Rusty and Katie behind. I was nervous about Rusty stopping any forward progress simply due to worry. Mom helped my case by insisting on Katie staying behind.

The little Cessna reacted to every strong breeze. It felt like a matchbox on the wind.

"You ever been in a small plane before?" Hank asked.

"Yeah, a few times. Most of my flying is in helicopters."

"Do you know about this place you are going to?"

"Only a general layout."

"There's nothing there. That's why it's a wilderness area."

"That makes sense. It's what I expected."

"First thing I wonder is, why would this guy venture out into a place where there isn't anything to see or do?"

"He was doing something. Maybe I can figure out what it was."

Changing the subject Hank said, "You're nothing like your old man."

I laughed but I kind of disagreed with him even though, more often, I disagreed with my dad.

"I'm more like him that you think. Where he is driven in social circles, in business and being successful, I'm driven on the trail."

"But look at you. You could have been anything. You could have gone the college route and been anything you chose."

"Thanks. I chose the Marines and I am what I choose. I choose to run off into the middle of nowhere looking for people who got into nowhere too deep to get out."

"But this guy you're looking for. He doesn't do that. He never gets in too deep."

"And that's what makes this search so important. If something can happen to Chase, it's got to be bad. He would have no problem shooting his way out if it came to that. I'm having a real hard time figuring out what he could have met up with that even he couldn't handle."

"So you are going to go find out what it was. You?"

"I can't leave him down there. That's the only reason my husband let me go. I'd find a way. Or I'd be miserable. And if something happened to Chase and I hadn't tried, I'd be worse. He thinks I'll be in good hands."

"It doesn't sound like you will."

"Not if I can help it," I admitted.

The ground crept by slower than I thought possible. I was trying to plan how to get started. The first glitch was going to hit really fast. Rusty's dad. Bill was going to take his responsibility very seriously. I had to get my contact information and a rental car and somehow lose Bill. When the plane began descending my stomach did little flip flops all the way down. I wasn't sure if it was from flying or from nerves. I love Rusty's dad. He was about the best father-in-law a girl could hope for. But that was part of the problem. I was going to have a hard time crossing him, and I didn't plan on going into the Otay with an army of officers and volunteers behind me.

The ground came at us so suddenly I jumped. I was used to all kinds of transport and comings and goings. I pretty much got in and didn't jump out until I saw smoke (which *had* happened once) or the plane stopped and the others inside moved around. Hank taxied the plane to the side and pulled up next to a small hangar. He pointed to a building off in the distance.

"You'll probably find your ride in there," he said.

"Can I pay you? Dad said he would but I'd feel better if I could pay you myself."

"Can't let you do that. How would it look to your dad if I took it from you? Just take care of yourself. Don't make me sorry I did this."

I fingered the little medal I kept in my pocket reminding me of another man who was counting on me to take care. The medal had a story, just like all medals do. If I could do what it took to earn *my* medal, then I could do this. I'd find Chase. If he had a chance I'd find him.

I wandered around looking for Bill. He was not in the building Hank pointed me to. Even for a small airport there was a lot of walking to do to locate one person. I tried the parking lot and found there were several parking lots, too.

"Does he come here often?" a guy in greasy coveralls asked.

"No, well, I doubt it."

"Then try the museum. If he doesn't know where he's going he'll park there. If you don't find him come back here."

"Thanks, but I'll find my father-in-law."

"Oh. Okay."

I headed for the building that looked museumish. I glanced around the parking lot. What kind of a car would Bill drive? I tried to remember the cars at Bill and Bev's house. Oh yeah, it was a red Saturn Vue. Golf clubs in the back. A sticker that looks like a golf ball went through the window. Combination lock on the door. Okay, he's here somewhere. I found a step to sit on where I could watch the car. It didn't take him long to round the side of the building and he knew where I was before he appeared. He was starting to think like me. He wanted to get his thoughts lined up. I was glad I hadn't appeared stressed. Inwardly I wanted to be on the trail. Inwardly I was worried about how I was going to get this guy off my tail before I hit the trail. I had things to do before I could start. Outwardly I was waiting calmly, looking for my ride. I scooted over so he could have a piece of the step. He sat down and put an arm around me.

"It's good to see you. Rusty couldn't come?"

"Two-seater plane. I'm sorry. He'll be down as soon as he can. I just hope Katie doesn't give him a hard time. She doesn't have much patience when it comes to travel. It'll be an all-day drive for him. Can you drop me off some place where I can rent a four wheel drive?"

"Nope."

"Aw, come on. I need to hit the trail."

"You've got nothing to hit the trail with. What's this?"

"The camping gear I could scrounge from my old bedroom back home. It's a camp stove and a Bivouac sack."

"You can't go on a search like that."

"I know. I've got a plan. I just need wheels."

He dropped the keys into my hand. "Then let's do it," he said.

"You can't go."

"Why?"

"Because… will you not look when I tell you to not look?"

"I think I see why your family calls you trouble. I'll look when I think I better and I'll not look when I think I better find something better to do. But you're stuck with me. I told Rusty I'd stick with you like glue."

"For how long?"

"For however long it takes."

"And Bev?"

"She knows. She's counting the minutes until that baby comes through the door."

"This could take several days. It's going to be boring."

"I doubt it."

"Okay," I said with a sigh of resignation. "Take me to Chase's house. Or get us outfitted with a radio."

"The radio's closer. What are you looking for at Chase's house? Information? You'll get that from Monty."

"Not the kind I'm looking for. I'm looking for something else at Chase's house. I'll make sure he gets it back."

Chapter 5

"Well, well, I thought I'd never see you again," Slick Whitman said when he ran across us at the station. "Why didn't you return my calls?"

"Because Rusty did. We didn't get your messages for a few days because we were out of town. I hitched a ride from up north to get here."

"Do you know what you're getting into?"

"No, I know I'm in for a tough track. Chase is always hard to track. I expect this to be nearly impossible. Why did you call me?"

"Because I'm a lousy, no good SOB. And I don't want to lose Chase. Even if we sometimes disagree, I need his brain."

I left the radioing to Bill. The guys always knew more codes and protocol than I did so I stuck to my job and I left them to their gadgets and codes. The one code I enjoyed sending: ten sixty-five found, ten forty-five A. Missing person found, condition, good. If it was anything else I let the guys analyze the situation, and come to their own conclusions. I was the tracker. They were the patchers. I wondered what I was going to do with Bill. He was neither a tracker nor a patcher. He was a cop. He was in good shape but he wasn't used to hiding in low cover.

Bill pulled up to Chase's house and I looked the place over.

"Stay here while I circle the house," I said.

All the tracks I found were at least four days old and that made sense. It matched the story I'd gotten so far. Angry eyes glowed from under the trailer and followed me around. I waved at Bill that he could come out and he slipped out of the Vue smirking at me. He'd let me play my little tracker games. I went to the front door. Locked. I descended the steps, opened a plastic bin on top of a table and filled the ceramic dish on the tabletop.

"What are you doing?" Bill asked.

"Feeding the cat. He's used to hunting but we can at least feed him while we have the chance."

"Chase has been missing for nearly a week and you're worried about the cat."

I walked around the trailer again looking for a way in. I thought, being in cop mode, he'd be careful not to leave any ways in, but this was an old trailer out in the middle of nowhere, who would think to break into it?

The bathroom window was open a crack for ventilation. I looked at the window doubtfully. It was small. It was Winnie the Pooh small. I was worried about getting stuck halfway. If I could get my boobs through…. Another thing about it was it was high on the wall. A rickety, old patio cover stood next to the window. A rusty nail protruded from a post, probably to hang a lantern from. I dragged a bench over, climbed onto the bench, used the nail as my next foothold and pulled myself onto the roof of the patio cover. As soon as I put my weight on the roof it caved in and I fell through, landing on my back on the bench with a big *oof!*

"Is this where I should quit looking?" Bill asked. "Are you okay?"

"Keep a tab for me. One patio roof."

"Can I run home for the movie camera? Bev bought it to take movies of Kaitlyn but I think Rusty needs to see this."

"If this is the most trouble I get into, he'll be happy."

I climbed back up, only putting my weight on the crossbeam next to the bathroom window.

"Okay, you can quit looking now," I said. I pulled out my pocketknife and cut the screen. "Add one widow screen to my tab."

"Is this breaking and entering?" he asked.

"That's why you aren't looking. I doubt if Chase presses charges."

I pulled the screen aside and pushed on the sliding window. It looked even smaller from up here. I crouched on the support and leaned over using the window frame to support my hands. I leaned cautiously until my head went through the window. Okay, Bill, don't look. I had to turn my head sideways to get it through the window. This did not bode well for the rest of me. I pushed with my feet and looked into the bathroom. The window overlooked the shower, a tiny three foot square water closet. I backed out.

"Hands need to go first," I explained.

I put my hands over my head, turned my head sideways and pushed my way through. Hoo boy! Boobs next. I grabbed the far side of the shower and pulled and squirmed. My feet left the roof, sticking out the window. I would have laughed if I could have drawn breath. It took a lot of wriggling and pulling and I'm sure my feet were giving Bill an amusing show on the outside. Oh man, it was a squeeze. I thought I was stuck for a while. I couldn't move and I couldn't breathe. The top of the shower was slippery from having shampoo bottles left up there. The slippery top rim of the shower was my undoing, and my salvation. My hands slipped off with a jerk and my top half followed. With a pop I fell into the shower. I automatically splayed out my feet so I ended up hanging from the window by my ankles.

"Cassidy!" Bill called.

"When you hear a crash, it's okay!" I yelled back. "It's just me landing head first in the shower."

If you've never been in a three by three by seven foot box on your head, you don't know what you're missing. I let go with my feet and tumbled into the shower headfirst. I ended up on my shoulders with my feet up by the showerhead. When I relaxed they slid down the wall to the faucets. My foot caught on a faucet handle and water dribbled from the showerhead and up my back. I lucked out when I happened to lean a little too hard against my back and the door popped open depositing me in the tiny bathroom. I got up, brushed myself off and took stock of the situation. Considering I was hitting the trail with my father-in-law and there was no cover, I did the wise thing. I used Chase's bathroom. Then I turned off the water in the shower. After I flushed and put myself back together I went and opened the front door. The cat looked up from his bowl and growled at me. I took the bottle off his water bowl, filled it up and put it back. I put my hand out to pet him but the cat hissed and laid a row of scratches down my finger.

Bill followed me back in. Let's see, where would I put camping gear if I lived in a place like this? I headed for the bedroom closet. I opened the door and peered inside. No clothes in the closet. I looked around on the floor. There were piles of clothes on the floor. I looked for camouflage. I found a patch of khaki and pulled. A pair of cargo pants came forth. I tried them up to me.

"Cassidy, what are you doing?" Bill asked.

"I can't track in girly clothes and I only had girly clothes at the ranch."

"I'll take you to a store," he offered.

"There isn't one that will have everything Chase's house will. We need to hit the trail. Look for Chase's search pack. How much gear do you have?"

"A tent and sleeping bag. A change of clothes. Rusty said you'd take care of the rest."

"Are you armed?" I asked.

"Reluctantly."

"Should I be?"

"Yes," he said decisively.

"I don't want to."

"I know."

He disappeared into the front of the house. I found a shirt to go with the pants. I closed the door and put the dirty camouflage on. I had to tie the waist of the pants tight. Everything was very loose. I found a set for Bill, too. He was deep into the coat closet.

"Bingo," he said, then turned and looked at me. His expression changed from victory to disapproval. I tossed him the other set.

"No." he said.

"Look, if you're coming with me, you're not wearing slacks and a polo shirt. I know you're used to doing stuff like this in uniform but this isn't a spiffy mission. This is a crawling-through-the-desert-dirt mission. On a crawling-through-the-desert mission you have to be ready to become part of it."

"You think I can really fit into these?"

I held up the pants, no elastic waist. Hmm. "If they don't fit we can trade."

He took the clothes from me grumbling, "What did that damn fool son of mine get me into?" Then after a short time in the bedroom he called out, "Okay, trade pants." I laughed on the other side of the closed door. I cracked the door and handed Chase's pants through. He stuck the pair he had through to me and I put them on. Now I needed to find a belt. He stepped out with his belly hanging over very tight britches.

"I hope becoming part of the desert doesn't involve bending over," he said.

I went back to the coat closet and pulled out Chase's search pack. The fact that it was still here told me a lot. I pulled out a daypack. Everything search related was as camouflaged as possible.

"He wasn't expecting to be out more than a night or two," I reported. "Do you know if he has more packs than this? This is obviously his search pack. If he was expecting to be gone longer than a night or two he would have this pack with him."

I began emptying the pack making sure it held what we would need. I compared his stove to mine, shook the tank to make sure we had a few days' worth of gas. My old stove had more gas so I packed mine. The pack was very similar to mine in its contents. He kept it stocked and ready to go with the normal three days' worth of food. I didn't care for his choice of breakfasts, but I'd get by, and it would be fun watching Bill make do with a chunk of pemmican for the morning. When I took stock of the contents I looked further in the closet. Chase's house was like a search and rescue treasure trove. He had more gear in that closet than I ever imagined using on the trail. But perhaps his border patrol work had more use for two foot long flashlights and automatic weapons. There was a headlamp, rock climbing gear, a GPS. I pulled stuff out of that closet that I couldn't even identify. I packed the camp shovel, glad to have it. I opened the daypack. It held one more day's worth of food. I put it in the big pack.

"Okay," I said. "Tell me. Are you going to be one of those macho guys who has to carry the big pack?"

"What do you mean?"

"If you need to carry the big pack I need to pack them different than if you'll let me carry it. If it helps any, you'd actually be doing me a favor by taking the daypack. If I carry the frame pack the weight is on my hips instead of my back. I can move easier in the frame pack. It's what I'm used to. It's mainly a matter of appearances. The guys hate it if I appear to have a heavier pack. So if you're a macho guy who has to keep up appearances you can have the frame pack but, if you don't care, I'd rather have the bigger pack."

"Tell you what. You pack the gear and we'll see how it balances out."

"Deal."

I tied one sleeping bag to each pack. Then, since the daypack wasn't built to carry a tent and sleeping bag, I tied the tent to the frame pack. I put the food in the daypack, the stove in the frame pack.

"Shoot, water," I said and got up to find Chase's idea of a water supply. I examined the pack. Sure enough, the pack had a water reservoir built in. Leave it to Chase to have the latest gear. Still, there were two of us. We were out of luck as far as more water went. It wasn't like Chase to go to the store and buy water if he could just fill up a pack. We found a two liter bottle that once held Dr Pepper, rinsed it out and filled it with water. While I was in the kitchen I found a couple of forks and added them to the pack. It would be lousy packing the water like this but we needed a ready supply for cooking and drinking. I placed the bottle against the back of the daypack, filled up the reservoir on the frame pack and crossed my fingers that it would be enough. I made sure we had matches. Then I remembered there was a river to the south, if worse came to worse, so I searched for a water purifier and didn't find one. That was odd. I knew Chase had one. Well, we'd have to make do without. I hefted both packs. I tried on the frame pack. Though it was top heavy for me, it was lighter than I was used to.

"Try the daypack. We can shift some more stuff if you want to," I told him.

He put the daypack on and glared at me.

"Try the frame pack, you'll see it's easier even if it looks awkward."

He took off the daypack and put on the frame pack.

"Buckle the hip belt and settle it in place."

I dug into the closet one more time and pulled out an old compass. I had to keep track of directions. I didn't want to wander too far south. I tucked it into the pocket of Chase's baggy pants.

"I think we're set. Is there some place to get some real food on the way to the Otay?"

"Let's just go home," he said.

"You really want Bev to see you like that?"

He looked himself over and said, "You've got a point. Is it that bad?"

"She'll just wonder why you're wearing Chase's dirty clothes, but are you sure you want her to wonder that?"

"I don't even want to go in a restaurant in Chase's dirty clothes."

"No problem, we can just drive through."

"What do you usually drive through for?"

"A Western Bacon Cheeseburger and a slice of cheesecake."

"And that is?"

"Carl's Jr."

"You sure that's the way to start off a search?"

"I'll start without lunch. I just thought it was safer to conserve our resources."

"Right. Why do I feel like I'm ten again and I'm playing army games in the back yard?"

"It won't feel like a game when we get there. It'll be much too slow for a backyard army game. You know, tracking isn't a very interesting thing to watch. It means standing there while someone studies a patch of dirt. This is Chase we're tracking so it's going to be particularly slow."

"It's okay. I have faith in you. Even in these silly clothes, with borrowed gear. I know you can find him."

I sure wished I had that much faith in me. I wasn't at all sure I could find Chase this time, though I was proud of the way I found him last time. That time it *had* been army games. Or rather, a friendly match of wits between the two of us. I hoped it would be as easy now as it had been then. Then I sighed, it hadn't been easy then.

We threw the gear into the back of the Vue, and Bill headed south. We passed a few fast food places. I watched them disappear hoping he wasn't set on Carl's Jr. I'd settle for anything that wasn't backpacker food. A convenience store sandwich. A frozen burrito left on the dash to warm. Anything.

"Bill? Just stop at the next place," I requested.

"Why? Are you hungry?"

"Not particularly. I'm just worried about running out of town and not getting anything. I eat so much backpacker food that anything sounds better. AM PM, Harry's Liquor Store, anything."

He grinned Rusty's lopsided grin at me.

"Don't worry. I'll stop."

I quit watching out the window for the last chance saloon and trusted Bill. The city thinned away and was replaced with rolling hills and scrub. The rolling hills gave way to some of the driest desert I'd ever seen. I'd eaten cactus for lunch once or twice. I'd rather have a bacon cheeseburger, with crispy hot fries and cheesecake. If I couldn't have cheesecake, then maybe a milkshake. Sigh, I was making myself hungry just thinking about it.

"Where are we?" I asked after more desert had gone by than city.

"Highway ninety-four."

"How far is it?"

"To lunch, or to Chase's car?"

"Either."

"Five miles to lunch. I don't know how far to Chase's car."

"Okay I can live with that."

"It's not far off the ninety-four," he said. "The border can't be twenty miles away. We're going around the east side of the wilderness area. You didn't have your gear. You flew into Gillespie Field alone. Is everything okay?"

"Yes! Everything is fine. I've gone a month without getting into trouble. Katie is crawling and coming close to saying her first word. She's still a pickpocket. You'll see them both when this is all over."

"What will I see?" he asked. "What'll I see in my son's eyes? Will it be quiet relief? How about pure joy? Please don't make it fear. Sometimes I wish his eyes weren't windows to his heart."

"Me, too. How about we track Chase into the desert and get this done today."

"Sounds good to me," he replied.

"I wish it was that easy."

"Me too."

"We can always hope."

"Is this okay?" he said motioning to a junky looking road kill café.

"Um, yeah, I guess, no drive through."

"I don't think they care what we look like here."

"This reminds me of the first place Rusty took me to. It wasn't anything like this. It was a typical pizza place. We eat there every once in a while now. But I'd just been car jacked. I still had glue on my wrists from duct tape. I'd slept on the floor and been roughed up. Rusty took me to Zeke's and acted like a perfect gentleman. He didn't seem to see the bruises, or the tape marks."

"He saw them," Bill said quietly.

"Well, it was nice of him not to point it out."

"He called me after that happened. He called me while you were still being held, too. He had to talk or he'd go straight back and bust in the door. I must have heard, 'Dad, how can I just sit here?' a dozen times. But he knew you had a plan. Something just told him to trust you. Afterwards he called back to let me know everything had gone according to plan. Then he asked me what he was going to do. You knocked his socks off. He called me every once in a while. First he said thigs like, 'she's just a kid. She's not ready.' He knew how old you were but in his eyes you were like a run away. He'd seen plenty of those. You needed somebody but you wouldn't accept anybody."

"I didn't know that. All I knew was he kept checking up on me. He made sure I was okay, made small talk. It took me a long time to come around. I was a widow trying to figure out what I was supposed to do with my life."

"You were a widow? At twenty-five?"

"Yeah, twenty-four. I was a little nuts when Rusty met me. If I hadn't learned so many survival tricks I would have died before he met me but something kept me going. And when he called I quit running for the mountains. I wanted to hear his voice, even though I felt guilty wanting to hear his voice. Rusty saved me from myself." I needed to change the subject so I said, "I want a big old greasy hamburger before we hit the trail and this looks like the place for it. Let's go."

He shot me a thought filled look and reached for the door handle.

Chapter 6

The place was just as rough inside as it was outside. The walls looked like unfinished lumber roughed up a bit with a hammer. There was a pool table and a dartboard and twenty types of beer on tap. A man behind the counter had on a stained, white apron. He seemed to be the only person in the place.

"Sit anywhere," he said. "You got plenty to choose from. You want the local news sit at the bar. You want me to shut up find a table."

Bill and I looked at each other.

"You know anything about an agent lost in the Otay?" Bill asked.

"He ain't lost. Chase don't get lost."

"Okay, I'm good at the bar," I said.

We sat down and Bill ordered Dos Equis. I ordered a Coke because it looked like iced tea might be dangerous there and there was no sign of a shake machine. The tea looked like it would have been made by setting a jar of water and a teabag out in the sun until they had an order for it. No thanks. I wasn't going to be the first one to drink from that old jar.

"If Chase didn't get lost, what do you think happened to him?" Bill asked.

"I think he had a deal gone bad," the man said.

"What kind of a deal?" Bill asked.

"Now that's for Chase to know, ain't it?"

"I don't know about that. If it'll help find him I think it would be wise to tell us."

"Why? What are you going to do about it? Go out there and find him?"

"Well... yeah," I answered.

"HA! HA, ha, ha, ha, oh that's a good one, little girl, that's a good one. Even Chase says there's only one person who can find him if'n he don't want to be found. Only one." The man bent over the bar and looked me in the eye. "And you're not it." He shifted to Bill. "And you're not it either."

"Who is then?" I asked. I was perfectly willing to call in this expert tracker if they would find Chase. I thought the guy was going to say some Indian's name. Elan's father or grandfather. Elan's great grandfather had taught Chase to track but the man said with an air of respect, "Trouble."

Bill's grin spread slowly until it stretched ear to ear. I had to give him credit. He didn't get the guy riled up. He didn't brag. He just wanted more information.

"Does this guy have a name? Lots of guys down in these parts are trouble."

"Doesn't live in these parts." His voice got low, like he was telling campfire stories meant to scare off the little kids. "But this tracker *can see the invisible*. He moves *like a ghost*. He's a *legend*. Anybody Chase speaks of like that becomes a legend right quickly. Chase is a bit of a legend himself. So if he says this Trouble can find him, then we're just waiting for Trouble to show himself. Somehow I doubt we ever meet this guy, now that Chase is gone. That'd be a pity."

"Did Chase come in here often?" Bill asked.

"No, not often, but over the years he's stopped in when he's in the area. He don't talk much but what he says, one just knows tween the lines."

"I know what you mean," I said. "So, how will you know this 'Trouble' when he shows up?"

"Why, he'll move like a ghost and I won't hear the door open or close and I'll only see him if'n he wants to be seen."

"O…kay."

"And of course he'd have to find Chase, or at least bring me the story of what happened to him, because this tracker can read the ground *like it was a newspaper*. He can tell you the day's events just like you was watching the news on TV."

"Right, I'll keep an eye out for him," I said. "Tell me, if Trouble were to walk in here without you seeing and he sat down at this bar and ordered something what would it be?"

"The house special," the guy said.

"What's the house special?"

"Road kill burger, just like always. It ain't really roadkill, it's buffalo, only it tastes a little different so people think it's roadkill."

"Okay, I'll have that," I said.

"Make it two," Bill said.

"Okay! Here goes!" the guy said and then he hit the play button on an ancient, grease covered tape player. We heard the screeching of tires, a light thump, then a screechy woman's voice said, "Oh! Yum! Fresh Meat! Greasy Joe, go bring that poor critter in!"

Bill shook his head and then took a long drink of beer.

"Do you ever drink?" he asked.

"Rarely. And never before I track. I want to be alert. And I don't go to bars because I attract felons and then Rusty has to arrest them. If we find Chase, can we come back and give this guy a little Trouble?"

"If you find Chase and manage to stay out of trouble doing it you can do anything you want."

"Deal."

"Think you can add a slice or two of bacon to that road kill burger?" I called out.

"Do I gotta go run over the pig first?" he asked.

"No, any old bacon will do."

"Right."

I was pleased when he set down a huge platter. The road kill burger filled one side of it and onion rings were stacked on the other half. I took two big onion rings and added them to my burger, then added a little barbecue sauce. Bill watched my actions with interest.

"I have to remind myself you're my little daughter-in-law. If I blink it's almost like I'm here with one of the guys."

"Maybe I'm reverting to my military days."

"You're Kaitlyn's mom. You're Rusty's wife."

"Bill, I don't care how you think of me. Even Rusty isn't sure how to think of me. I'm used to it."

"So, what's the plan?" he asked.

"You take me to my starting point. We strap on our packs. You follow me until we get to the end of the trail. If we get to the end of the trail and there's trouble, use that radio."

"That's it?"

"That's the plan I usually follow. Seems to work."

"Will you tell me about your work as we go?"

"Sure, I'm used to storytelling on the trail. If I stop suddenly, just have patience. I'll get back to you as soon as I figure out what I'm stuck on."

I pushed my plate away with half a road kill burger and a large pile of onion rings left. I was stuffed.

"You want to take that with you?" Greasy Joe asked.

"No, I better not. No fridge. Plus, it might attract critters."

"Where are you going?" Greasy Joe asked.

"I told you, we're going to find Chase. We're following him into the Otay Wilderness."

"You'll be back. You won't follow him further than you can throw a cow."

"We'll see."

"If you can find Chase I'll cook you another road kill burger for free."

"It's a deal. If I find Chase I'll be back and you won't see me come in and I'll just appear at this bar."

"You do that," he said.

Bill paid our bill and we got into the Vue again.

"That was fun," I said.

"He still doesn't believe you."

"That's good."

"You ready to hit the trail?"

"More than ready. I have two thousand calories to hike off."

"You have Chase's tall tale to live up to."

"I'm not blaming Chase unless you know something I don't. Chase isn't apt to loosen up with a drink or two is he?"

"Chase? No matter what, you have to read between the lines. If anything you have to connect more dots after he's been drinking."

"So, where did this tall tale about the mysterious Trouble come from?"

"Chase must have started it. Then I bet the locals blew it up. You can see the locals can chew on a story for a long time."

"Let's go see. Let's see if we can keep my reputation intact."

Chapter 7

He started the car and continued southeast until he came to an unmarked turnoff. It was a jostle moving from the pavement to the dirt road, then he pulled to a stop. We stared down the road. I was used to roads like this but this was new territory for the Vue.

"You got four wheel drive?" I asked.

"No, but we'll be fine. We'll take it slow."

Slow it was. A bulldozer would have gotten us there faster. It would have been fun to drive, too. But a bulldozer hadn't been over this road for years. The Vue was great on the highway, but this road was a challenge. Of course, I wasn't going to blame Bill, but it was possible he just didn't know how to drive on a rough road. He bumped straight over the washouts. He didn't approach obstacles at an angle to lessen the impact. I expected him to straddle a large bump and get hung up.

I enjoyed driving roads like this in my Jeep. They often led to places where animals didn't expect to see people. They led to good tracking. I hoped this one did, too. It took a lot of patience on my part to not backseat drive. I just sat back and rode it out just like I did in the airplane. Just don't pay attention, Cass, if there's smoke, bail out. When the car quits moving and the others get out it's time to get out, too. If we got stuck the walk wasn't that much farther.

A jackrabbit bounded down the road ahead of the Vue and I took that as a good sign. A land with active wildlife was a friendly land. It might be harsh and dry but it supported life.

When Bill pulled off the road and stopped I almost thought he was giving up. There was nothing in sight but desert. We'd managed to make it three miles closer to the Mexican border.

"If I throw a rock southwest, I'll hit the Otay," he said.

I looked out the window. Desert as far as the eye could see. Scrub. A few scrawny trees in the distance. Miles of aridity. This was a thirsty land, like nothing I'd ever hiked before. The water in my pack shriveled at the sight.

"How far to Chase's parking spot?"

He pulled the door handle and got out. I quickly followed. If this was our starting point I wanted him to stay off the tracks.

"Wait!" I said, "I need to look at the tracks without adding any new ones to the mix. Just point me in the right direction."

He pointed to the side of the road just ahead.

"Can I watch?" he asked, "I'm interested in how you do this. I've seen trackers work before, of course, but they tend to be a secretive bunch. Plus, I just want to see how your mind works."

"So now I am Demothi, too?" I asked.

"What?"

"I'm just kidding. Demothi is the Indians' name for Chase. It means 'talks while walking'. You want me to tell you what I see, *like I am reading the daily news*. I just think it's funny. I'll tell you what I see, mostly because you know Chase better. So if you have anything to add, by all means, speak up."

"Okay."

As we walked towards the parking spot I asked Bill, "I don't see any gun club. Start thinking about why Chase chose this spot when he planned on going to the gun club."

"I have no idea. Could be whatever brought him here, the story changed and he decided this spot held more promise."

"More promise for what?"

"Something brought him here. He didn't just suddenly get the urge to hike the Otay. If he did he'd have brought supplies. Plus if he was out here for recreational purposes we wouldn't have these hints of a motive behind it."

"I wish we had a map of the area. It would be helpful to know where we are and what might be out there."

"Well, we aren't exactly at the north end. We're in the far eastern part. The Otay Wilderness stretches for about ten miles west. The border is about two and a half miles south of us."

I walked the road watching for Baja Bug tracks. When I found a set of tracks that pulled well off the road I slowed down. It was plain that the Bug had been towed away a couple of days ago. Tracks from the searchers avoided the Bug, except for a quick inspection. The tow truck driver had reason to walk around the car so most of the sign had been destroyed. I pointed tracks out to Bill.

"See the boots? Only a couple venture into the Bug. Most mill around outside the perimeter. Those are the BORSTAR guys. This is the tow truck driver. He wasn't careful at all. He had no reason to be. BORSTAR got what they wanted from the scene. I usually count on the first couple of steps after a person leaves a vehicle. They tell me a lot. The first step is usually a good one, with plenty of weight in it. It tells a lot about the attitude of the person. If they just place their foot outside the door and come to a standing position they were calm. If they are rushed or nervous there will be a lot of dirt moved around. If they know where they are going the steps go that direction in a sure manner. If they don't the steps will stay in one spot for a while as they take in their options. This guy didn't leave me much to work with but hopefully we can make up for it when we find Chase's tracks. See this line?" I asked pointing, "I bet that's Chase. We'll know for sure as soon as we get away from the parking spot and pick up Chase's tracks."

"There's not much to it."

"Nope, the truck driver walked all over it. But it isn't the search team's boots and it isn't the truck driver's shoes, not enough tread. If Chase was going for stealth he wore his moccasins."

"In these rocks?"

"If you've grown up in them you learn how to walk, even over this rocky ground, without hurting your feet. I'm wearing *my* moccasins. There's a technique to it that becomes natural after a while."

"I can't even see them under Chase's pants."

"Picking up Chase's trail here shouldn't be too hard. The BORSTAR guys will start us out the easy way."

I walked a small circle around the parking spot until I found the footprints of three men heading away. Then I looked more carefully for the tracks they followed. While Chase was within view of his car he was only mildly careful, which meant he only hid his tracks unconsciously. Unconsciously hidden tracks were easier to track than what I knew he was capable of. Bill didn't really understand what I was doing.

"Why don't you just follow the search crew? It's a piece of cake."

"I'm not tracking them. I'm tracking Chase. They are easy to track but they don't tell me anything about Chase."

"But I don't see anything in Chase's trail."

"*You* don't. I'm soaking up all the hints I can."

"What are you getting off this trail?"

"Well, he's not worried about being spotted yet. He is just walking. The hints kind of build up in my subconscious as I go along. I don't know how to explain it. They get into my brain and work their way around. If something is important little facts from the trail will start niggling at me to stop and think. I know, it's weird. I've learned when to take them in and when to stop and listen to them."

"How do you draw facts out of sand?"

"First of all this isn't sand. If it was we'd have a much easier time of it. This is bad tracking ground. See all the little rocks? They support the foot so less of the ground gets the weight of the track. It's why you don't see a track. But I do. Partial tracks. See this line? It's the outer edge of Chase's moccasin. I sure hope the ground is easier to read when he starts thinking about his trail."

"This is his easy trail?"

"Yeah."

"I'm with Greasy Joe, there's no way. If BORSTAR gave up and this is the easy part..."

"Ah, but when we get to the hard part is when it gets interesting. That's when the puzzle begins. We're not giving up. There's always a next step, always. It might be subtle but it's there. All I have to do is find it."

Bill seemed to switch modes for a little while. There seemed to be many facets to his study of me. His main reason for coming out here was to keep me out of trouble. He knew I had a talent for it, but he'd never seen it at work. Breaking into Chase's house had helped a little in that department but the me who stood before him now seemed a whole different person. This Cassidy was level headed, not prone to chasing whims, focused. I think he was still reminding himself I was his daughter-in-law. And I think he thought we were on a wild goose chase. But we weren't. We were following very specific clues.

When we'd gone a hundred yards or so I decided we had plenty to draw from so we went back to the Vue and strapped into our packs. We stood there for a moment looking at the big pack versus the little pack and he finally nodded that I could have the big one if I really wanted it. Then he put on the daypack with a guilty look. I balanced the big pack on my small frame, pulled everything snug, shifted it until it settled onto my hips and jogged back to where I'd left off. Bill checked over the SUV making sure it was locked up and well off the road, then he headed out to catch up with me. He didn't need to worry about getting left behind. Tracking is a slow process and I was never out of sight on that flat, treeless land.

I dived into the trail and let the tracks talk to me as Bill asked me questions about tracking back home.

"My toughest track?" I asked when the topic came up, "There's no such thing as a toughest search. Any search that ends in a fatality is the toughest search. Any search that covers rocky ground is the toughest search. Any time it's a little kid, it's the toughest search. The fatalities hit me hard. Sometimes I have nightmares about them for weeks. It's not just the fact that the search ended in a death. It's that the tracks talk to me. When the person gets weak or scared it reflects in their tracks and it works its way into my mind. I begin to feel what my missing person is feeling and it can drive me to track without eating or drinking. Sometimes Landon has to remind me to eat and tell me when it's too dark to see because I become so engrossed in the trail I just keep on. Rocky searches are painstakingly slow and take a lot more patience, study and thinking. They drain me. When I track kids or women who don't know their way in the woods I am just driven. The guys can hardly keep up with me. It's a tense chase, more than a search. So this job is rarely easy even if the tracks are easy to follow. There's always something pushing me to do more than I think I can."

"Then why do it?"

"Because I can."

"Why not let the guys do it?"

"Sometimes I do. But if it takes a tracker. If time matters. If someone is in danger. I can't stay away."

"Like today?"

"Yeah, like today."

"You expect trouble?"

"Trouble expects me. Just the fact that I'm here tempts trouble. But… seriously, I don't think Chase would still be out here unless he ran into trouble."

"Yet you charge ahead."

"I wouldn't exactly call this charging ahead. We're not even walking and it's going to be slower when the trail gets tougher."

I could make my way track by track as far as the BORSTAR guys had. When they got stuck less than a mile from the car I began tracking them to see what they had tried. They had tried a familiar approach where they branched out looking for new leads. Two guys circled around left and right and the third guy zigzagged across what they thought the trail would do. They spent quite a bit of time looking for Chase's trail but it was gone. It was gone for me, too, but now it was time to put on my thinking cap, pull on Chase's moccasins and think like him. Then I needed some help from my old tracking mentor so I put myself, in Old Frank's boots too. I went back to the last track and studied it. Bill stood there arms crossed over his chest, head cocked to the side, wondering what I could possibly see there. I traced the visible part of the track so he could see it. I backed up and traced what could be seen of the previous track.

"This looks like the ball of his right foot. The curve is right for it if he's wearing his moccasins. It's only a line though. This other track looks like the outer edge of his left foot. It's straighter." I pictured Chase making the tracks. It seemed to be a fairly normal walk. He was light on his feet. I pictured the two tracks being laid and let my imagination fill in the third track. I looked at the spot I thought it would fall. Nothing. Not surprising. I looked to the right and left of where I thought it would fall. I got down on hands and knees and looked at it sideways. I still didn't see a track. But I saw a rock. And I saw a slight shifting. The ground was barely disturbed on one side of the rock. Just a couple of tiny cracks in the soil adjoining it. I pictured the two tracks being laid. I pictured the third track coming down on that rock, which way would the rock tip? Maybe. Maybe that was the next track. If that was the next track where would the fourth one be? I imagined Chase balanced on one foot on the rock the other foot moving forward, coming down… coming down… where? Not on the next rock. A plant grew over it. He might brush off some dry leaves. He might break a brittle branch. He wouldn't leave that clue behind. So the ground drew my attention this time. Again, I got down on hands and knees. About this time Rusty would be handing me gloves, but Rusty wasn't here. I could catch a slight indentation. I drew a line next to it and then stood up to see if the line followed a footprint shape. Three steps. If the whole track was like this I was in trouble. The tracks would fade before I could get to them. Even these relatively fresh ones barely existed. I explained my findings to Bill as I went. I wanted him to see how small sign could be. That all you had to do to see it was change your perspective both in mind-set and in angle. A little fine tuning and tiny things became more obvious.

"Is Chase hiding his tracks here?" Bill asked.

"I don't think so. This is just natural walking to Chase. When he really searches for ways to hide his footprints it gets tougher. Look at this. This is clever. He used an animal burrow to hide his toe print in. When he took his foot out he scraped the dirt so anybody else would simply think an animal had been digging there. If you look down in the hole just a bit you can see the toe print of his moccasin."

"What makes you look in places like ground squirrel holes for tracks?"

"I put myself in his shoes. What would I do if I was walking carefully this way? It helps a little that we think alike."

"So you would think to use a hole in the ground to hide a track in?"

"Anything can be used to hide a track. Look. See this stick? It hides the side of Chase's foot. He placed his weight so the line of the track would follow the line of the stick. If I move the stick, there it is."

"How can a man walk that way without thinking his way through? It would drive me nuts," Bill said.

"Not if you just had a knack for being sneaky and grew up that way," I answered. "Try tracking me. I'm not hiding my tracks. I'm only thinking about finding Chase's next footprint. You'll see, it comes pretty naturally with time."

An old yucca stalk hid three steps. The stalk was splintered from being stepped on. Most people wouldn't think about seeing a splintered stalk lying in the middle of the desert. They would think it was weathered. But it was splintered in just such a way that told me it had been walked along.

"I do believe you are living up to your reputation," Bill commented.

"We're just getting started. Are you bored yet?"

"Hardly. I'm taking notes. This is very educational as long as you keep talking. As soon as you stop talking it all gets invisible again."

"Just never lose the last track. If you can keep the last track you have something to go by to find the next one."

"You draw a line in the sand and call it a track. I know it means something to you. I can see which way it points."

I put an obvious track in the dirt. I traced about four inches of the ball of the foot.

"Can you see that shape as the ball of my foot?"

"Yeah."

I traced the side of it.

"So what part of the foot is that line?"

"I get the point. I know what you are doing I just don't have the track to go by."

"Then you will just have to trust me. But I don't go on to the next track unless I'm fairly certain."

The light was beginning to fade. A plane flight, a trailer raiding, lunch and a rough track had used up the day.

"See if you can find a good place to set up camp," I told Bill.

"What am I looking for?"

"Just a flat place with fewer rocks than you want to clear out of the way. We need a tent spot and a cooking spot. It doesn't have to be anything fancy."

I found the next few tracks while he looked around. There wasn't much more I could do that evening. Chase's tracks were hard enough to spot in the day time.

Bill found a spot, just a flat spot on a hill. He'd cleared two tent sized spots but I really didn't need a spot cleared for me. I had the bivouac sack, which was little bigger than a sleeping bag. I helped him set up his tent and then I tossed out the sack and unrolled the sleeping bag inside it.

"That's your tent? You'll freeze!"

"I'll be fine. My sleeping bag is rated down to minus five."

"You can't move in that thing."

"It's just for sleeping in. I don't need to move much to sleep. Have you ever been camping before?"

"Not since I was a kid and mostly in the back yard."

"Well, this is a little different. Have you ever eaten freeze dried backpacker food?"

"No."

"You're in for a treat," I said sarcastically. "You mean Rusty never went camping and hiking as a kid?"

"We rented a cabin a few times. We never roughed it like you're used to."

"He could've fooled me. He sure took to it when he went camping with me."

"It's amazing what a guy will do for love."

I scrounged in the pack and pulled out the foil pouches of backpacker food.

"This," I said holding up a couple of them. "Is your dinner. A typical serving is one pouch. We'll make do with two pouches per night. I can't eat a whole one. I only finish them off because we also have to pack out all trash, no matter what form it's in. It's easier to pack it out in your stomach than in the trash bag. So if you finish a pouch and you're still hungry let me know. I'll be glad to give you part of mine. So... choose your poison."

He chose Mesquite Grilled Beef and Rice. Wow, where did Chase buy his backpacker food? I was used to spaghetti and beef stroganoff. I read the labels. Sweet and Sour Pork. Chicken Fajitas with Spanish Rice. Chicken Parmesan. I was dining upscale on this search. I chose Sweet and Sour Pork just because it sounded so weird for a backpacker meal.

I dug out the old backpacker stove I'd found in the closet back home. I hadn't used this stove since I was about seventeen. I had checked it for gas. We should be in good shape. Should be. Yeah right. I looked it over verifying it worked like my current stove and like most backpacker stoves the world over. I put my finger over the little hole and began pumping it up. Bill wandered over to his home away from home.

"This is nice," he said. "If I don't freeze this'll be fun."

Chapter 8

I pumped and pumped and it never felt stiffer like it should have. Usually it took about ten pumps and I could feel the pressure building. Oh well, if it's not pumped up enough it'll just fizzle out, I thought.

"What is this stuff?" Bill asked as I struck a match.

"What…" FOOM! "Stuff?" I asked.

Flames engulfed the stove followed a trail of gas to the daypack and before we knew it the camp was on fire. NO!

I whipped off my coat and smothered the flames around the stove then I followed the little trail of flames stomping them out as I went. I flipped the daypack over and tackled the flame free side smothering those flames as well. Bill hopped around camp stomping out little spots of fire. It only took a few minutes to put out the fire and we both stood back in shocked silence. I picked up my coat. It was ruined. The lining was melted and the insulation was either melted or falling out in clumps. The stove was useless. The daypack had a gaping hole in the front, making it worthless as well. Two backpacker meals were now shrink wrapped in the melted foil pouches.

"What do you think? Are they still edible?" I asked.

"It depends on who you ask and how hungry we are."

"I agree, we better not discard them. We might need them scorched or not. Did the plastic water bottle survive?"

"Looks like it. I think you tackled the pack just in time. Are you all right?"

"Yeah, but I don't know why. I'm just glad the fire didn't get away from us! This kind of puts a damper on our search. We're down to one pack. Our stove is useless. We might be shorter on food and my coat is only good for a shop rag. Not even that. It sheds too much for a shop rag. I've never had to prepare backpacker meals with cold water. I sure hope it works."

It worked with disappointing results. It took longer for the food to rehydrate and even when it was edible it was cold. We fished out bites from the foil pouches and ate only because it was time. The rest of the search would be similar.

"You think we ought to hike out and resupply?" Bill asked.

"No, I'm on Chase's trail and I'm sticking to it. If we take time out we'll lose the trail. If you want to resupply you have two options. You can hike out and leave me with the radio. Or you can call Monty for a drop. If it was just me I'd keep going with what I've got. I've made do before. It's just part of having the trouble gene. But if you want to go back, I think you can still find the car."

"No. Rusty warned me you'd give me the slip if you had half a chance."

"I wouldn't leave you in the middle of the wilderness," I said. Now that I know you don't know what you're doing out here. "I'm not going to ask for a drop unless we truly need it. I'll eat cactus before I'll call for a drop."

"Not in the wilderness area."

"Shoot. Is everything protected?"

"Probably even the rocks."

"So we call for a drop before we eat cactus."

"What are you going to do without a coat?"

"Be cold. Don't worry, there's ways to stay warm. It's been comfortable during the day. It's only nights that get cold. I'll get by. It's just a pain that we now have to haul around all this useless stuff. There should be a rule that you only have to pack things you can use."

I placed my stove in the burned up pack, then I rolled up my useless coat and stuffed it in the useless pack. The coat plugged the hole enough to keep the contents inside. We could still strap a sleeping bag to the underside of it. I figured we'd get by okay.

It was getting really dark now. The stars pierced the sky. Each tiny light was crisp and as I watched the sky filled with more stars than I had ever seen before.

"Are you sure you'll be okay in that little sack?"

"Oh yeah," I replied. "I think it's better than a tent. I get to watch the stars."

He smiled in the dark. "You really like this, don't you?"

"Yeah, I do. I like the open free feeling of being on the trail. I like the new sights, the night sounds, the breeze and the feeling of the sun when I hike. I like the bite of cold when I first get up in the morning and the warmth of a cup of hot chocolate. Guess I'll miss out on that tomorrow, with no stove. When I track I get up at first light. We can't cook so we can hit the trail early. Have you ever had pemmican?"

"No, well, I've had beef jerky."

"This is different. Chase made it. It's got meat and berries in it. It's breakfast. It's handy because you can eat it on the trail."

"Something tells me these pants might fit by the time we get out of here."

When it got dark it also got cold. I slipped into my sleeping bag and sat up talking to Bill but he eventually got tired of pacing the camp and went to his tent. I listened to the night sounds and watched the stars until I got drowsy, then I zipped the sack closed and went to sleep.

We woke up to a bitter cold morning. Even Bill was stamping around trying to stay warm. There was no frost on the ground but that was just because the desert was too dry for frost to form.

I handed Bill a chunk of pemmican, and he looked at it doubtfully.

"Go ahead," I told him. "There's more to it than it looks. You'll like it. That chunk will last you an hour and you'll feel like you've eaten."

He munched on it tentatively. We quickly broke camp and hit the trail but hitting the trail didn't help much in the warmth department. Tracking Chase was such slow work we never could warm ourselves through activity. We ended up freezing until the sun was well up in the sky. Every fifteen minutes or so Bill offered me his coat and I refused it. I learned on survival trips to just tune out the cold.

Chase's trail was just as hard to read as it had been the day before. I was thankful for the still night. The desert is notorious for wind and a bad windstorm would have wiped out the trail completely. The sign led me down into a little fold in the flatness and I noticed the angle of Chase's footprints changed. He was walking differently somehow. I slowed down even more taking careful note of the subtle differences from the day before. His weight was centered on his toes more, indicating he was crouched over. Was he trying to stay out of sight of something? The fact that he headed for low ground indicated he was trying to lay low and not present a profile. The walking was much easier on the firm ground above so the choice of lower ground was noteworthy. He crouched even lower, the ball of the foot taking most of the weight. Weight forward and…to the right?…or left? I examined the stance. I examined the surrounding countryside wondering what Chase might have seen. Nothing stood out.

The day wore on painfully slowly. The tracking was tedious, hands and knees work. I've heard of injured people crawling through the desert for help. But I've never heard of anybody crawling through the desert studying the lay of the sand there, except a few experienced trackers. To me it was natural. If you can't see the tracks from above, maybe you can see them from the side. Looking from the side brought out subtle differences in the height of the dirt. Shadows were different from that perspective. It must have looked awfully peculiar to Bill but it was the only way to get an eye on Chase's tracks.

Patches of hard pack were common. In some cases I could count on Chase using it and catch up with him on the other side. Other patches were so broad he could have gone any direction once he entered it so I had to follow track to track, on hands and knees, looking for slight indentations, or little scratches from pebbles. Chase left very little evidence of his passing.

Suddenly the tracks turned and I found a place where Chase had stopped and lain down on the slope of a low rise. I bent down to get an idea of what he was seeing.

I removed my pack quickly and instructed Bill to wait there. Then I jogged up the slight rise that had caught my eye when I'd bent down. It was perhaps a hundred yards away. I watched the ground as I went and after I topped the rise I saw tracks. Not Chase's tracks. This was different. These people had no inkling that their tracks told a story. They went about their business here leaving plenty of evidence of what they had been doing. I celebrated this breakthrough silently and bent to the task at hand. This was going to take some deciphering. I walked the perimeter of the area trying to figure out what these people had been doing. At first glance it appeared three people had been beamed down from a UFO to get sick together. What? I guess I might be sick after a trip in a UFO, too. Once I figured out what happened I was even more puzzled. Three people, one single man, and a couple had walked to the area, met there, sat in a circle and gotten sick. Violently sick. I followed each trail into the scrub. The evidence was clear, and it was not a pretty picture.

Now, I know I grew up in a cave. Growing up on the ranch was a very sheltered life. My school was filled with a bunch of farm, ranch and small town kids. We had a few delinquents but it wasn't cool to be one of them. So I was totally stumped when I came on this site. I jogged back to where Bill waited.

"Put the pack down and come look at this."

"Will I see anything?" he asked.

"Nothing you want to see. But I need your cop experience."

"Uh oh."

He followed me over to the area and I began just reading the ground to him.

"Three people. They came from the north. A single man." I pointed out the man's tracks. "And a couple. Here's the woman's tracks. They met here and then sat in a circle. You can see that they shifted around, like they were uncomfortable sitting on the hard ground, so they spent some time here. Then one by one they ran off into the desert and got violently ill."

Bill folded his arms over his chest and rocked back on his heels, then followed me to the sun-dried splats on the ground. He stared at the ground, knelt down to examine the mess. I couldn't tell if he was frowning or smiling.

"Well, I'm glad you don't know what you are seeing. If you'd experienced it you'd know right away," he said.

"Okay, spill. Um, I mean, don't. Educate me on this practice of walking miles into the desert just for a cookie tossing party."

"Peyote."

"You'll have to educate me a bit further."

"It's a little cactus."

"I thought you said we couldn't eat the cactus out here."

"They didn't get it out here and believe me, it wouldn't be much in the way of nourishment."

"So, why here?"

"Think of it kind of like seeking out the old man on the mountain."

I know I had a ditzy blonde look right about then. I wasn't connecting the dots.

"The old man in the desert has... cactus?"

"What else would the old man in the desert have?" he asked, amused. I think he was enjoying one-upping me for once on this trip.

"Okay, I guess I can accept that. Three people walk four miles into the desert to eat cactus and get sick. Somehow that doesn't appeal to me, as much as I enjoy a nice hike I don't think I'd do it to get sick."

"In some circles it is a cheap recreational drug. In others it takes on a more spiritual nature. The drug induces a deep introspective state. I haven't taken the time to find out if anybody has actually learned the meaning of life from ingesting peyote. Somehow I doubt it."

"So, Chase came out here to catch some druggies?"

"He wouldn't have tried that alone. He probably heard some rumors and he came to observe, maybe build a case. It's not something we'd encourage him to do."

"Not even Slick?"

Bill paused with a disgusted look. "I wouldn't put anything past Slick," he said.

"Slick knows more than you think. He called to get me down here. He wouldn't have called without a very specific reason."

"Like I said, I wouldn't put anything past Slick."

"So," I said summarizing our findings. "We have three people who think that by coming out to the middle of nowhere they can gain some insight about the meaning of life. And they choose to eat cactus to do it. And Chase came out here to watch them do it and build a case?"

"I'm ninety-nine percent sure about the peyote. We'll have to go back and track Chase to find out what he was really doing out here."

"Uh huh. Right. So let's do it."

I could feel Bill laughing at me as he followed me back to the packs.

"It's hard to tell how long Chase laid here," I said. "He's used to staying still in one spot for long periods of time. It could have been minutes or hours. How long does a peyote party last?"

"It doesn't take long to ingest it. Most people can't keep the stuff down long. It's just plain disgusting. It's tough and slimy and stinks. But the effects can last most of a day."

"So it's possible Chase didn't go very far for a while."

My eye was naturally drawn to the ground. I still had a search on my hands. I followed Chase's tracks to the end of the sandy stretch and then buckled down for more tough tracking. Chase was being very careful. He watched the group from different angels and on the far side of the group he found a hidden spot and made a camp. Camp to Chase is different from most people's idea of a camp. Since it was winter I thought he at least had a bivouac sack like mine. But he might not. One thing about winter in the desert is that most of the critters you need to worry about are holed up under a rock: rattlesnakes, scorpions. They don't like the cold. So it was possible Chase just tossed out his sleeping bag. He might have had a stove. Or he might have gotten by on jerky, trail mix and pemmican. To me his camp just looked like a person sized flat spot. He kept tabs on the group, eventually making a complete circle about them and getting in quite close when the land made it possible to close in without being seen. When the group split up and left he let them get ahead and then followed the single man.

"Rusty says you profile as you track. Tell me about this guy."

"I assume you mean the guy that isn't Chase."

"Yeah."

"If I concentrate on him I'm likely to lose Chase."

"Tell me what you think so far."

"He's five-six, five-five. He weighs about a hundred fifty pounds. He's got a short stride. He's not rolling in dough. His shoes are very worn. His pants are too long. He's used to walking in the desert. He smokes. He's right handed."

"You got all that out of tracking Chase?"

"The two trails are side by side."

"How did you know the guy was a smoker?"

"By the cigarette butts he tosses to his left. That's also what tells me the guy is right handed. If he drops the butts he drops them on the right but if he tosses them he tosses them to the left. Seems to fit a right handed man. He's lived in the area all his life. He's not particularly neat. He's a desert rat."

"Mexican? Indian? White?"

"I'm guessing Mexican. He doesn't walk like the people I've tracked with Indian influence. If he's Caucasian he's short. It just doesn't seem to match up for him to be a white guy."

Chase followed the guy north and into some hills until he came to a road. A road? Well, that explained how a group of three people seemed to magically appear in the middle of the desert.

"I thought there were no cars allowed in here," I said.

"Guess we'll see. Which way did Chase go?"

"He stopped here for a while. Then he found the tracks of a vehicle of some kind. Other cars have covered his tracks and the tracks of the car he's following. I imagine he's trying to sort through his options. He knows there's no use following this car."

"It's probably a truck or jeep of some kind. The border patrol that uses this road would drive Jeeps. What do you say we radio in and get the twenty of one of those Jeeps and see if we can get a lift back to our car?" Bill suggested.

"You can if you want. I haven't lost Chase yet."

"Cassidy, this is a road. He probably got picked up."

"Something happened. If he got a lift they would have taken him to his car. He never got there. That means he's either out there or something happened to him. I'm staying on this trail as long as I can. Whatever his last contact was with the ground, I'm going to see it."

I followed Chase's tracks down the road to the east. At first the tracks disappeared beneath the tire tracks of the border patrol but then they wandered closer to the side of the road. Chase seemed to be bummed out. His tracks were careless, very unlike Chase. For some reason this disturbed me. It made him seem particularly vulnerable, more like an old man and less like a retired cop. Bill saw the change in me, but he didn't say anything. Observing the shift in Chase's mood made me more determined than ever to find him. I had to see him be Chase again. I'd drop in this desert and Bill would call for a pickup before I'd give up. I kicked rocks as I tracked silently.

Reading the tracks, the story unfolded in my mind: Chase walked dejectedly down the narrow margin between the road and the little heap of dirt that marked the drop off down the hill. The road had gone up hill until there was a drop off to my right. The desert was greener here, more scrub, and occasional bushes struggling to gain tree status. The fold in the land caught precious water and the plants took advantage of it. The road evened out and I was taken by surprise when Chase's tracks suddenly stopped in a defensive posture. I marked the spot, though I knew I could find it again. I took off my pack and jogged up the road, knowing I'd see nothing that would tell me what was going on. The tracks on the road looked normal. Something niggled at my mind that someone had been driving awfully fast for a road like this but I argued with myself that the border patrol knew this road inside out. If anybody would drive fast on this road it would be them. Shoot, I felt so wishy-washy. I was letting Chase's trail get to me, so I went back to Chase's tracks.

"What is it Cassidy?"

"Chase saw something. Stand with your feet like this," I said drawing lines in the dirt, "and you'll recognize it right away. Weight forward."

He nodded recognition. I continued reading the tracks carefully. The defensive posture, then a few carefully placed footprints leading off the road. A crouching in the brush. He had waited there for several minutes letting the vehicle get past the next bend and out of sight. Then he climbed back up onto the road. He continued east but he kept an ear open and turned to watch his back frequently, and with good reason.

I was walking quickly down the road keeping tabs on Chase, cataloging intricacies, adding them to the jumble and then I was brought up short. There was a wild scramble for cover where Chase lost his footing and tumbled down the hillside, but that wasn't what brought me up short. What really caught my attention was a small nick in the bark of a tree. It was a scrubby old thing hanging on from one rare rain to the next. I sat underneath the tree wishing I had my own insight into the workings of this place.

"Good, I could use a rest," Bill said.

"Rest then. I can't. I need to corral my thoughts."

"Can you corral them out loud?"

"We can't hope to catch up to Chase if they caught him."

"You need to fill me in a little."

So I repeated the past half hour's tracking to him.

"Maybe he's just being overly cautious. You know Chase," Bill said.

"He's not being overly cautious. He needs to watch his tail now, which means the tracking is going to get really tough."

I took out the little 9mm Bill had loaned to me. I verified that it was much like my own 9mm back home. Bill didn't like to see me check my weapon. He knew what kind of a mindset triggered such an action.

"I sure hope I don't have to use this," I said. I got up and took a closer look at the nick in the tree. "What do you think?"

He hadn't noticed the nick but he'd seen bullet holes in various surfaces in his years on the force.

As we stood there looking over the scene a green and white border patrol jeep drove up and pulled to a stop.

"Bill Michaels?" the agent said through a rolled down window. "What the hell are you doing way out here?"

"Taz." Bill responded, "We're looking for Chase."

"We?" Taz squinted out the window and then got out. He walked up with a long whistle and tipped his cap to me. "Damn, Bill, you robbed the cradle this time."

Bill smiled. "This is my daughter-in-law, Cassidy. Cass, this is Tazio Navarro."

"Good to meet you," I said holding out my hand.

"Ma'am," Tazio said. "You followed this crazy man out into the middle of the desert? What kind of spin did he put on it? This'll be a fun camping trip, you'll see."

"Actually, it was my idea to look for Chase. Bill's along to stop me from doing something dangerous. But so far we've only followed Chase through the desert. What kind of weapons do these guys carry out here?"

"What kind of a question is that for a girl like you to be asking?"

"It might be useful to know when we catch up to him," I said. "This shot was aimed at Chase. I'm guessing some small rifle. Whatever it was it sent Chase diving off this road for cover."

"Cassidy's a tracker," Bill explained.

"You'll never find Chase by tracking him. If he's on the run…"

"We've tracked him this far. I aim to follow him until he quits leaving tracks."

"Don't knock it," Bill said. "We've followed him all afternoon yesterday and half of today. It's been slow and it's been mind-numbingly tedious but we're still plugging away at it."

"So, which one did you marry?" Taz asked. "Not Cody. You're too calm and level headed to be Cody's girl. Tony? You're not old enough to be Rusty's wife. He's what? Over thirty now?"

I almost laughed when Bill slipped into grandpa mode.

"She's Rusty's. They have a baby girl. You want to see her picture? She's cute as the dickens."

He pulled out his wallet and presented Taz with a picture of Katie when she was just old enough to sit up by herself.

"She's a cutie," he said. "Why is there a watch in the picture?"

Huh? I looked at the picture. Sure enough, dropped beside her in the picture was a silver watch. Bill and I looked at each other.

"Umm, she's got a talent for stripping people of their possessions. She'll outgrow it. I hope. Watches and cell phones are her favorites," I confessed.

"Her parents are both cops of one kind or another and they have a pickpocket kid," Bill said.

"You wouldn't happen to have a rope in that Jeep, would you?" I asked, "We need a one way ticket to the bottom of this hill."

"I thought Bill was the crazy one. Yeah, I've got a rope." Then addressing Bill, "Are you sure I should let her use it?"

"If you don't, she'll just take on the hill without it," he answered.

"Wait'll I tell Paco a woman is on Chase's trail. Watch, I bet he drives out just to give you a hard time. He gave up on Chase the first day. Paco's good. He's who we call on first. If it's important and Paco and Gunnar can't handle it, then we call in Chase. Between Paco and Gunnar they managed to track

Chase maybe a mile. Paco's not going to like a woman upstaging him."

"He'll get over it," Bill said. "Tell him Trouble's on the case. If he doesn't know who Trouble is have him go talk to Greasy Joe."

Navarro didn't admit one way or the other about knowing who Trouble was, but he nodded gravely and got out his rope. I made my way down the hill first, following in the wake of Chase's fall. It took a while for me to make it to the bottom because Chase's fall didn't take him far, then he stopped to compose himself before he angled his way down. He was still in a hurry and the difficulty of the incline made his tracks easy to follow. I had to take his route, dragging the rope along with me. When I ran out of rope I let the end go slack. After about fifteen minutes Bill joined me. He followed the rope down until I called to him from the side, then he, too, angled to the side.

"Thanks, Taz!" he called up.

"No problemo," Taz called down. "Two days?"

"Yeah."

"Two days what?" I asked.

"Until we run out of provisions."

"Why did you tell him that?"

"I figured we'd be out by then."

"Maybe. Maybe we'll call for a drop. Sending Navarro to Greasy Joe was like tossing gas on a fire. Every little town on the 94 is going to be waiting for the outcome of this search."

"Plus a few in Mexico."

"One reason I wanted to come out here alone was so I could lay low. Now, my presence will be announced ahead of me. You of all people should know it's easier to find Chase quietly."

"I also know these people tend to be superstitious. If they think of Trouble the way Greasy Joe does they will be nervous. And they won't be expecting trouble to come in the form of a young woman. It may work to your advantage."

Chase kept up a steady pace until he was forced to stop. The further he went the more his tracks faded but when he stopped I had a new puzzle to piece together. Usually I come onto a resting spot with relief. As long as my missing person was resting it gave me time to catch up. But this time I wasn't pleased.

"Did you bring an evidence bag?" I asked Bill.

"I'm a concerned dad, not a cop," he answered.

"Couldn't you be a little of both?"

I took off the pack and rummaged through it coming up with an empty backpacker food pouch. I got out the camp shovel and scooped up the blood soaked soil next to Chase's resting spot. Bill watched grimly. Chase wasn't just a fellow retired cop to him. Chase and Bill had served on the same force for twenty years or more and Chase had remained a family friend in the following years. He knew Chase's tracking took him to dangerous dealings but so far Chase had managed to save his skin and work his way out of any fix he got in. I had a feeling Chase's reputation spread quietly, so quietly that Bill had only an inkling of Chase's real activities.

It was important that I take my time at this site. It was possible to tell from the sign just how seriously Chase had been hit.

The radio crackled, "Unit fourteen to Trouble."

Bill and I looked at each other. "You get it," I told him. "We don't want everybody up and down the border to know Trouble is a woman."

"Trouble here," Bill said.

"I've got casings up here."

"Ten-four, we're on it. How many?"

"One at the first location. Three eighth of a mile down the road. Nine millimeter. Not much use from this distance."

"Useful enough."

There was a long pause. He got the information he needed. That was one thing I always marveled at in radio communication. The less said the more information got through.

"Unit fourteen out."

As the guys were going through this short conversation I was studying the ground. Chase was going along pretty strong. No blood on the ground. He flopped down in a small clearing that was sheltered from the road above. He sat feet outstretched, resting at first, then he had squirmed around, I assumed trying to get a look at the site where he'd been shot. He twisted to his left. No sign of him dropping his drawers. All the blood came from his left. I saw no signs of tucking in or pulling his shirt off. Maybe he lucked out and it was a superficial wound. As I pictured the actions that went with the sign I concluded he'd been shot in the left arm. I hoped it was his arm. The other option was his head. If he was off balance his head could have dripped that direction. Head wounds did tend to bleed a lot. I was betting on the arm though. It gave me more hope. I folded over the top of the bag and stuffed it into the bottom of the burned daypack.

"I'm guessing the shot got him in the upper arm. Let's hope it's not serious. Have you ever been shot?" I asked.

"I've been shot at. I've had a few close calls. Never been shot."

"I'm glad."

There was that pause and I knew he knew.

"You going to tell me about it?" he asked.

"Maybe. After this is all over. Rusty was there if you don't get it from me." Another pause. "Okay, I'll tell you on the way home. I don't want Rusty to have to tell it."

"Why won't you tell me now?"

"I think you can figure that out for yourself." The truth was I didn't want Bill to know how much I was willing to risk.

When Chase got his bleeding under control he set off again quickly. He continued to angle downhill until he came to the bottom and followed a wash to the east. He didn't step into the sand in the bottom. He followed off to the side but I got the feeling he was making a run for the Bug. At least I hoped he was making a run for the Bug. It had been parked just a few miles away. We could be getting close. He hadn't made it back to his car.

Oh, man, if I'd known what really happened at that point I would have thrown in the towel. As it was, I didn't. I just tracked carefully and hopefully, track to track to hidden track. I kept an eye out for bloodstains. They were rare. Each spot made my heart skip a beat and I had to console myself. It's just a drop, Cass, focus.

Chase's wound troubled him. His steps felt tense and pained. I don't know how footprints tell me the feelings behind them. It just leaches into my brain and I find myself empathizing with the person I am tracking. I had to constantly slow myself down because my mind became tense and hurried just like I imagined Chase feeling.

Bill dropped behind and when he caught up he pressed some jerky into my hand. I'd forgotten to eat again. In a way, I'd rather not eat. I'd rather save the provisions, but I also knew I was likely as not to track until I dropped. I chewed without thinking about what was going into my mouth. What was this? Pemmican? Jerky? It didn't matter.

The closer to the Bug I got the antsier I became. Come on Chase, you can do it. Whatever happened between here and the Bug, you can handle it. Show me where to look. I felt like a kid wondering if the kryptonite would really kill Superman. Nothing could kill Chase. Not if I could help it. And at that moment I knew what I was putting Patrick through with each bout of trouble that came my way. Nothing could kill Aunt Cassidy. Aunt Cassidy was sneaky, she was a survivor. It made me feel oddly defiant and fragile at the same time.

The wash turned south and Chase started south but when a gap in the hills led west he followed the cut. When he turned west his caution tripled. At first I worried. How would I follow Chase through this place? He was hard to read all along but suddenly his tracks disappeared. We were so close! Chase! Don't do this to me.

I had to sit down again. I took off the pack, paced in a circle for a few laps and sat down putting my head down on my knees.

"You okay?" Bill asked. "You've hardly eaten today."

"I'm okay. I'm just frazzled. I need to clear my mind so I can concentrate on the next part of the trail. It's going to be slow. The next quarter mile is going to take longer than the track from the road."

"Let's just hike back to the car. We know he was headed there."

"Problem is he never got there. I need to know what happened and I need to get a feel for what shape he's in."

He stood there thumbs hooked into his too tight camouflage pant pockets.

"We're not going to find him, are we?"

"I don't think so," I choked out. "Judging by his trail he should have reached the Bug no problem."

Bill sat down, too. We were both about as low as can be. Our grasp on a very dear friend was slipping away. We were both willing to do anything to get him back, yet the possibility of that happening was getting slimmer and slimmer. I had to guard my feelings very carefully. I was sitting there, walls up, bricks carefully stacked, mortared together, with nice clean caps on top. Plum-lined. They weren't leaning. Eight foot walls against the unknown. And then Bill leaned forward.

"Cassidy, kid, come here, you don't have to take it all on yourself. We're in this together," Bill said and he held out an arm. I couldn't move. If I moved I'd cry. "It's okay. I'd rather see you be the girl Rusty would have married than this GI Joe/Skipper tracker woman. Come here. I'm so thankful to see that heart of yours. I knew it was there behind all the stubborn determination."

I crawled through the desert sand until I was beside him and sat with him. He put an arm around me. The tears came quietly.

"We'll give it our all," I cried. "We'll stay on this trail until… until his feet aren't touching the ground any more. We've done more than BORSTAR ever thought we could."

"You did. You did more than BORSTAR thought *anybody* could. You would have done it without me."

"I was shot because I wouldn't give up on a search that I knew was swiftly turning into a trap. A man was in trouble. I knew he was in trouble and I followed his trail until I was just inside the trap and then they sprang it. Rusty and the rest of the team were closing in when it happened. Rusty must have seen it happen from a distance. I was shot in the side but they had to finish bringing the guy in before anybody could help me. It was scary for Rusty. When I heard the officer-down code I told Victor to go help. I didn't even know they were talking about me," I rambled on about the shooting because it was easier than thinking about Chase's fate. "I ended up in a hospital in LA but the wound wasn't serious. It was just very tense until surgery was over. I was out cold so it was rougher on Rusty."

"I wish we'd known."

"We weren't married yet. When these things happen it's the first few days that are tense. We're so busy trying to come to grips with the present. We don't mean to leave you out. A couple of times I didn't think I'd make it back. I was lost in limbo. Bill, I don't know how many more of these rough spots I can take. I've fought my way back from near death too many times. A person can only fight so many battles before they lose one. I'm not afraid. But sometimes I get so tired thinking of fighting for the rest of my life. I can't do it. I want to hold my baby. Teach her to say daddy. I want to be there when she learns to walk. I want to give Rusty a son. And I really want to find Chase. Chase can't be gone. I lost Old Frank. I can't lose Chase, too. Just knowing he's down here, keeping tabs on us, gives me comfort. He might be ornery. He might look scary to little kids, but he's got a heart. Patrick is convinced nothing can kill Chase, and I know it's not true. I wish I could think so, too."

"It's okay. Even if we don't find him. We'll have tried. He couldn't ask for more."

"Yes, he could. There's always something more. Until we find him, there's always something more."

"Don't worry about that yet. One step at a time."

We sat quietly for a while. I felt like I wasn't holding up my part of the comforting. After all he had a friend in trouble, too. But maybe helping me helped him, too.

"Are you hungry?" I asked.

"Sort of. I've been semi-hungry since we hit the trail but I just decided this was a forced diet."

"I know how you feel. I'm like that most of the time on the trail. We're close to the car, you might as well eat. We'll be restocking soon."

"Restocking?"

"Yeah, we'll come up with something to keep us going."

I know he was hoping to go home when we reached the Bug. Maybe we would. I hoped not. If we went home it meant the end to our search... and the end of Chase.

I couldn't quit.

When we rose to finish the track neither one of us was really ready for it. Bill took another piece of jerky, tore off pieces and ate as he walked. I went back to the last known track and got down on hands and knees puzzling together this last little bit of our search. If I'd known how close we were to the car I would have lost it right there. The little gap in the hills only separated us from the road for a third of a mile. I could look down the gap and the other end of it was where the road was. But I didn't know that crawling along. A track hidden on a rock, three lost in the leaves of a little scrub oak. Impossibly hard ground mixed with the careful footsteps of a seasoned scout. When I looked up to see where Chase might be going and I saw the gap open up and the road in front of me I cried inside, "No! Lord, please don't make this be the end. Give me something."

It's funny how I don't really have a religion as such but when I need there to be a god out there I call on him. You're in control up there! And I don't like the way this is going. Change it! You write history, rewrite this one. Please? This can't be it. But it was. That was it. And I did find out what happened to Chase.

He snuck through the gap and his caution intensified when he came in sight of the road. The gap dropped him down to the road about a quarter mile north of the Bug, but he stayed well away from the road. His steps reminded me of stalking deer. A few cautious steps, watch and wait... freeze, a few more cautious steps. He must have known the man he was avoiding. He knew discovery could mean deep trouble. He was within sight of the Bug when all hell broke loose for Chase. It was the moment I dreaded. I didn't know if I could read it. But I had to. I had to know. So I read the story written in the sand to Bill. From the first dive for cover. I stood over it dumbstruck at first.

"There must have been another shot," I said somberly. "Chase hit the dirt. He's trying to head back into the hills to find cover. Here he found his feet again. He's trying to hide his tracks and run as fast as he can. He needs to put distance between him and the guy who is after him. He's thinking if he can top the hill he can get out of sight on the other side. Then while the guy is looking for him he can sneak back to the Bug.

"We were so close to the end of his trail when we started. If we'd have only known.

"He made a mad scramble over the hill but his pursuers came from the direction of the car. Here are a few more bloodstains. I hope it's from the old wound. He laid under these bushes hoping he wouldn't be seen."

"Those bushes wouldn't hide a rabbit," Bill said.

"Yes they will, and they will hide a man, too, if you stand up on that hill and look down you only see the tops of the brush. What's below them is seen so little the eye skims right over it.

"I can sort of predict, based on Chase's actions, where the guy is. See? He lays here until he has a chance to move. When he does move he goes up hill and south. Only ten feet, but I can picture the guy coming over the hill from the south heading east, so that drives Chase west and south. He's working his way closer to the guy but he's hoping they pass around each other so he can make a run for the car. Another wait and another shift in position. He doesn't stand. He's crawling to stay below the level of the brush. He knows to stand invites a bullet."

As the two men made a big curve around each other the other man came to stand below Chase and the brush offered less cover. Now it really had come down to stalking.

I was tense watching the scene unfold, wondering how long Chase could stay out of sight. He had nearly crawled to the top of the hill and made his escape when his tracks were discovered and I had to read as the man followed until he caught sight of Chase and aimed, fired, then ran after him. I searched the ground frantically for signs the shot had hit. Chase got just over the hill and waited for the man to follow. When the guy topped the hill Chase charged him. The man stood to fire again but I couldn't tell if he did. Chase tackled him sending the gun spinning off into the brush. A fistfight ensued. There were hardly any tracks in the fight. The men were hardly ever on their feet. Chase had two distinct disadvantages. He was older and he was wounded. Chase was eventually subdued and forced back down to the road where he was taken away. Taken away. What would they do to him? I went back up the hill reading the fight again, trying to drag out any information I could out of the scratches and skids. I was feeling desperate and I knew Bill was about to call me off. I plopped down in the dirt, ready to give up. This was a case for the police or border patrol now. There was nothing more I could do. Then I noticed a flat spot in the dirt, a smear of blood and scratched into the sand was: Tecajc Bus.

"Cassidy…Cass, come on Kiddo, you've done what you can. Let's report in to Monty and…"

"I'm not through yet."

"There's nothing here to do. I know you don't want to give up on it. Neither do I, but we don't have any choice. Let's go home, call Monty. He'll take it from here."

"Leave me here," I asked.

"I can't do that. How would you get home?"

"You're going to call Monty. He'll send his trackers down to examine the site. I'm not through here."

"What could you possibly do here?"

"I need to think. Chase left clues behind. He knew where they were taking him…"

"Home. Come home with me. I've got a son waiting to see you. I've got a grandbaby to hold. I bet she's grown like crazy since the last time she was here. Come home with me. We'll come back tomorrow if it's that important to you."

Chapter 9

I numbly followed Bill to the Vue and we drove back, stopping at Greasy Joe's on the way. It was getting towards dinnertime and the place had four cars out front. We entered and found a place at the bar. Greasy Joe was busy in the kitchen but when he saw us sitting there he came out.

"Well, if it ain't the great trackers! I told you, you wouldn't find Chase Downing. He's a wily one. But don't worry. I heard Trouble was on the case. He'll find Chase."

I was too bummed out to answer. Bill had other plans.

"So, what's the latest on this Trouble character?"

"They say he's in the Otay. Bet you didn't see him."

"No, we didn't see *him*," Bill admitted.

"You can't because he moves like the wind."

"Chase isn't in the Otay Wilderness. We did figure that much out," I said.

"Then where do you think he is?" Greasy Joe asked.

"I don't know, but Chase knew."

Talk stopped. Things got real quiet and then a miracle happened. A guy on the other side of the room slammed down his beer bottle and in a very American accent slurred out, "Uno mas Tecate, por favor!"

The order drew my eye and there, sitting on the table was a beer bottle with Tecate proudly displayed on the label. An idea flickered in my brain and grew into a spark. I went to the end of the bar and picked up a pen and wrote out Tecajc on my little, square bar napkin.

"Bill, look, Chase wrote this word in the dirt on that hill. If I was hurt after a fight my writing might not be the greatest. Could it be, he was trying to write Tecate?"

Bill looked at me. I shot him a questioning look back.

"Yeah." he said.

"Why would he write the name of a beer in the dirt? Somehow I doubt it was his dying wish."

"Tecate is the name of a border town about fifteen miles from here."

"What are we waiting for? Let's go!"

"Tomorrow. I'm determined to spend a night in my own bed. We'll see what Rusty has to say. Now order some dinner."

Greasy Joe stood over us at the bar, greasy pencil and greasy pad in hand.

"The usual," I said. "And Tecate."

Greasy Joe hit the button on the tape player and three people in the room groaned at the sound of the screechy old woman's voice. I didn't blame them. It was getting old to me, too, and I'd only heard it once before.

"I'll have to see an ID," Greasy Joe said. He squinted at it, looked at me, ran his greasy fingers over it. Looked at it front and back and handed it back to me. Greasy Joe looked to Bill.

"I'll have a Tecate, too. But I'll have the babyback ribs just so I don't have to hear that recording again."

Greasy Joe went back into the kitchen to cook.

"So, tell me about Tecate."

"Not here. I'll answer any questions you have later."

"The fact that Chase knew where they were taking him seems to indicate he knew who was after him."

"Shh, later."

I sat back in frustration.

"How 'bout them Dodgers?" I asked and he smiled.

"This is San Diego."

"Okay, so how 'bout them Padres?"

"It's winter. Ask me again in April. How's that grandbaby of mine? Is she big?"

"She's bigger, but she isn't big for six months. She calls Rusty Dada now. Rusty loves her to pieces. I've never seen him as content as when he's rocking her or walking around with her on his shoulders. He's a natural born dad. Her Christmas picture came out really funny. I think Rusty has a copy for you."

"Is she still a pickpocket?"

"Yeah, in fact the reason her Christmas picture is so funny is because she lifted a flask off of Santa Claus and Rusty took it away. She wanted the flask so she's looking anxiously at it. My dad said she looks like an old man at a peep show. We had an interesting Christmas at the ranch. We found out that Santa Claus likes Hawaiian shirts and Studebakers but he didn't fly a Studebaker for his Christmas rounds. We found out reindeers can fly because they have ADAPT."

"ADAPT?"

"Oh hell, I'll never remember what all the letters stand for. Advanced Disgravitational something, something, something."

"Disgravitational?"

"Yup, we're lucky Patrick didn't push for it to be added to the dictionary or the reindeer could have been hunted to extinction to aid space exploration."

"Cassidy? Are you okay?"

"Yeah, I've just got an interesting family."

"So I see."

"Just wait until Katie's imagination gets going."

"I can't wait."

Greasy Joe set down our plates and my road kill burger already had two strips of bacon, two onion rings and barbecue sauce added. He might be greasy but he was also observant. It didn't take long for conversation to die down as Bill dug into his plate of ribs.

Bill was up to his elbows in barbecue sauce. I was still hoping I had a good hold on the gargantuan burger and was fixing to take my first bite, hoping it wouldn't slide and make a mess, when an older Mexican woman came up beside me. She was barely over five feet tall. Her hair was up in a neat bun. She wore an old calico apron. I was guessing she worked for Greasy Joe.

"Are you Trouble?" she asked quietly.

Bill paused and cast me a warning glance.

"Oh yeah," I scoffed. "Just look at me. Do I look like trouble to you?"

"I think trouble comes in ways we don't expect."

"I'm Chase's friend, and I'm hoping I can find him."

"You? Chase is a friend to you?"

"There's more to Chase than most people think. He's a kind man."

"If you see Trouble, advise him to follow the river." It was almost a whisper. I ran through the clues I had and my hopes rose considerably. Go to Tecate, follow the river, look for a bus.

When we got in the Vue again Bill started putting the key in the ignition and stopped.

"How do you do that?"

"Do what?"

"How do you walk into a place and have people walk up and dish out information that some people would kill over?"

"It's just what happens when I go to a bar. Ask Rusty."

"It's a deal."

Chapter 10

He started up the Vue and pointed it toward San Diego. I could see the contrasting emotions play across his face as he drove, relief that he was going home with a trouble free daughter-in-law mixed with concern over what had happened to Chase.

I felt like a yoyo. As the miles stretched between Tecate and me I felt like one snap of the wrist and I'd be right back. On the other hand, I couldn't wait to see Rusty.

The forty year old Cape Cod house was always a welcome sight. I relished the homey feeling that would envelope me as soon as I walked in the front door. A place where family showing up was cause for a party. I dearly wished Chase would sense a Michael's get together, like he always did, and find a way to be here tonight. But I couldn't get my hopes up. If anybody knew the real chances of that happening it was me.

Bev was sitting on the couch and Katie had her arms buried in between the couch cushions when we walked in. I was sure the couch was cleaned out by now but Katie thought there was always hope.

"That was quick!" Bev said a little too brightly, "I expected you to be gone for a few days."

The talk brought Rusty down the stairs.

"The tracking was rough," I admitted. "It took us a day and a half to track Chase's afternoon."

"You're looking good," Rusty said. "The news must be good."

"No, we didn't find Chase, and it doesn't look good for him, but I know what to try next," I said. "I'll be going back out tomorrow. I need to sort through my supplies."

"You need to talk to Monty," Bill said. Then he scratched his head and looked to Rusty. "Do people always just walk up to Cassidy and offer information?"

"What did she do this time?" Rusty asked like a dad reserving judgment on an unruly teenager.

"Nothing. We stopped to eat somewhere and talk flowed, then this woman walked up, asked if she was Trouble and, when Cassidy didn't admit it, the woman gives her a tip to pass on to Trouble, if she ever ran into him. Gossip along the border going in said only Trouble could find Chase. Word coming out was that Trouble was somewhere around there. Trouble's reputation is about as blown up as Crocodile Dundee. Cassidy is a legend. Only thing is they are expecting this big mean guy."

"I'm not sure about that, remember he moves like the wind. He can see *the invisible*. Sounds more like a ghost. Whatever those people are expecting, I'm not it," I said. "Only that one woman was open minded enough to think that I *might* be Trouble."

Rusty grinned. Bev handed Katie to Bill, put her hands on her hips and looked at us disapprovingly.

"And what is this you're wearing?" she said.

"Neither one of us had the right clothes for tracking so we borrowed some from Chase. We've got a couple of his packs and I owe him some backpacker food. Oh, and we definitely need a different stove and I need a new coat before we go back."

"It was that cold out there?" Rusty asked.

"Um, no, it was that hot. We had a little mishap with the stove." I turned to Bill. "We need to have that evidence analyzed as soon as possible. I'm positive it is Chase's but it would be good to know for sure."

"I'll take care of the blood. Slow down for just a few minutes. Tomorrow won't get here any quicker or slower if you sit down and visit."

Bill headed for the door.

"It's in the burned up pack," I called after him.

He brought in both packs so I could go through the contents. He unzipped the burned pack and pulled out my coat.

"Good lord!" Bev exclaimed, "What did you do out there?"

"Minor trouble," Bill assured her. "Cassidy had the fire out before I could even think."

"I thought you went along to keep her *out of* trouble," Bev said.

"What can I say? Trouble happens fast. She's had more experience dealing with it. In all my years as a cop I never set my campsite on fire."

Well after dark Slick Whitman stopped by. He took the blood sample and he put a rush on the lab, but what he really wanted was details.

"You were able to track Chase?"

"Very slowly, but, yeah."

"Well, well," he said leaning back in the big easy chair and looking at me like he was reassessing my worth.

"Did he find…" he stopped abruptly. He was fixing to paint himself into a corner and he caught himself just in time. The slip did not go unnoticed by Rusty. "Tell me what you saw."

"Not until you give me some names," I said, bargaining with him.

"No."

"Okay, I saw a whole bunch of nearly invisible tracks leading west, almost due west. Until we came to a spot where Chase stopped to watch something." I paused.

"Yes?"

"You tell me. What did Chase find out there?" I pressed.

Rusty was enjoying this. And he was taking notes like crazy. He knew both sides knew something and his detective mind was trying to piece both sides together.

Slick didn't like being put on the spot. It felt like a poker game with all the little nuances to go with it. His eyes narrowed and I knew there was something in *his* hand. Should I fold? Or should I up my bid?

"Whatever it was," I said. "He was able to observe it for some time. He worked his way around the place, it must have taken him hours."

"Did you check out what it was that he was watching?"

"I did."

"Where was it?"

"I told you, just about due west from his parking place."

"Within the wilderness area? Because there is a strip of land in the middle of it that is not designated."

"I'd be interested in seeing it on a topo map," I said. "I can show you where it is."

"Tell me what you saw and I'll do one better. Can we use your computer, Bill?" Slick asked.

"Sure, though I don't keep it updated with all the latest."

"That's okay."

Bill led Slick into the back of the house. They were gone about half an hour.

Katie got fussy so I changed her and fed her. I was holding her, giving her a bottle that I hoped would put her to sleep when Slick came back. He motioned for me to follow him up the stairs. I turned Katie over to Bill and followed.

In one corner of Bill and Bev's bedroom was a small desk set up with an old computer.

"We had to download the program," Slick told me. "I don't know if you've seen it before. It's been around for a while but it's been upgraded recently. I think you'll like it."

On the screen was a view of southern California. The picture was roughly pieced together satellite photos.

"Satellite images of the earth," Slick said, introducing me to the computer. "You can select a place and zoom in on it as close or far away as you want. Well, almost. I think you'll find it useful."

I sat down in Bill's computer chair and took the mouse. This was cool!

Slick showed me how to zoom in on an area and I soon had the Otay Wilderness at the tip of my fingers. I found the road leading from Greasy Joe's to Chase's parking spot. I zoomed in on Greasy Joe's and counted the cars in the parking lot. It had been a busy day. I counted three cars and two pickups in the little parking lot, and a big rig parked illegally on the highway. I followed the lines to where we had left the Vue and zoomed out a little. My tracking mind was taking off with this new concept. Satellite photos at a click of a mouse! I wanted to look up so many things! I wanted to see just what I had traversed when I went after Homer Gent, the crazy man who doggedly walked from his campsite most of the way home simply by walking due west. I wanted to see the country around Elk Meadows. I wanted to see the big shale mountain and learn the little nooks and crannies of it. I wanted…I wanted to find a bus near a river in Tecate! Yes! I could do that! But not now. I was still playing poker with Slick.

I zoomed out to show only the area we covered on foot. I traced Chase's route on the screen.

"He stopped right here, circled around like this. See these little folds in the land? He stopped and laid in each of them watching *this* spot."

I almost expected to see tiny cars moving on the highway and people walking down the sidewalks, a tiny tracker out in the Otay Wilderness, but of course nothing moved.

"Why that spot?" Slick asked.

"That's what I kept asking myself. I wondered why anybody would choose that particular spot as a gathering place."

"A gathering place?"

Oops, I had slipped.

"How many somebodies were there?" he asked.

"Name?"

"Juan Garcia."

Rusty gave out a disgusted grunt. "He just told you, basically, John Doe. You go to Mexico and ask for Juan Garcia and they are going to look at you like you're nuts and ask which one. Everybody will know a Juan Garcia who is a butcher, a baker, a beer bottling plant employee, their neighbor. There's no end to the Juan Garcias down there."

Slick glared at Rusty.

"Three." I told Slick. I didn't know what his ultimate goal was but he did want to get Chase back, too. "One man that I am going to assume was Mexican, and a couple, a man and woman, who I think are Caucasian. Chase wasn't concerned with the Americans. He followed the Mexican. Name?"

"No."

I ended up showing Slick the whole day and a half's worth of tracking and I never did learn a name but I figured I didn't need one. I had an ace up my sleeve. The bus. I was the only one who knew about the bus.

"What kind of a vehicle did the Mexican drive?"

"I don't know. The border patrol Jeeps covered over all the tread."

"You really covered all this ground following Chase's tracks?"

"Yeah."

Slick backed up a bit. "What exactly was this 'gathering' that Chase had staked out for most of a day?"

I looked to Bill. He'd know how far to trust Slick. Bill knew what would help Chase's cause and what would simply be giving in to Slick's manipulations.

"Peyote," Bill said knowing Slick would fill in the rest.

Slick leaned back and folded his hands over his stomach with a satisfied look. I wanted to slap him but I refrained.

"Name?" Bill asked.

"Juan Garcia."

I'd keep my ace. It might come in handy later. There were a few things Slick still didn't know. We didn't even get into the events that happened at Greasy Joe's, so Slick only suspected Tecate figured into the situation. He didn't know about the woman telling me to follow the river. He didn't know about the bus. If Rusty wasn't here sitting so close, with a warm hand on my shoulder I would have packed up and snuck out as soon as people went to sleep. As it was I really wanted a night with Rusty. A night with Rusty would be worth the wait and I'd be ready to take on the world tomorrow.

Slick got up and headed for the door. Guess he found out enough to satisfy him. When Bill and Rusty followed Slick out I lagged behind. I zoomed in on Tecate, found the highway, the border crossing. They even had little dots I could click on and see what the border crossing looked like. Tecate looked like a pleasant town, very modern. All the pictures that showed businesses also had Tecate Beer signs posted on them. I clicked on all the little pictures so I could get a feel for the city in general. Then I zoomed in and checked the border crossing. There were only three cars going in and several more coming out. Not too busy. I wondered what they would ask when I made the crossing. I found the river and followed it from the border crossing west. It curved south and then headed west again. All in all I was only looking at about three miles, max. I watched for a bus. There were busses on the streets, lots of cars but I was sure the bus I was looking for wasn't a city bus or a tour bus. Chase wouldn't point me to a bus that I couldn't find. This bus was stationary. When I found a gray bus shape and a yellow bus shape I printed out the picture. Bill definitely needed a new printer. I could barely recognize the buildings. I got a pen and traced the river and major streets and I mentally noted the places where I'd seen busses. If the wrong people got hold of the map I didn't want them to know where I was headed.

I went through the contents of the backpack and added the map to a pocket. I doubted I'd have reason to use the camping gear but if I had to flee into the desert it might come in handy.

Katie was down for the night, well most of it, and Rusty and I were laying on one of the mattresses up in the attic room we loved because it wasn't stiff. When we slept up here we were family over for a visit. When we stayed in the guest room we felt like we were, well, guests.

"Why did you come back?" Rusty asked.

"Honestly? Your dad made me. But now that I'm here, I'm staying because I need you tonight. I'm going back, but I wanted tonight. I know you had a rough drive. Was it impossible?"

"Impossible? I wouldn't be here if it was impossible. But I don't want to hear *Pop Goes the Weasel* or *Fox in Socks* for a long, long time. Katie likes *Pop Goes the Weasel*. It's all yours now."

"Gee, thanks."

"That bottle that Patrick gave her kept her busy for a long time, too."

"I want to see you," I said sitting up next to him. "Even as I'm tracking and worrying about Chase you're always in the background of my thoughts. You drive me crazy. I wonder what I'm doing out there. I'm complete again when I'm back with you."

I felt guilty asking for him when it was I who was always taking off with little regard for his feelings. So I wouldn't push, but I also knew he had some minutes to catch up on. He reached up.

"Come here, I want to feel you close, just here. We've got time."

This was a step in the right direction so I stretched out on top of him and let him run his hands up and down me as I rested my head on his chest. I felt a gentle smile when he felt me relax under his hands and I knew what was next, gentle teasing, tantalizing fingers. Just the thought of them tensed me up so he backed off. When I was relaxed again from the touches and just tense enough to take the next step myself he pulled me into a deep kiss. Oh yeah. Electricity raced down to nether regions. My stomach did a little flip-flop as his hands found me, then my hands got into it, too.

"Oh Rusty, you feel so good to me, come here. Please?"

"Not yet," he said. "Slow. Slow is sexy."

Arg! Slow was hard, too. I slowed down and he laughed at me.

"You're always in such a hurry," he said quietly into my ear. "Savor it."

Savoring it created such a mixture of aching and longing. I couldn't tell which one was bigger. When he could see me teetering on the edge he turned his attention to erotic teasing until my nipples were hard and I wanted to wrap my legs around him and hold on for dear life. Touches moved down, ever down until... No! Keep going! Oh, how that man could torment me. The most luscious torment I'd ever felt.

I felt a little tipping and a wonderful kiss and realized I'd fallen asleep on top of him. My hair was damp with sweat. He lay on his side watching me before teasingly kissing one nipple, then pulling me close and going back to sleep.

A cry in the night and I didn't want to move. I knew it was my turn, though. Rusty had his hands full for two days. The least I could do was get up in the night. I got up and pulled on some pants and a shirt. I smoothed my hair down hoping Bill and Bev hadn't answered Katie's call, too. The crying eased up and I wondered what was going on. Katie usually had three levels of crying. Calling, fussy crying, hungry something's wrong crying and frightened, attention grabbing crying. Night crying reached level two and pretty much stayed there until she was tended to.

"You better hurry," Rusty said. "She knows how to climb out."

That got me moving. We'd pushed two big chairs together and made a little mattress out of comforters. I rushed down the stairs and tripped over Katie on the next to the last stair. To avoid giving Katie a tumble I leaped over her stumbling right into the coffee table and skidding across the top of it to land between the coffee table and couch.

"Waaaah mamamama!" cried Katie.

"I know, I know, I agree," I said pulling myself up.

Cody rushed out of his room and down the stairs. He stumbled over Katie too, and into the coffee table he went, running right into me coming over the top of it to get to Katie quick.

"Oh shit!" he cried.

We landed in a tangled heap. Footsteps rushed down the stairs.

"Stop!" I yelled. "Freeze! Baby on stairs!" The footsteps slowed. A shadow bent down and picked up Katie. Another shadow felt for a light switch. Blinding light filled the room.

"Babe, what are you doing?" Rusty said and I turned scarlet when he added. "If you wanted to go for round two you could have said something."

Cody blushed, too, even though we both knew he was kidding.

"You're right," I said. "She figured out how to climb out."

Bev handed Katie over to Rusty and made up ice packs. I ended up with a goose egg on my head and Cody ended up with a split lip.

"I have a date tomorrow," he whined.

"Me, too," I said, "with Chase. At least he'll think I look normal."

Feeding Katie had turned into a family affair. Bev warmed a bottle even though Katie liked it just fine cold. Rusty sat with me still grinning at my carelessness. I gave up on the ice real quick. Cody didn't. He was determined to be ready for a nice kiss on his date.

"What's the plan tomorrow?" Rusty asked.

"I drive down to Tecate, find Chase, get help if I need it."

"You make it sound so easy. How are you going to find Chase?"

"I've got directions," I said in a joking manner.

"Babe…"

I've got directions, a map and pictures, I thought.

From way up the stairs Bill called out, "You try and sneak out by yourself and Taz will stop you at the border."

And I thought meeting up with Taz was a stroke of luck.

Chapter 11

I never did get back to sleep. I looked at the clock. I got dressed quietly, loaded up the Explorer silently which was quite a task considering all the baby toys we'd hauled down from the ranch. I put my pack in the back and tiptoed up the stairs.

"I'll take my chances with Taz," I said quietly as I kissed Rusty good-bye.

He was on me in a half second. I was amazed that he could bend my arm behind me just far enough to disable me without hurting me.

"Rusty let go."

"You're not going alone."

"I'm not taking your dad along. If I'm stuck with Taz, so be it."

"Who is Taz?"

"Tazio Navarro, border patrol."

"You'll never get through."

"I'll take my chances on that, too."

"You have no hope of finding him."

"Yes, I do. If there's one thing I do have it's hope."

"Let *me* go," he said.

"No, I need to stay out of sight. I'm not going to go walking around asking where Chase is. I have a destination in mind. I've done these things before. If I find Chase and I can't do anything I'll bring in help."

"Babe, this isn't some game…"

"Believe me, I don't consider this a game. Chase's life is on the line."

"And you think you have a better chance than people who are trained for it?"

"At first. If it proves to be too much, I'll give it to them."

"Stay here, tell Monty everything you know. Leave it to them."

"I have a reputation to uphold. Chase started it. Now he's stuck with it."

"Screw your reputation."

"I have a reputation in that department, too?"

"Cassidy… you walk out that door and I'm going to be on the phone before you get to the end of the street."

"Okay. I love you."

He grabbed me by the arms and gave me a fierce kiss. I thought I was going to have finger shaped bruises encircling my arms. When he let me go, I gave him a kiss of my own, gentle, passionate, sexy. I wished he had a punching bag to work on as I got into the Explorer and drove away.

The sun was well up in the sky by the time I reached Greasy Joe's. I didn't stop, though I was tempted just to give them a dose of the real Trouble. Trouble was also smart enough to know there could be uniforms out there ready to pull him over. I laughed to myself about how distorted my name had become. It kind of gave me a boost. It was like putting on a costume and being *Trouble*, the camouflaged avenger. Though I toyed with the idea, I knew my limitations. But I also knew when it came right down to it I was capable. I could do this. At least I could try.

Highway 188 took me south into the American side of Tecate. I pulled off on a side street and got out. I walked to the corner and looked south into the border crossing. It was quiet. Two agents per station. People walked back and forth passing the building without being stopped. I debated. It looked like it was easier to sneak across on foot but I might need wheels over there. I pulled out and approached the border cautiously. I saw a man that I thought was Tazio. I got in the other lane.

"Nationality?"

"American."

"ID?"

I handed him my driver's license.

"What are your plans for your stay in Mexico?"

"Shopping. My brother collects beer t-shirts."

"You've come to the right place. Drive carefully."

Whew! I pulled forward. I got to within license plate reading distance and Tazio yelled, "Stop her! That's Trouble!"

A Mexican walking by whipped around, "Señor Grande!" he said, shocked.

Three agents ran for their Jeeps and I hit the gas. Damn, if there was one thing I didn't want to do it was get in a fender bender or get pulled over in Mexico. I wove around trying not to get lost, but trying to lose the border patrol. About six blocks down and three over I came to a line of cars parked diagonally on the street. Across the street was a huge building I could use for a landmark. I screeched into a parking place and grabbed my pack. Time for Trouble to be invisible! Who cares if they find my truck, as long as they can't find me.

Stealth mode in the city is a challenge. Especially dressed in camouflage and a backpack. People stared at me. I hid behind buildings, watched for uniforms and headed south. The big building turned out to be the beer plant.

Hide, look, walk as quickly and normally as possible. Hide, look…Damn! Pretty soon there were border patrol Jeeps everywhere. Uniforms walking briskly searching the streets on foot. I doubled up on caution.

Up and down the street men were whispering and glancing around nervously. Señor Grande and Traviesa were whispered on the street corners. I was immensely grateful the local folks were not expecting Trouble to be a young woman in camping gear.

Hide, look, wait.

There goes a Jeep.

Wait some more. Look. Go for it! Wait! I ducked into a little gap between buildings and got out the satellite picture of the area. Oh wow! The beer plant was nearly on the river! I looked around for a street that would take me south just a bit more. When I spotted it my heart sank. I had to cross a large, busy intersection. I began to wish I looked more like a tourist. I was back in Chase's too-big camouflage. For some reason the idea appealed to me to find him using his own gear. It was something Chase would take note of. I made my way from building to building. When the intersection lay before me I sat back in the shadows waiting for the light to change. When it did a border patrol Jeep was sitting at the light. I had to wait through four cycles before I had a chance to cross.

Patience was one of the things I was good at when it came to stealth. It was hard to be stealthy in a hurry. Calm focus was the key. When the light changed and there were no border patrol Jeeps in sight, I walked quickly across. The light changed when I was only half way across. I was stuck on the island knowing the border patrol was going to watch me cross the rest of the way. Please, no Jeeps. No Jeeps. She went thataway! Think invisible. Trouble is invisible, right?

Oh man, a border patrol Jeep pulled up to the light. I put my back to the agent within. That didn't help much because I looked just as out of place in the bulky pack as I did from the front looking like an overloaded runaway. The light changed and I walked as calmly as possible across the street. When I looked before me there were no buildings. Just a long wide-open bridge. Shoot. Wait! Bridge! Bridges cross rivers! I abandoned the street in favor of what might at one time have been a river. When I got to a big mesquite bush in the middle of the dry riverbed I sat in its shade and looked again at the image. This was the river all right. It looked wetter farther upstream.

I wondered who exactly had called Tazio Navarro. If it was Rusty he might not even mention the river being in my plans. I wracked my brain trying to remember if he knew about the woman's comment in Greasy Joe's. If Bill called then they would know to watch the river. I was sunk if Bill called. But perhaps Rusty called not wanting to wake his dad so early and thinking his call would be enough. At first there was no cover at all along the river. I nervously opted for a light trail on the side of the riverbed furthest from traffic. I turned my eyes downward and pretended to be a hiker. A little boy went riding by on a beat up, old bicycle. The front wheel squeaked and the hand brakes were nonexistent. He sped past, skidded to a halt, and turned around. He dragged his feet to stop in front of me and I got ready to run. I didn't understand much Spanish and he only spoke a little English but we attempted to converse.

"Senorita!" was followed by a string of Spanish words.

"No hablo Español," I said. I did know that much.

"You buy mi wheestle? Is muy cheap. Three dollar."

When I looked closer he had about a hundred of the little ocarinas strung around his neck. Hmm, a whistle might just come in handy. If anything I'd look more like a tourist if I had one on me. I chose one with Indian looking patterns on it.

"You buy more? Two for fie dollar."

"No only one. Uno."

I reached into my pocket for the little cash I had on me and pulled off three ones.

"Gracias señorita! Gracias!"

"You're welcome."

"You look shops? Go wrong way."

"No, I look for mi amigo. I look this way. Es bueno."

Boy did I know how to butcher a language, or what?

"Buenos dias!" he called back as he rode away, whistles clanking musically as he pedaled. I blew on the ocarina. I could only get a sound out by blowing very softly. It wouldn't be heard far. I hung it around my neck and it bounced against my belly as I walked.

At first the river bed was open and sandy. Modern houses bordered the riverbed. A broad divided highway was to the north. After a while the riverbed narrowed. Then the plants in the riverbed became greener. At last I began seeing long puddles of stagnant water. It didn't give me much hope of replenishing my supply but I thought I'd be okay for a day or two. The plants had grown up near the puddles and provided a good deal of cover for me to hide in.

The buildings got older and more run down the further west I went. This was what I was watching for. As I walked along I watched for busses permanently parked. I saw old RVs. I saw rough concrete one room shelters. I saw plywood structures little bigger than a shack. Children played in the streets, many without shoes. They played soccer in the street, happy to be together. I'd seldom seen people so poor. Women in colorful skirts and blouses stood talking in small groups. I thought it odd that they wore plaids and flowers, stripes and polka dots all in the same outfit. Most of the older women also wore an apron with two big pockets. I wondered what Katie would find in those pockets. I wanted to hide in the brush and watch this totally foreign world go by in front of me. There was a gap in the houses and I saw a group of women making tortillas together. It was fascinating to me. Tortillas were things I bought at the grocery store. I never thought about women rolling them out by hand on a table in a village somewhere, but this was a staple here, I knew. Snapshots. I was very thankful to carry home these snapshots of life.

A baby about Katie's age crawled out of a doorway and a child of about five rushed after him and hauled him back. How I wished I could walk down their streets and read the prints in their dusty roads.

In the middle of the shantytown I spotted the roof of a bus. How was I going to get to that bus? I sat beside the river calculating how far in it was. I was guessing three short blocks south and about five little shacks to the east.

How dangerous could a village be? It was just like a neighborhood in the U.S. except it was in Mexico. It might be a rough neighborhood but the people looked friendly. I knew I'd stand out but I wouldn't worry about a foreigner walking the streets of my city. So I made my way to the closest little street. It took me about thirty seconds to regret the decision. Eyes appeared in doorways. People stopped what they were doing and watched me walk by.

"Un chica Americana," the kids said.

There were whispers. One brave kid followed me. He asked me a question in Spanish and I answered, "No hablo Espanol."

He ran off and pretty soon there was another kid by my side staring up at me with big brown eyes.

"What you do here?" he asked.

"I'm looking for a friend. He's an old man. Very tan, long hair, short beard. Have you seen a man like this?"

"Americano?"

"Si."

"I no see heem. You no stay here es muy big trouble you stay. Is danger. Peligro. Tonight I stay my home. Tonight es muy mal."

Very bad.

"Why?"

"Señor Grande come. Señor Grande bad man."

"Mexican? Americano?"

"Un gran Americano, terrible."

"I don't think so. Why would a bad man come here?"

"I no say English. Pero este hombre es…es…you go home now."

"I'm not going home until I find my friend. Does everybody know about this Señor Grande? Why haven't I heard of him, if he's American?"

"Señor Grande he is perseguidor. He find men, bad men."

"Perseguidor? What's that?"

He put a hand over his eyes like he was searching the horizon and made sneaking motions. "What you say? Hunter? He man hunter."

"Bounty hunter?" He didn't understand the phrase, so I tried again, "A man who hunts people for money."

"But Señor Grande no find them. Señor Grande, he keel them. You no see heem coming. In dark he come and…" he made a throat cutting motion with his hand.

Wow, the little blond tracker had grown. I was a weretracker. Not only did I turn into Dangerous Tracker Woman, now I was the dreaded Señor Grande de Tecate.

I passed a large home made out of old garage doors. In spite of the crude construction, each panel of the home was painted bright, cheerful colors. The roof was tar papered to keep out the rain.

The boy continued to follow me. So I tried a new approach.

"I see so many different kinds of homes. Cement. Wood. Is that a bus over there?"

"This my people es pobre. Use todo, all building…"

"It's okay I get the idea. You use any building materials you can get."

"Si."

"But, a bus?"

"Es un casa grande. Tres rooms. Cocina."

Three rooms and it was a grand house.

"How many people live in a house like this?"

"My house, one room. Six live one room."

"And the bus?"

"Aye! Two family and two… two… what you say. Child who parents die."

"Orphan?"

"Si, two family have gran house, take in or… orphan so they not starve."

It didn't sound like a place where Chase would be held captive.

"You get enough to eat?" I asked.

"Some day. Some day mi hungry todo de dia."

It cut me that he reverted to Spanish when something touched him.

"Are you hungry?" I asked.

He hung his head. "You have canny? Dulce?"

"No but I will share my food. You've been a big help to me."

I reached over my shoulder and unzipped the pocket of Chase's pack. I pulled out a Ziploc bag and saw that it contained jerky. I pulled out another and it contained pemmican. I held out the bags.

"Which do you like? Jerky? Carne? Or pemmican?"

"Pemmican?"

"It's like a meat and fruit hard bread. It's good for you. Pan carne."

I reached into the bags and handed him one of each. He ran off eyes shining. Though I was glad he got something useful out of the encounter, giving him food was a big mistake. I ended up with a trail of children tagging after me. I didn't have enough to go around. If I gave it to them I'd be forced to cook my dinner. I was hoping to not have to cook. The activity would draw attention to the river. And how was I going to get back to the river with a parade of kids following me? Getting rid of them proved easier than I thought. First I asked if one of them spoke English. When one stepped forward I said that I was looking for an old American man. I gave them a description of Chase. Then I asked, "Who will help me look for my friend?"

The kid translated and hands shot up into the air. I started with the kids who looked like they could actually do the job and handed out jerky and pemmican until I ran out. When it was gone I held up the empty bags, "Es todo, I'm sorry."

I had to swallow a big lump in my throat as they dejectedly turned away. But one little girl looked at me curiously.

"Que pasa con su cabesa?"

I fingered the large bump on my head.

I meant to say that trouble struck me, but then it occurred to me that they were suspicious of anything to do with Señor Grande so I told them that Señor Grande had struck me.

Her eyes got real big, there were whispers all around, scared looks at me, like I was jinxed, and then they quietly disappeared behind heavy blanket doors. I felt like a heel. I wanted to go home, buy a case of chocolate bars, come back, and hand out candy to them all day. I was sorry I fueled their fear of Señor Grande. I didn't want them to be scared.

Now the whole village was on edge. They were glad to see me leave. I walked down one long street and found a way over two streets where I could make my way back to the river by passing the gran casa that was an old school bus. I doubted this bus was the one Chase told me about. There were curtains in the windows and real toys under the bus. That reminded me that it was just a few days after Christmas. I felt sorry for the kids and all I had left to give them was money so every once in a while I unobtrusively dropped a coin into the dusty road where they could find it. When I got to the end of the long street I watched my tail as I made my way back to the river.

The other bus was farther down the river in a sparser little village. Luckily this other bus was on the outskirts of the village so I could observe it easily from the river.

As the bus came into view it gave me the creeps. I didn't want to be *this* close to it, I thought as I stood on the riverbank gazing through the sparse, yellow branches of a desert willow. Well, there wasn't much I could do about it. The river offered the cover I very much needed.

I went to great pains to find a spot that wouldn't be seen from the bus or from the few shelters on the street. Street was a misnomer. It was a couple of wheel ruts worn through the normal desert sand. I made sure my waiting spot was not where anybody would want to go to get water or wash clothes. I couldn't imagine anybody drinking or washing in that water but, on the other hand, if it's the only water around what were they supposed to do? So I chose a spot carefully. I got out my camp shovel and dug a foxhole just deep enough and wide enough to lay down in. I hunkered down in the foxhole, camouflage and blond hair about all that could be seen from above, and I watched the bus. My observations seemed to back up my hunch that this was the place. First of all, who would live this poorly, yet have wrought iron bars over their windows? Secondly, as the wind whipped up, a horrible stench floated my way and I knew why these people had no close neighbors. I seemed to remember a little snatch of conversation I had with Bill. He said something about peyote. He said it stunk. Two out of two. Things were adding up.

I could hear voices within. Barely. They were all Spanish, no understandable words from this distance. It was a long, cold wait. One person left. No cars approached. No cars were parked near the bus. The man who left headed for town on foot. He was dressed poorly. He reminded me of my days in Afghanistan after we had all turned dust colored. His clothes were faded. His red plaid shirt was barely recognizable as red or plaid. It was tucked into tan pants that were too long for him. His shoes... his shoes looked like the footprints I had seen in the Otay. The footprints *almost* drew me out of the foxhole. They were like a magnet. They pulled at my curiosity. I had to see. But instinct told me not to move out from cover yet. There was at least one person in the bus that wasn't Chase. Rusty would have been proud of my restraint.

When darkness fell things got mildly worse. As the sky dimmed thousands of mosquitoes buzzed about. I hunkered down in my foxhole and pulled my shirt up just below my eyes. Still, I could hear the little kamikaze bugs around my head and they eventually started biting through my t-shirt. After the mosquitoes had a chance at me, and the sun went down, the night grew cold. I hadn't replaced my coat before I left. I'd spent the time with Rusty's family, holding Katie, hoping I wouldn't need much in the way of camping gear on this little outing. I'd given up all my food that didn't need cooking, but I didn't want to fire up my stove this close to the bus. I was used to ignoring hunger but it took a little of my concentration to do it. Still I watched.

A dim light came on. There was a bump that sounded like a plate being set down on a table. A silhouette moved past the window. A woman. That was good news. If there was only a woman in there I wasn't as worried about getting caught.

Suddenly a small child ran up the road and stood before the bus steps. He banged as hard as his little fist could manage on the side of the bus and the woman opened the door. I strained my ears to hear but there was so much Spanish flying by that only a few familiar words caught my attention. Un chica Americana, Señor Grande, aquí, un hombre Americana, viejo. I thought that meant old.

I had a little tattletale! A very helpful little tattletale.

When the kid went home and it was just the woman in the bus I hid my tracks in the little clumps of grass that dotted the land between the river and the bus, then I slid silently underneath the bus and lay in the dark listening. All was quiet. When I didn't see people moving around outdoors I got braver and inched forward until I was under what should have been the engine of the bus. I knew that only a thin wall of fireboard separated the engine from the cab of the bus so I was hoping I could hear through it, but when I looked up I was amazed that the motor had been stripped out and I could see right up into the bus interior. The front of the bus had a rough kitchen built into it. There was a gas stove and an ice chest, a homemade table, and mismatched chairs. A wall separated the kitchen area from the back of the bus.

I wondered what use the Mexicans had made of the big bus engine and counted my lucky stars they were frugal and resourceful people. I shrank back from the opening, knowing if I could see them, they could also see me. I found a musty old blanket under the bus and pulled it over me as I waited, observed and fought off the urge to shiver. The stench was even stronger here and I had to guard my breathing and remember not to use my nose.

Three men approached the bus and I froze even though I was pretty sure they wouldn't notice me. They were talking and walking at a brisk pace and the first one pulled the bus door open with a jerk. I heard the woman inside get up and walk to the door. The three crowded in and sat in the wooden chairs. I could tell by the way the legs scraped on the floor of the bus. I wished for a few more years of Spanish classes and kicked myself for sloughing it off when I'd had the chance to learn it in high school.

They talked in worried but animated tones. Something was going to happen en la mañana. Tomorrow. The woman seemed relieved. I worried that it involved Chase. I wanted to see him, know I was in the right place, but I was worried about getting caught and losing our chance.

Under the bus I could tell that all the Mexican activity was at the front of the bus so I crawled to the back of the bus and poked around. I found a toolbox. Opening it quietly, I took stock of my options. Beside the toolbox there was a jack and some oily rags. Apparently someone here did have a car.

I slid out from under the bus and used the jack for a foothold. If I stood on it on one foot I could just see inside the bus and what I saw appalled me. It was filthy. Nothing had been done to make the closet sized room habitable. A rough blanket was tossed on the floor. The frame for a bus seat remained bolted to the floor and a chain was strung loosely through the legs. I almost expected to see a large fierce dog on the end of the chain, but what I saw was a very beaten old man. His eyes were still puffy and his cheek had been laid open. His lips were swollen. He appeared to be asleep. I put my finger to the side of the bus and scratched the side: scratch, scratch, scratch, pause. His eyes popped open. He glanced around without moving. The sound was so soft he wasn't sure he'd heard it right but he trusted his senses. He knew the sounds of this place and that scratch was not normal. I did the pattern again. His eyes zeroed in on the window I stood at. All he could see of me was a shock of blond hair and my eye, but recognition registered on his face. It was quickly replaced by worry. I studied his situation. Chain through the bench frame. Cuffs? His hands and feet were tied with thick rope. Drat. Cuffs would be easier. Thinking about his hands brought me to check for gunshot wounds but I couldn't see that much in the gloom. There did appear to be a large stain on his sleeve but under the conditions he was living in the stain could be anything. Oh Chase.

I had to prioritize. I couldn't rush into this. Could I get some information from him? I held up my hand in a gun shape and looked at him with a question. He gave me a barely perceptible nod. I had to assume they were armed. There was a movement in the front of the bus and I stepped off the jack and slid underneath.

While I was down there I assembled some tools. I found bolt cutters and about half of a socket set with a ratchet handle in the toolbox. I imagined how big the bolts would be that held down a school bus seat. I put several different sizes in my pocket. I grabbed a pair of pliers in case I didn't have the right size sockets. I left the bolt cutter and the socket handle under the hood of the bus and took the sockets and pliers with me. After carefully checking the windows for eyes I stalked back to my foxhole. I lay in it stewing. I had to do something. It sure would help if I could eat. I could think clearer if I had dinner. I considered walking farther away from the bus and firing up the stove and then I remembered that my stove didn't work anyway. It was a fire hazard. It was… hoo boy, it was a hell of an attention getting device! Once the idea of a distraction entered my head I thought of other ways to create a diversion. Yes! This could work. It could be dangerous as hell, but it could work. One more trip to the bus and I'd be set. I was glad it was a dark night as

I made my way back one more time. I grabbed the oily rags from beside the toolbox. I found a roll of duct tape and a pack of cigarettes in the toolbox. I grabbed the cigarettes because I knew arsonists commonly used them and I was planning a little fireworks display.

It took a good half hour to make all the preparations for my little stunt. I found a group of trees well away from any dwellings but within sight of the bus. An old rusty car helped hide me from passersby. I got out my 9mm and took out all but two of the bullets. With the pliers I carefully pulled the tip off each bullet and emptied the gunpowder in a line onto my computer printout, praying I could find the beer plant without it. With the gunpowder neatly lined up I rolled the paper tightly and wrapped the whole thing with duct tape. It looked like a silver label cigar but I wouldn't advise anybody to smoke it. I stuck a cigarette in the top of the assembly and set it aside. Distraction number one.

Next I moved to a different location farther away but close enough that the people at the first distraction would be drawn away from the bus. I took the filler cap off my old camp stove and stuffed the oily rag in the top of the tank. I duct taped the rag in place, then lay a cigarette at the end of the rag. Distraction number two.

I wasn't sure about the timing on this. Which one would blow first? I hoped the gunpowder would blow first and I was hoping for a small fire that would take some time to put out.

I lay in my foxhole and waited for instinct to tell me when to act. I forced myself to stay alert, catch every sign, each flicker of light in the windows, each movement within the bus. I got out the little ocarina and played a low trill. Something to catch the ear without drawing them out. Something to pique their curiosity. I waited until the trill was forgotten and then played it again. After a while two of the men left the bus and stumbled through the darkness toward the village. One man and the woman were still inside. Two people. And a gun.

Time crawled. I was itching for action, anything. Every tick of the clock felt like Chase's life hanging by a thread. But patience was key. Timing was everything.

Finally instinct told me it was the time. I wasn't sure what changed, but something in my caution clicked. Instinct didn't always sense the same things my eyes and ears did. Instinct worked on a different level.

I ran back to the gunpowder bomb and lit the cigarette with a match I found in the pack. Then I stalked my way over to the other bomb and lit that cigarette, too. Before I could get halfway back to the bus, circumventing the bombs, the first one went off with enough bang to rock the nearest shelter. People stumbled out of shelters and speculated about the explosion as they stumbled through the desert, suspicious of the strange events of the night. Several men ran that direction, the take charge men.

I ran toward the bus. The man stood in the doorway, unwilling to venture out. Hell. I was desperate.

I screamed. Now, I am not ordinarily a screamer. I'll take just about anything silently but I needed a scream to get this guy moving so I screamed bloody murder. "Aiiyeee! Señor Grande! Señor Grande is here! Aiiiyyeee! Help! Help!"

The man rushed out. The woman stood in the doorway. Gosh but these people were unshakable!

"El ninos! Señor Grande is after the ninos! Señora! Look! Vive!"

"Que ninos?" she asked.

I had just about used up all the Spanish words I knew.

"Chiquito ninos! Tres!"

She hurried after the man and I pretended to follow her then dove under the bus, crawled up inside with the bolt cutters and rushed to the back. I took a quick look over my shoulder and saw a good sized fire where I thought the old car was.

"Damn you Cassidy! What are you doing here?" Chase whispered angrily.

"Shut up and help me. We have about five minutes before that woman is going to come back!"

I threw my weight into the bolt cutters and cut the chain, then went to work on the ropes. The ropes were harder to cut than the metal had been. It occurred to me that Chase could still run with his hands tied so I switched to the feet. I put all my weight into the handles but the multiple strands made it tough work.

"Get out of here!" Chase hissed.

"When I get you loose go for the hood of the truck. Not the door. Go through the front of the bus."

"What?"

"They'll expect us to come out the door. They won't look under the bus."

"You don't have time! They'll kill both of us if this doesn't work!"

"Then help make it work! We have one more explosion's worth of distraction. Come on!"

About that time there was a big flare up out in the desert. There were shouts and the sound of running outside.

Damn these ropes!

"Go for the knot. If you can get one part of the knot the rest will go."

"Hold on! I got an idea!" I said. I dashed for the front of the bus and scurried underneath. Where is that saw? I frantically pulled tools out of the toolbox. There it was! A hacksaw! I scrambled back inside. The rope gradually parted under the rough teeth of the hacksaw. When it finally gave way Chase yanked on the ropes until they came loose. My heart was hammering in my chest. I just knew people were going to bust into the bus at any second. I didn't want to use those last two bullets. Oh please, don't make me use those shots!

"Chase?"

"Yeah?"

I handed him my 9mm. "I can't do it. There's two shots left."

"Let's go. We'll worry about the hands later!" he said.

We made a mad dash through the front of the bus, dropping down to the ground and taking in the action around us.

"Where to?" he asked.

"The Explorer is parked across the street from the Tecate plant."

"What?"

"I had border patrol after me! I had to go on foot to lose them!"

I dived into the foxhole and grabbed the pack.

"That's *my* pack!" he exclaimed, "And... and my clothes!"

"Shit, I'll explain it all later! Run! Follow the river!"

I heard splashing and sputtering.

"I didn't mean that literally!" I said urgently.

"I couldn't see it!"

There was a volley of Spanish behind us. Damn! I wish I knew what they were saying.

We ran like Señor Grande himself was on our heels. A crowd of Mexicans chased after us and still we ran. We had a good head start on them. I was just hoping we could get ahead of them enough so they couldn't see us in the dark. When we passed the shantytown small groups of people stood looking into the west wondering what the commotion was. Children hid and whispered to each other. Was it Señor Grande?

"I can't run anymore!" Chase called out to me.

I looked behind us and I didn't see people running. We stopped. He was gasping for breath, bent over at the waist.

"Are you okay?"

No answer. It was too dark to see much of anything so I thought we were pretty safe.

"Chase? Are you okay? I know you've been shot. Judging from your tracks I thought it was your arm. Am I wrong? Is there something else I should know?"

He looked over his shoulder. Flashlights advanced.

"Aw hell."

I looked to the bridge. One car went over it. It wasn't a high traffic time of the night. I was wishing it was a border patrol Jeep. We could use one right now. I tried to judge the distance. It looked to be about a mile away.

"Chase, you see the bridge? It's only a few blocks from the bridge."

"I can't. Got to stop."

I looked around. Where was the nearest cover? We were at the rich end of the shantytown. We climbed the bank and ducked in between two houses to land in the little dusty road I'd walked earlier in the day.

It was late at night but tensions were high and children and adults alike were up and talking about the goings on in the west. A glow still lit the sky, barely discernable. Just visible enough to cause questions.

"Senorita! Senorita! Wait!" A little boy approached us. "You lost this time?"

"No, we're looking for a place to rest."

"You rest here, my house, mi casa."

"I can't. Bad men are after me."

"Señor Grande?"

"No, you don't need to worry about Señor Grande. Señor Grande is friendly. He's not scary."

"Who is Señor Grande?" Chase asked.

"Don't ask. I'll explain later."

"You hide mi casa. They no look there."

"No, if the bad men find out your family would be in trouble."

We stumbled on and the kid ran off. Pretty soon a Mexican man came after us and we almost took off running again but the kid was with him.

"Vamanos aqui!" he called and Chase pushed me in that direction. He led us to a small shelter made of plywood walls. Sleeping pallets had been arranged but no one was sleeping. "Gracias Senorita," the dad said.

"What's he thanking you for?" Chase asked.

"It's amazing what a hunk of beef jerky will buy," I responded. We huddled in a corner and worked Chase's ropes loose. He rubbed his wrists to get the circulation going again.

The boy squatted in front of us eyeing us warily.

"Did you see Señor Grande?" he asked.

"Can you understand my English?" I asked and he nodded. "Can you keep a secret?"

"Si!"

"The answer to your question is long. Do you want to hear the story?"

"Si!"

"This is my friend, Chase. You remember I was looking for my friend? He and I are both trackers. Perseguidor. We look for people but we do it for good. To help people. Chase is very well known in southern California as a tracker.

Many people admire his abilities. One day he told someone that only one person could find him if he needed to be tracked. That person, in English, is named Trouble. In the U.S. the reputation of this 'Trouble' was talked about in cantinas and restaurants up and down the border until this person named Trouble was admired by all. When the story crossed the border to Tecate the Mexicans called him Señor Grande, or Traviesa. The truth is Señor Grande is not mean. He is friendly. And in fact he isn't even a man. He is me. Chase told people that only I could find him but nobody expects a woman to be a tracker. So, with the reputation of Señor Grande bigger than real life, I was able to sneak in and find my friend."

"Usted? You are the terrible Señor Grande?"

"Yes."

The boy looked to Chase. Chase just shook his head. He didn't believe the story either.

"Don't look at me like that! You started it! Greasy Joe blew it up and now I'm some weirdo freak who can *see the invisible* and walk *without making a sound*. I can leap tall buildings in a single bound! All I can say is it paid off, even if it isn't true."

The boy puffed up his chest like the rooster who walked by the open door.

"I talk to Señor Grande! I help the great Señor Grande and his friend. Gracias senorita!"

"So, now you aren't scared of Señor Grande, are you?"

"Si. But today you nice girl. Tomorrow I don't know."

"Just keep quiet until we are on our way," I advised him.

I turned my attention to Chase's arm.

"Is this the only shot that hit? How does it feel?"

"Useless."

"Drive straight to a hospital useless? Or stick on a band aide useless?"

"Rest in the dark until morning useless."

"Are you sure?"

"Yeah. Why'd you come after me?"

"I had to."

"How'd you end up with my pack?"

"I didn't have gear. I'd already flown down from the ranch to get here. I didn't have time to go shopping, so I broke into your house. I owe you a porch roof, a bathroom screen and a daypack."

"Forget about it."

"No, I aim to replace them. Oh, and I fed the cat. He's probably ready for more water, though."

"You really are Señor Grande," he said and fell asleep sitting against the plywood wall. After a while I curled up next to him and let sleep take me. I woke with the sun. Chase slept on.

"Mi mama ask what you eat."

"Nothing, we'll be fine. In fact, I wish I could give you something to thank you for your help. I have nothing to give. I only have camper food."

"Camper food?"

"Yeah, you just add hot water and it makes a meal." I dug in my pack until I found one. I showed it to the boy.

"Water? Hot?"

"Yes, you want to try it? Ask your mom. You can have it."

He took the pouch and ran off to talk to his mom. Chase sat up. "You're going to have the whole village after you," he said.

"I know, but I only have one more. I gave away all your pemmican and beef jerky on the way in."

He laughed, "They need to change your name to La Madre, only they won't because they think you're too young for the title."

When the little boy came back with the pouch of backpacker food he offered us some.

"No, no, you eat it. Is the coast clear?" I asked.

He cocked his head at me and Chase asked him the question in Spanish in a way he'd understand.

The boy answered in Spanish.

"He said yes, but we should leave as soon as possible."

"It's a deal. But as soon as the danger is past I'm coming back."

"You're kidding."

"No. I owe these kids. And they can use a helping hand. I'm going to buy a case of candy bars and cookies and I'm going to go around handing them out. What is your name?" I asked the boy.

"Juan Garcia!" he said proudly.

"Which? How will I know you to bring back some candy for you?"

"I am Juan Garcia! Son of Juan Garcia!"

Chase grinned at me.

"Okay, Juan Garcia, you watch for me. If you see Señor Grande call your friends. I'll bring candy back."

"Si Senorita!"

"Are you ready to make a run for the truck?"

"Do we have to run?"

"I hope not. It's not far. Maybe a mile and a quarter. If we drop down to the river we can see the bridge."

We trudged up the dry riverbed until we reached the bridge and I led Chase up to the surface streets. We found the truck where I had left it but as soon as we approached a uniform closed in on us.

"Well, well, any luck shopping?" he asked.

"None at all, in fact I almost lost the shirt off my back."

"You have anything to do with the commotion last night?"

"Me? No, it was Señor Grande. He did it."

"How do you know who Señor Grande is?"

"Let's just say we are very well acquainted."

"Call home," he said and turned on his heel.

"You must me starving," I said to Chase.

"Call home."

"I will. I'll call as soon as we stop. I have one stop to make on the way home and I need your help."

"You. Need my help?"

Chapter 12

Greasy Joe's was quiet by the time we got there.

"You got me into this fix. Now you will get me out of it. When you hear the road kill recording you can come in."

"And what am I supposed to do?"

"Just call me Trouble."

He grinned lopsidedly. It reminded me I still owed Rusty a call. I opened the door as slowly and quietly as I could. The bell remained silent. I looked in. Greasy Joe was bent over a notebook on the bar. He had a pencil perched behind his ear. He was figuring. I stood in the doorway and watched him in deep concentration. I took a couple of silent steps. He gave a frustrated look at the clock and I froze. He looked right past me but I didn't see any recognition cross his face. He jabbed the pencil into the notebook and walked to the door of the kitchen. While he had his back turned to me I advanced four more long, silent steps. He made a note on a calendar, scratched his greasy head and went back to the bar.

"Damned slow today," he mumbled to himself. "Sure could use some excitement."

He bent over the notebook and scratched his head again. I took two more steps. I was now standing at the end of the bar. He wrote something down and looked at the next thing he had to take care of. I crouched below bar level and inched closer.

"A seven letter word for *disturbance*," he muttered.

"Trouble," I said.

"Wha! Who said that!" his pencil tumbled off the bar.

I stood up, sat on the nearest barstool and said, "I'll have a Tecate and a road kill burger with all the fixings."

He didn't move for a second. "How… how… how'd you get in here?"

"I walk without making a sound," I said in a Cassidy version of his campfire voice.

"But how'd you get in here without me seeing you?"

"I move like a ghost and you don't see me unless I want to be seen."

"You're freaking me out, lady!"

"Do I get my road kill burger? You said I'd get one free if I found Chase."

"But, lookie here. I don't see no Chase."

"Hit the button."

Still looking freaked out, he pushed the button and the screechy woman's voice came on. When it finished Chase tapped Greasy Joe on the shoulder and said, "Make it two."

Greasy Joe almost jumped out of his skin and ran away.

"How's it going, Trouble?" Chase asked.

"Same ol', same ol', sneaking into foreign countries. Creating explosions. Running for my life through the night."

"Me, too. What about you Joe? Anything exciting happen while I was gone?"

Greasy Joe's mouth opened and closed a few times and he said, "Road kill burger?"

"Yep," Chase said. "And make sure the beer's cold. I haven't had a cold beer in a week."

"Thanks," I said. "I'll let you two catch up on the news. I'm going to check in with Rusty."

"Cass?" Rusty said on the first ring.

"No, it's Trouble, Traviesa, Señor Grande de Tecate and I'm fine. We're on our way home. I'm going to drop Chase off at the hospital. I bet he won't let them keep him though. I bet he shows up for dinner."

There was a long pause. "Do I want to hear the story?"

"No. But you probably will anyway. We'll be heading out as soon as I eat my free road kill burger."

Greasy Joe looked at me with newfound respect when I walked back into the bar.

"How was I to know Trouble was a girl?" he asked in his defense.

"It's okay. I thought it was funny. Not quite what you pictured, was I?"

"We were watching for The Terminator or Rambo or something. When we heard Trouble was on the scene and we hadn't seen hide nor hair of him we started leaning towards you being a ghost."

"I've been called a lot of things but this is the first time anybody has thought I was a ghost."

"Did you really track Chase?"

"I did, and that's what told me where to look to find him without tracking. If you hadn't written *Bus* in the sand you would have been a goner."

"How did you find that one bus in all of Tecate?"

"I did a little technological tracking. Did you know you can do urban tracking by computer? Slick didn't know what he was doing when he showed me that program."

"You talked to Slick and still managed to get in and find me? How?"

"He didn't tell me everything. So I didn't tell him everything. He told me just enough to give me the tools I needed, but he didn't know it at the time. I think he's still stumbling around in the murky depths of police red tape."

"This road kill burger is going to be the death of me," Chase said with a burp.

"Nah, this is my third one in a week."

"Third? How can you stand it?"

"It was that or backpacker food."

"You don't have to order the road kill burger."

"Yes, I do. I have a reputation to uphold. I was told; if Trouble showed up here he'd order the house special road kill burger. So that's what I aim to do."

Greasy Joe didn't charge us for the road kill burgers but I left him a tip to cover both, plus a little. I was thankful to him for adding to the story of my adventures. I was looking forward to telling Bill about it.

I dropped Chase off at the hospital and nearly kept him at gunpoint until he was checked in. I promised him a ride home if he needed it later. Then I drove once again to the Michael's house. Rusty was watching for me and met me on the sidewalk before I could even get to the front door. For once he hesitated to hug me.

"Ughhh! You didn't eat any of that stuff did you?"

"I was a little busy to eat anything."

"That's good. Why don't you take a nice long, hot shower?"

"Is it that bad?"

Even Katie backed off. She reached for me happily until I got close and then her little nose wrinkled up.

"Okay, I get the hint. My nose must have died from being in that bus with the stuff," I said and Rusty and Bill both froze. Golly, I needed to think before I spoke. A shower suddenly seemed to be the safest action I could take.

As I stood in the warm spray I sure was glad to be me again. I didn't want to be Señor Grande. I didn't even want to be Traviesa. I even balked at being called Trouble. I wanted to snuggle on the couch with my husband. I wanted to play on the floor with Katie. I wanted to see all the Michaels family happy and together. I wanted Chase to walk in without being heard and sit down for a nice long story telling evening. And I wanted some of that fudge I saw on the dining room table.

I finished my shower and put on some comfortable, feminine clothes. I curled my hair and put on some make-up. I gathered up all Chase's clothes and washed them so I could give them back. Dinnertime came and Chase still hadn't shown up.

"Are you sure he's okay?" Bev asked.

"He was shot and roughed up but it was nothing serious. We stopped at

Greasy Joe's to eat and make a point. If he'd been hurt seriously I wouldn't have stopped."

"It's not like him to stay away," Bev said.

"He's probably tracking your activities around his house," Bill offered.

"Then he's sitting on his back porch laughing," I said.

"That's very possible. It was like watching an episode of *I Love Lucy*."

"I thought I was going to get stuck in that little window!" I laughed and Rusty and his mother exchanged questioning glances. Bill and I exchanged knowing glances.

Chase didn't show up that day, or the next. Bill called the hospital and found out Chase had been treated and released. Slick was unavailable. I was tempted to drive to his house but I thought Chase would rather stay on his own timetable. People don't usually go to Chase. They wait for him to come to them. I worried about the cat. I knew it was a tough old cat but even a tough old cat needs water.

We passed the two days enjoying the family time, chasing Katie, and shopping for candy. All the grocery stores were selling Christmas candy cheap so I bought as much as I could, preparing for a run down to Tecate. There was a little boy down there waiting for me.

On the third day the doorbell rang and I jumped up to get it. I hoped for Chase but the man on the other side was not Chase. It was Slick. Uh oh.

"You were withholding information from me," he accused.

"I told you everything you wanted to know."

"You're lucky you didn't kill both of you pulling a prank like that."

"I'm lucky trouble was on my side for a change."

"On your side? Seems like you met as much opposition as you could."

"No, it could have been much worse."

"How bad does it have to get to make you back off?"

"If I didn't have options I would have backed off."

"You see options in some of the darndest places."

"I'll second you on that one. You've seen Chase since he got back?"

"I have."

"If you see him again, tell him I have two days left. Tomorrow morning I'm making a candy run to the kids in Tecate. The next day I'm going home."

"You're making a candy run. The great Señor Grande is making a candy run for the kiddies."

"Yeah. I doubt you'd understand. But there's one person in Tecate who would."

"Who's that?"

"Juan Garcia. Thanks. Juan was a big help to me. He saved our skin."

His eyes narrowed. He didn't take the thanks seriously.

"I know you came here for a reason. What can I do for you, Detective Whitman?"

"You did it. I just wanted to know if Trouble was alive and well. I see you are so I'll be going. You'll hear from Chase before you leave. He's still trying to put pieces together. He doesn't understand why."

"Why what?"

"Why you'd risk everything. He was down to one day. He thought he'd die, if not in the morning, at least soon. He was to be turned over to a rich man down south. Someone got tired of Chase's interference on the border. There was a price on his head. He was counting the minutes until he quietly disappeared into Mexico, never to be heard from again."

"En la mañana. I caught that phrase while I had the bus staked out."

He extended his hand. "Thanks," he said as a kind of peace offering.

I wasn't sure it was wise, but I shook his hand with a nod of my head. He turned and walked down the sidewalk to his car.

"He respects you," Bev said from the dining room. "Take Chase, squeeze all the scruples out of him and you get Slick. But he does respect you."

Chapter 13

We stopped at the border crossing. Tazio Navarro walked up to the window.

"Good morning, Taz," I said from the passenger side.

"Buenos Dias, Señor Grande," he said.

"You're Taz?" Rusty asked from the driver's seat.

"Yeah. ID?"

We handed over our driver's licenses.

"Have to ask," he said. "What are you doing in Tecate this time?"

"Delivering candy to the kids in the village by the river."

"No explosives? No firearms?"

Rusty produced his weapon and the permit to carry it. Taz glanced at me.

"I don't carry unless I have to. I don't want the kids to be scared of Señor Grande."

The Explorer really stood out in the dusty village. I directed Rusty to the little wooden box Juan Garcia lived in. We got out and I knocked on the wall gently. I was a little worried about knocking the whole thing over. A woman looked out.

"I'd like to speak to Juan," I said.

She rattled off a bunch of Spanish and I got lost.

"Your son. Chiquito Juan." I said holding my hand out about Juan's height.

Rusty laughed at my attempts at communication. Hey, I wanted to say, it worked the first time!

The woman walked down the street about four houses. There was a bunch of Spanish and then a group of about five youngsters ran up the street.

"Señor Grande! You come back!" he called.

Little heads appeared around buildings and in doorways.

"Tell your friends I bring candy. Muchas dulces."

I opened up the back of the Explorer and sat inside handing out candy bars to any kid who approached. Juan stood aside watching the goings on happily. I was sure some of the kids came to the truck twice but I didn't care. I couldn't tell them all apart.

"Mas amigos!" I told Juan and he ran off to find more kids.

"Cassidy, why are you doing this?" Rusty asked.

"Because it makes me feel good. You do the same thing. You have a drawer full of toy cars at work. Each of these kids would have a toy car, too, if I had access to that drawer."

"Tell them the story of the great Señor Grande!" Juan asked.

The kids jumped up and down and asked for the story, too, so, sitting cross-legged in the back of the Explorer, I launched into the tale and Juan translated for the little kids. Even Juan's mother stood listening, as did several neighbors.

At first I thought the kids who came first got more candy than the late comers but I quickly saw that these kids were so used to making do they broke off pieces of their candy bars and traded the pieces so they could sample different kinds. They savored the sweetness and shared with others who came late. The candy got passed around until all the kids were a sticky mess and moms all over the village would be mad at me for getting all the kids onto a sugar high at the same time. It was time to go. The kids were hyper. Señor Grande was laid to rest. It was a good day.

That night, right on time, the doorbell rang. We all fell into our usual rolls when Chase dropped by for dinner. Rusty and I got up and scooted our chairs down. Bev got an extra place setting from the kitchen and Cody answered the door, then got a bottle of beer from the refrigerator. There was a difference this time, though. Everybody moved about with a feeling of relief that we got to do it one more time.

"What have we got tonight?" Chase asked. "Please, don't say beans and tortillas. Hey, rug rat, you've grown," he said to Katie.

"Ba bye!" Katie said.

"Are you hungry?" Bev asked her, "You want bites?"

"Ba Bye!" she said again.

"We've got bites!" said Bev. "We've got bites of pork chops and mashed potatoes, salad. I even have a pie for desert."

"Sounds wonderful," Chase said.

His arm was in a sling and his face was still swollen but he was looking more like Chase.

"Patrick has called me every day since Christmas," Chase said. "How much should I tell him?"

"I was at the ranch when we heard what happened. They know what a trouble magnet I am, and this was relatively minor trouble. Just don't tell him how to turn a camp stove into a Molotov cocktail or the gunpowder from bullets into a stick of dynamite."

"Is that what you did?" he asked.

"Um," I said looking around the table. "Yeah, that's why I was down to two shots."

"Cool!" Said Cody, "Will you show me?"

"No. How'd the date go?"

"What is it about girls and commitment? Why can't we just have a good time and not worry about the details? I mean, she's a nice enough girl and all but that doesn't mean I want to spend the rest of my life with her."

"How old is she?" asked Chase.

"Twenty four."

"She cute?"

"They're all cute."

"When you're done with her can I have a go at her?"

"Chase! You're old enough to be her father!" Bev said.

"So? Women my age are set on sitting around making afghans and quilts and going on RV trips to Las Vegas in the winter. The young ones are looking for adventure and a man of character."

"Well, you *are* a character," she said. "We've been waiting three days to piece all the parts of this little adventure of yours back together."

"Little adventure. It's been going on for months. Did you get a good look at the guy in the bus?" he asked me.

"I saw three men. I don't know which one you're thinking of."

"Juan Garcia, part Indian, part Mexican, part rattlesnake. Fancies himself a teacher. What he's really doing is starting people on the road to drug addiction. Kids in California start on weed, this guy has easy access to peyote. He poses as an Indian, plays a Mayan flute for the tourists and then lures unsuspecting kids out to experience a genuine Indian ritual. Once he brings them back it's pretty easy to con them into a high without so many side effects. Of course the price is a little steeper... you could say I've been documenting. Garcia was onto me and I was onto him and we were all happy doing this little Otay waltz until some big honcho down south gets tired of me and decides I've got to go. He offered Garcia a lump sum to bring me in. I thought it was an interesting little twist. Guess I could have taken it a little more seriously."

"Why would a guy that sells drugs live in a dump like that?"

"The money doesn't go to him. It goes south. Garcia's always in debt and they like to keep him that way. I think I'd be doing him a favor to have him arrested. It's a touchy situation, though. He seldom does any major dealing north of the border and he's out of our jurisdiction south of the border. How'd you get roped into this mess?" he asked me.

"Slick."

He swore. "Slick calls you just ignore it. Do you hear me?"

"I'd do it again if I had to. So don't make me have to. Why did you have to blow up my image into some supernatural tracker dude?"

"I didn't. Joe asked me who could track me and I just said you could. Joe must have expanded on it a little and the story grew with each telling. You didn't help much by living up to it."

Bill grinned, "You did?"

The storytelling went on late into the night. Cody thought it was funny how distorted my image became when it crossed the border. Bev was horrified to think how close I came to being discovered. Rusty was never going to let me out of his sight again after hearing about the chase back to the border. For some reason he only thought blowing up my stove and making fireworks was right up my alley.

"What made you think anybody would see those two words in the sand on a random hill in the Otay?" I asked.

"The only person I could count on to find them... was you. And I thought you'd go out with BORSTAR. I never dreamed you would piece it all together yourself."

"Just goes to show you how unobservant I was," Bill added. "I didn't even see it. I didn't know Cass had read anything in the sand until she asked me why you'd write the name of a beer up there. I didn't know about the bus."

"Why does Garcia have people walk down into the Otay? Why do they meet in that spot?"

"They don't always meet in that spot but the gist of it is if they want insight from the peyote it must come from nature and to listen to nature you have to immerse yourself in it. The part of the Otay they were in isn't wilderness area so technically it's kind of exempt from the rules of the wilderness area, plus it's just far enough away from everything that they can do what they want without anybody noticing. Go down to Tecate, wander around the shops, talk to the guy with the Mayan flute. He'll give you his little sales pitch."

"If it's that easy why hasn't anybody picked him up?"

"He's also got cop radar."

"Oh and I'm not cop like enough, am I?"

"You can't touch him south of the border. And he doesn't do much we can get him for north of the border."

"Has anybody tried buying other drugs from him when they are in the Otay?"

"Cassidy, drop it. It's none of your concern."

"He was enough of a concern for you to hike miles into the desert just to spy on him."

"He's... kind of a hobby of mine. It's like Wile E. Coyote and the Roadrunner. I've been shot at by that guy more than I ever was in uniform. I have this ultimate goal of arresting him but I never catch him at anything worth hauling him in for."

"How can you arrest him if you're retired?"

"I maintain volunteer status. And stretch the rules a little."

So we had Chase back and we had a sleazy drug dealer loose and there was nothing we could do about it. At least we had Chase back.

Chapter 14

It had been an interesting Christmas. I'd gotten to visit both my families. I'd learned a great deal about Santa Claus and Mexico. I'd gotten a taste of the outdoors and seen a little action. I was still in one piece. Life was good.

Rusty went back to work and we fell into the humdrum life of a typical American family. Katie and I jogged around the block every day. There was a spot where the road was uneven and Katie waited for us to hit that bump and then she laughed at the sudden dip. In the evenings Rusty came home and played games with Katie while I fixed dinner. Every few weeks I baked cookies. I took a bunch to the station and then went to the library. There was a homeless woman there in the mornings. I had met her a few months ago and learned that she knitted slippers for people at the homeless shelter. So whenever I made a cookie run I also made a yarn delivery at the library. My neighbor, Hazel Mireau, had dumped a large box of yarn on me when she heard Bertie could use it. On days that I made a cookie/yarn run to town I also visited the gym, hoping to stay in shape for searches.

One day I was getting ready for just such a cookie/yarn run when my cell phone rang. It was Schroeder. That was a surprise. If I was called on a search it was usually Lou "Strict" Strickland who called. I wondered if something had happened to Rusty on the job. I answered feeling tense and worried.

"Hello?"

"Cassidy. I wanted to give you a heads up that you might be needed soon."

A rush of relief went through me.

"How soon?"

"Not today. Thought you could use some advanced warning so you can line up a sitter."

"Yeah, thanks. Why not today?"

"So far the search is all urban. You'll get a call back if it goes the direction we expect it to."

"I was getting ready to go to the station anyway. Can I listen in on the goings on?"

"Sure."

"I'll be wracking my brain about who can babysit."

It was about half way to town that an idea for a babysitter whapped me upside the head. Bertie! Bertie was homeless by choice but I bet if she had a chance to do a good deed, get a shower, do some laundry, and have a roof over her head for a few days at a stretch she would jump at it. She loved Katie. I mentally did a little happy dance.

When I got to the station I searched out Rusty. I knocked and peeked in his window like usual. He knew the knock and answered the door. I got my hug in and entered his office.

"I need to run an idea past you and, if you say yes, I need to run."

"No," he said.

"You haven't heard it yet."

"I know but usually if you need to run it past me it involves firearms and…"

"It's not like that. Schroeder called to tell me they might need me soon for a search they are working on in town. Have you heard about it?"

"Yeah. It could be a tracking case for you."

"We need a babysitter and my idea is to get Bertie to babysit."

"Bertie?"

"Bertie Bag Lady."

"How do you know Bertie?"

"I met her in the library when I was doing some investigating. She loves kids and babysitting would give her a chance to get a shower, do laundry, earn a few bucks, get her off the street for a day or two. What do you think?"

"Sounds great. What's the catch?"

"Well, I'd hate to put her to work and then drop her off at the homeless shelter every night. Could she just stay in the guest room until the search is over?"

"So you want her to work for room and board by babysitting?"

"Can you think of a better solution?"

"No, unless Hazel wants to do it."

"I think putting Katie and Hazel together for a full day straight is pushing it. Plus it doesn't help Bertie. The whole point to asking Bertie is to give her a chance to get off the streets."

"Talk to her. She and I will figure out nights if she agrees to it."

"Oh yay!"

"Do I get a cookie?"

"Yeah, show me where they are working on the search. I asked Schroeder if I could listen in."

I walked into the command center. There was a map laid out and lists of people with checks by them if they had been contacted and questioned. Leads had been followed up on and possibilities had been scratched off a list.

Bringing Katie and a bowl of cookies into the room didn't help much. The bowl of cookies got passed from hand to hand without much of a break in conversation but Katie was amongst friends. Friends with lots of pockets. Friends with radios and interesting patches. As Katie made her way around the room it was obvious this was not going to work. Every time they handed her off the next person in line had to empty their pockets, reposition their radio, take off hats and glasses. I was getting valuable information out of the meeting, but I needed to get Katie out of there. She was driving the whole room to distraction. I decided to go work on Bertie.

The library was less than a block away so I tried there first. Katie was not the best library visitor. She called out to anybody with a large purse, book pack or pockets. I spent the whole time there shushing her uselessly. We found the newspaper nook and Bertie was nowhere in sight. One problem with finding a homeless person is that they don't have an address. I looked at the clock. She wouldn't head for the shelter for several hours. I walked out to Main Street and looked up and down it. Hmm. I went back to the station and started asking around.

"I'm looking for Bertie, the bag lady. Any idea where she is this time of the day?"

"Try the gas station at the end of the street."

"Okay, thanks. Um… what's she doing there? Or do I not want to know?"

"I'm just speculating, but she probably uses the restroom. And the chilidogs and frozen burgers are so gross there they get thrown in the trash real quick."

"She eats food from the trash?"

"Sometimes."

"Okay. Maybe I can help in that department, too."

I put Katie in her car seat and drove down to the gas station. Sure enough, there was Bertie sitting next to a trashcan. I pulled up into a parking place.

"Come eat lunch with me," I said through an open window.

"Can't."

"Why?"

"Nobody wants me in their establishment."

"Oh come on. We can find some place."

She stood up and looked herself up and down like she was wondering what she could do to make herself presentable enough for lunch out.

I got out of the Jeep and unbuckled Katie.

"Come on," I said leading her into the restroom. "What's wrong? Why won't they let you in?"

"Too dirty," she said.

"So? Wash up. It doesn't take much to wash up."

"It's not just my hands or my face. It's…it's everything."

Ah ha, time to put in my first plug for babysitting.

"If you had a place to wash, would you do it?"

"Depends. Takes me a week to save up enough money for a Laundromat."

"I'm not talking about a Laundromat. If you had a chance to wash for free. Would you do it?"

"I wouldn't impose on nobody."

"What if it would help that person? What if you washing your clothes and taking a shower would actually help them out too? Here," I said fingering the outer layer, "the outside layer is the worst. Take one layer off. You'll be in my nice warm car. You don't need all the layers."

She took off a threadbare blouse and a faded calico skirt. She still had old polyester slacks on under the skirt.

"See? This is easy."

"You think I'm dirty?"

"I'm just trying to get you to eat lunch with me. I'd take you however you'll go."

"Why?"

"Because I have a favor to ask."

"Don't need to buy me lunch to get a favor out of me."

"I know, but I want to. It's going to take some talking and lunch is good for talking. I brought some more yarn for you, too."

"Oh, all right. I'll go. No place fancy though. I can't stand them stiff places where a person can't even shake their own pepper."

"Me too."

There was a café down the street that attracted a large percentage of elderly customers. They were used to people of all kinds and we didn't stick out much at all.

"Now what did you want to ask me?" she said after she had read the menu several times and finally come to a decision.

"I need a babysitter, not often, but when I do need one, I need one quick. There aren't many people I can call on at a moment's notice. You and Katie get along great. You can use all the things at my house, the washer and dryer, the shower, the kitchen, as long as you watch Katie. I'll pay you so you'll have a little pocket money. If you will do it, it would help both of us. If Rusty works late there's even a guest room you can use."

The waitress came up and took our drink order. I ordered iced tea and a basket of crackers. Bertie ordered a root beer float.

"I can't say yes right away. There's factors you can't know about. Who will help Jerry? And will they give my cot away at the shelter if I don't use it?"

"It won't be often. It's not like a regular job. I get called out for a search when someone gets lost. Sometimes I can find them in a few hours. More often it takes me a few days. Who is Jerry?"

"Why, he's an old man, older'n me even. We have a date every other Friday. We go dumpster diving. We go on Friday because the pickings are better. Sometimes we can find a whole meal in one box. Sometimes we find clothes we can use."

"Well, Jerry is your problem, you'd have to figure that out for yourself. I think we can talk to the shelter and when they see you're doing something useful they'll want to encourage you in that."

"Could be."

"Usually if people are going to get lost they do it over a weekend and I get called on Sunday or Monday after the family gets truly worried."

The waitress brought our drinks and crackers and she took our order. I ordered small, not wanting to be ostentatious in front of Bertie. I ordered a turkey club with fries. Bertie knew exactly what she wanted. She ordered a side of bacon, a side of sausage, two eggs over medium. "Make them yolks soft, whites hard. I don't want no runny whites. It's gross." She added a slice of pecan pie and a side of fruit. I didn't question it, though I thought the order rather odd. Especially since I just pulled her away from a trash can where people dumped gross chili dogs and microwaved, frozen hamburgers.

I crushed a packet of crackers and emptied the contents onto Katie's high chair tray.

She held up a crumb. "Ba Bye!" she said and stuck it in her mouth.

"Yes! Bite!" I said cheerfully.

"Has she said her first word yet?" Bertie asked.

"No, she comes close. She has baby words for a few things. Ba-bye for bite, Dada for Rusty, Mama for me, baba for her bottle. Typical baby talk."

"Baba!" Katie said.

Shoot, I was hoping to save that for naptime. I gave her a sip of my tea.

"Why don't I give you a ride out to my house and you can see what you think?"

"If you lived in a two room apartment with a laundry room in the basement of the building it'd still be the Ritz."

"One reason I am asking right now is because I might have to go out in the next few days. The police are searching the city right now. If the search moves on to the desert I'll get called in. I'd like to be there right now, getting what information I can out of all their investigating but I can't. All the guys want to hold Katie and she was causing too much disruption."

"So, you got a meetin' you're supposed to be at?"

"It's not required, but it would be helpful to me to be there." Actually, the meeting was pulling at me and I was fighting it like mad.

Our food came in two trips. Bertie waited until her pecan pie was on the table and bowed her head quietly for a moment.

"When you're used to cast off food you learn to be grateful for what you got," she said and then dug straight into the pie. "You only live once, so eat desert first. I may not be around for the main course."

"Of course you will."

"I'm not taking any chances."

I broke up a couple of fries and dropped them all over Katie's highchair tray. Then I pulled off tiny bits of meat and bread. By the time I'd given her enough to keep her busy it looked like my sandwich had been attacked by a chicken.

"So, after lunch you want me to babysit."

"No, if you have something better to do you should do it."

"Yes, you do. You want to go to that meeting. You got the detective gene as bad as that hunk of a husband of yours. You can't get your hands on a case but you is itching to go work on it. Today's not Friday, is it?"

"No, today's only Tuesday."

"Good! Then I'll do it."

"You will?"

"Sure, it'll be fun."

"You remember the rules?"

"Empty my pockets, take off my watch, only wear earrings if I want my ears rearranged, no cell phone, not that I got one."

"Remember, Katie can crawl now, so you have to keep an eye on her every minute. She can't get out of her crib but she can climb out of the cradle. She's kind of outgrown it, anyway. Oh and she can climb out of the swing once it stops moving. If you want her to stay in her car seat you have to strap her in. She'll stay in the high chair as long as you're in the room and there's hope for more food. She'll play on a blanket on the floor if you put something under it first. Or you can use a quilt that my mom made that holds toys in pockets. She's still trying to figure those pockets out but don't trust her to stay in one place. Oh and…"

"Cassidy, I've had kids before."

"I know. You just haven't had *this* kid."

"A kid's a kid."

"I'll see what you think at the end of the day."

Bertie stacked all her plates up and pushed them to the end of the table.

"That was good!"

"Why did you order a simple breakfast when you could have gotten anything on the menu?"

"Because I haven't had fresh eggs for over a year. In the shelter all you get is huge vats of scrambled eggs. I just love the taste of the meat dipped in that rich golden yolk. I had chickens when I was a kid. We had fresh eggs every day. When rough times hit we could always count on having chicken or eggs even if we couldn't count on beef or bread or sugar."

I paid for our lunch and I drove her and her bags out to the house. She took off her shoes and left them on the porch but I think her socks were just as dirty. I wasn't worried about the dirt. I was the one in the family who went crawling around in the undergrowth looking for tracks.

"How'd a young thing like you afford a house like this?"

"Bertie! What a question to ask! But as it turns out we both had smaller houses before we bought this one."

I showed Bertie around, opening cupboards that had things she might need to use, and pointing out where baby things were kept.

I showed her where the washer and dryer were and where she could shower if she got a chance.

"Wowie, kazowie! Now that's what I call a shower. You don't even need a man with a shower like that!"

"A man makes it better," I said.

"Hell yeah, especially your man! Can I use it?"

"Just remember you're watching a baby. Go ahead and use the laundry soap, shampoo, conditioner, whatever you need. I'll write my cell phone number on the white board in the kitchen in case you have questions. Oh and, if by chance, you ever have to call 911 there's no need to give them an address. They all know where Rusty Michaels' house is, in fact they'll think I'm in trouble and send every department they have on hand. Police first, then the rescue squad, then the ambulance. You're sure you want to babysit?"

"Oh yeah! I'd do it just to try out that shower. Soon's that baby goes to sleep I'm going to be in there! I wish I had a camera!"

I wasn't going ask what her plans were for a shower and a camera. We walked into the living room and I just stood there holding Katie.

"Cassidy, it'll be a cinch. She'll be fine. We'll play and take a nice nap."

"You forgot something."

"What?"

"You've got your watch on. What's in your pockets?"

"Oh yeah."

When she had stripped down to two layers and the contents of her pockets were on the breakfast bar, along with her watch and all her bags, I handed Katie over.

"Rusty and I will probably be home around seven."

The guys were still pouring through facts, rumors and fake sightings when I got back. I sat there listening trying to fit pieces together but I'd missed a lot when I was with Bertie. I was lost until it got around to who had and had not seen our ten sixty-five. I still didn't have a name.

"Hold it," I said and Schroeder held back a swear word. "Map out the circles so it shows where they overlap. I'm willing to bet the circle that knows something will give you an idea where the problem lies. If you know the problem it will point you in the direction the person would seek a solution."

"What do you mean?"

I drew a large circle on the white board and wrote the first name in it.

"Who is this person?"

"Andario's girlfriend."

"Okay next. Who is Norma Chavez?"

"The girlfriend's best friend."

"Okay so we'll give her a circle overlapping Celia Dominguez."

"Who is Arleta Richardson?"

"She's his tutor in Trig class."

"How old's this person?"

"Sixteen."

"And he's in trig class? You're dealing with intelligence here. He's probably a thinker, despite the fact that he needs a tutor. At least he cares enough to have one. You're likely to find out he thought himself into a problem so deep he thinks he can't get out of it. Now, let's put the rest of these people in here."

Andario was a popular kid. We had circles all over the place but when we started crossing people off we found a little thread through the crazy life Andario led.

"Once you contact everybody do the same thing with the people who are left. See where the circles overlap."

"Cassidy, we've been at this for two days. Sit back and we'll hash this out."

I went to Rusty's office and found paper and pen. I went back to the meeting room and copied the chart from the white board. I took down all the notes I could. I listened. I added more notes. I made a chart of places Andario had been and the times he had been there. I found those places on a map I came to the conclusion that Andario did not have wheels. All the places he had been to he walked to, unless it was confirmed he was with a friend or parent who had a car. School, the mall, Tae Kwon Do class, those were normal activities and I scratched them off my list. These places he had walked to, though, they bugged me. And there was an empty space of time that was not accounted for.

Despite being shoved off to the side to observe, I noticed officers would come in, take a look at the diagrams and add the information they had gathered. I jotted it all down.

That one empty space still bugged me. Hours went by and still that space remained blank. And there were still a few people unaccounted for. The more I looked at the notes and the chart the more I felt that the key was one person. And it was that one, right there, the one with the name all alone, the circle not over lapping any of the others. This outside influence. Not a school friend. Not a church member. Not a friend of the family. Not...anything. Yet somehow Andario knew this person. The five hours before he disappeared nobody knew where he was, yet here was this one person. No one would think to go to that one person because they didn't know him. I sure wished I was a detective so I could get in a police car, drive over and talk to the guy. Rusty was on another assignment. The only name in the circle was Buck. No address. No phone number. No reference. That circle niggled at my mind. Who was Buck? Where had Andario met him? What kind of a guy was he?

As the circles filled in more and more with good solid information that made sense, I was more determined than ever that this missing link was the key. Friends admitted he was dealing with a lot of social tensions. Teachers admitted he was having trouble in school, but not alarmingly so. His family didn't know what was going on at all. The church described Andario as a leader, a kid who kept the others motivated to do well.

At first the police stuck him on the runaway list, but a sixteen year old boy on his own in Joshua Hills didn't worry them much. With their hands full of juvenile delinquents one good kid who just wanted out was trivial. What got their attention was a friend mentioning that Andario had talked about suicide. This caused a whole new chain of actions, so here we were, in a race against Andario's mind. But I was still convinced that this guy Buck, from who knew where, had the key. It bugged me so much I couldn't sit still in the meeting room any more. I decided to take a drive over to Andario's part of town. He tended to walk to places close to his house. Maybe he walked someplace nobody thought he would. Maybe he met somebody there. A city the size of Joshua Hills, I didn't expect to be able to walk to a shopping center or into a restaurant and see anybody who stood out. If they did I should probably run the other way. Normally if a person stood out to me it was because they were trouble. But maybe I was looking for a just a little bit of trouble, just not *my* trouble, Andario's.

A half mile from Andario's house were two strip malls. They didn't look promising. I doubted a high school kid would choose to hang out at a grocery store unless there was a particularly cute girl bagging groceries. There was a walk in hair salon, a Subway sandwich shop, a cigarette store, a Laundromat, a thrift store, a craft store and a bank. Across the parking lot was a Taco Bell, and a Burger King. I started down the line. I walked the grocery store knowing it would amount to nothing. The hair salon proved a little more useful.

"Good afternoon, how may I help you?" the receptionist asked.

"I'm looking for a boy, high school age, tall, black hair, brown eyes."

"You just described half the kids in town," she said.

A stylist walked up to the counter with a slip of paper in her hand, "Carl?" she said. A man got up and followed her to a chair.

"Do all your customers sign in with a first name?" I asked.

"Yes."

"Do you have many regular customers?"

"Oh yeah, lots of people come here because it's handy and they are in and out quick."

"Do you have a customer by the name of Andario?"

"I'm sorry but we're not allowed to give out information about our clients."

That meant yes. If they didn't recognize the name they would have thought it over and said no.

"When was the last time you saw Andario?"

"Miss, I just told you I can't give out information about our clients. Would you go to a place that talked about you to strangers who wandered in asking questions?"

"If I went missing for days at a time, and my family had contacted the police, I would hope my hair salon might bend the rules to help get me back."

"I'm sorry, if you were an officer maybe we'd help."

"Would it be worth an officer's time to come out?"

"I don't think so. Would you like a haircut? Style?"

I felt my hair. I guess I could use a trim.

"Sure."

"Name?"

"Cassidy."

"Okay, Cassidy, have a seat. It'll be about ten minutes."

I took a seat and found a magazine and learned what the top ten divorce cases in the country were, rated by dollar amounts and mudslinging. Just what I always wanted to know. I looked through a hair book hoping a style would jump out at me. There wasn't much I could do with my hair. No matter what I did I came out looking like Skipper.

"Cassidy?" a young woman with a familiar slip of paper called out.

I put down the hair book, got up and followed her into the salon.

"Cassidy, is that, like, the Sundance Kid? How do you want your hair?"

"No, it's as in Butch."

"Butch?"

"Yeah."

"You?"

"Yeah."

"Are you sure?"

"That's what my dad's always told me."

"Your dad likes it butch? But you're so *cute!*"

"He wanted a boy."

"O…kay…If you're sure."

I sat in the chair and she put a black cape around my neck. She spread it out carefully so all the hairs would fall the right directions, then she got out the clippers and turned them on. The buzzing sound caught my attention just as she was bringing the clippers up to shave the back of my head.

"Wait!" I cried. "What are you doing?"

"You said you wanted it butch!"

"No! I said I'm Cassidy as in Butch Cassidy."

"Whew, you never know in this job. If you went through with it I was going to suggest a tattoo but I don't think you're really the tattoo type."

"I don't think my husband would like that. I just need a trim."

I had a little bit better luck with the stylist than I did with the receptionist but I wondered if I was getting her in trouble with her boss.

"So, what have you been up to today?" she asked.

"I'm out looking for a friend of mine. He lives near here so I thought he might frequent the businesses here."

"Oh yeah? Who's that?"

"His name is Andario."

"Oh yeah, the human calculator. I ask him questions and he does the math in his head. He is amazing."

"Has he been in lately?"

"No, but you know how scruffy he lets his hair get. I bet his mother *makes* him come in. I think he looks cuter when his hair is a little long but he always gets it cut short. Then I don't see him for a month or more."

"Last time you saw him was there something bothering him?"

"I don't think so but I see so many people in a day one conversation blends into another. My day is one long conversation."

I didn't learn a whole lot but I left the salon feeling perkier. I thought I was headed in the right direction.

The sandwich shop didn't know Andario by name or description. I was relieved the cigarette shop asked for ID but they only looked for the age and for fake IDs.

"Every kid in the area comes in here eventually," the cigarette guy said. "I can't turn them in but I can turn them away."

I looked at the strip mall across the street. A little coffee shop drew my attention. Kids these days lived on coffee. I noticed the shop attracted a wide variety of people. Outside was a Jeep, a Mercedes, two old junkers and a couple of normal family type cars. The Jeep caught my eye. It was more beat up than mine. It had seen some action recently. There was dried mud on the tires and up the sides. The top was torn. The bumper sticker said, "This vehicle brakes for reloading." It had political bumper stickers for three elections. An Indian dream catcher dangled from the mirror.

The coffee shop was a modern place. They sold a variety of coffee and tea drinks, pastries, and microwave sandwiches. There were ten tables. Some had cushy wing chairs. A few had stiff backed chairs. Two kids sat at one table. They had scruffy hair and baggy jeans. One played a guitar quietly. His buddy had a skateboard and a book pack propped up against his chair. The pack was open as was a laptop computer. He was plugging away on the keyboard. A woman in business attire sipped a coffee with lots of whipped cream and drizzles on top. A man I took to be the Jeep guy exited the restrooms in back and made his way to a table with another laptop on it. He moved the mouse and clicked a few times, then settled in to read. A couple of guys at a table seemed to belong to the junkers. Students or house painters. I couldn't tell which.

"Doug? Wes?" a girl in a black coffee house apron asked. She handed the two house painters their coffees and they walked out and rumbled away in their junkers. They drag raced off in the same direction, probably on the same job together.

"Hey darlin'," the Jeep guy said.

"Hi," I responded.

"You look undecided. I come in here every day. I'll tell you how the girls narrow down the choices. Hot or cold?"

"Actually, I'm not here for coffee. But you helped me narrow down the choices. Mind if I sit down?"

He raised an eyebrow. He was obviously getting further than he expected. He was fiftyish, had long black curly hair, cargo pants, leather deck shoes. His shoes were not very worn. His shirt was chamois. Hmm, stylish outdoorsy.

"Go ahead, but hang on, I need to finish this thought."

He bent over this computer and typed a few paragraphs, read through them and closed the window open on his screen.

"Well, well, if you're not here for coffee you're what...applying for a job? You can do better, though Mark will take one look at you and hire you on the spot. All you need is a pretty smile and a cool head."

"I have a job. What do you do?"

"Writer. *Field and Stream*. Right now I'm working on a article about hunting moose in Alaska."

"Yeah? When did you go to Alaska?"

"Never been there. Doesn't stop me from writing about it."

"Do you sell many articles?"

"Nah, I do better at my other job."

"What's that?"

"Radio talk show host."

"You're kidding. How did you get into that?"

"Weird circles, loud, obnoxious opinions. What do you do?"

"I'm a tracker."

He sat back in his chair and gave me a "This ought to be good" look.

"Actually I'm tracking a kid right now. I'm just missing the tracks. If you come in here a lot you might have run into him. His name's Andario."

"This kid in trouble?"

"I don't know. That's what we're trying to figure out. His parents reported him missing. I just came on board today. I got tired of trying to keep up with the police and branched out on my own."

"What made you branch out this direction?"

"A hunch. A blank spot in Andario's life that nobody knows about but one person."

"You always just drive around town following hunches?"

"Depends on where the hunches come from. I don't make a practice of driving around town and asking people questions, because more often than not it leads to trouble. This hunch has been paying off so far."

"No kidding?"

A high school aged girl walked quickly up to the man in the chair. "Buck?" she said. "Here's your Foglifter. How many of those can you drink in one day? Dang! I'd be, like, jittery or hyper or something."

"Thanks, Amy," Buck said. "Actually she's always jittery or hyper or something."

No kidding. My hunch was paying off big time. It was my turn to sit back in the chair with a "this ought to be good" look, but I also ordered a white chocolate mocha cappuccino.

"When did you last see Andario?" I asked Buck.

He sat back, sipped his coffee, took the lid off, stirred it and blew on it.

"Tell me about this tracking you do. I like to write about the outdoors. You're obviously outdoors a lot. Tell me what it involves."

"There's enough articles about me. I don't need any more."

"Okay, tell me about that."

"I rescued a photographer. He did a pictorial on search and rescue after that. I rescued a newspaper columnist. He did a full page on the local search and rescue organization. Shoot. I was the tracker trapped in a mine. I was the tracker who found Sherri Champlain. I don't need publicity. I need to find Andario. So, when was the last time you saw him?"

"Last week. Tell me what's involved in tracking."

I figured this was one of those poker game conversations. No, this was more like dominoes. We each played taking turns. Maybe I'd get more points, maybe not, but at least he was giving a little. Okay, so I'd give a little, too.

"My search commander points me to some footprints. I find the next one, and the next until I find the person who left the footprints behind. It's as simple or as complex as you want to make it. The process is simple, the technicalities of it can be mind-numbingly difficult. What was Andario's frame of mind when you talked to him?"

"It depended on the subject at hand. Sometimes he was bright and intelligent. He loves a good joke and he can't put down a riddle. A riddle would drive him crazy for days. He had a cute girl. He had a good life. But he's a typical sixteen year old. He wants to find out what more there is to life. I told him he had it good, he was better off where he was. I told him to stick to school. I told him time was on his side. But."

"Why you?"

"Because I'm loud, obnoxious and opinionated. And people just naturally talk to me anyway. Tell me how you follow tracks."

"I'm sure you've noticed footprints before. You know how to follow them. You probably can tell something about a person by looking at their tracks, whether they're an adult or a kid, male or female. You take the same things you already know and put those tracks in different terrains and it gets a little trickier. Some terrains are almost impossible to track in. It's easier to demonstrate than it is to talk about it."

"So…demonstrate."

"I've got a kid to find. You left off with a qualifier. But. But what? He didn't want to stick to school? He was doing fine in school. He was doing fine at home. He has close friends at church. Yet off he goes. Where?"

"Only you could know that. You're sure he needs finding?"

"No, I'm sure he needs locating. His family needs to know he's all right. Is he?"

"I don't know."

"What makes you think he might not be?"

"How did you get into tracking?"

"I grew up doing it. I grew up where I could follow my curiosity and I was curious about how animals moved and where they went, so I followed their tracks. After a while I followed their tracks until I found the animal.

Then I got curious about how animals lived so I went camping and got to know them better. Tracking people is even easier than tracking animals. The more I followed tracks the more I learned. The more I learned the farther I tracked. What makes you think Andario might not be okay?"

"He might be fine. The kid I saw was stretched. Everybody expected too much out of him. He wanted to be free of all that. Tensions were eating at him. His kid mind blew it up into problems. His adult mind would grapple with them. It was interesting to watch. Made me glad I didn't have to go back to being a teen again. Imagine being a teenager these days. I sure wouldn't want to. So what does a teenage tracker do?"

I laughed, "Well, they sure don't date much. I trained horses, did a little cowboying, hunting, camping. School was just a way to lock me indoors. I had no social life beyond the ranch. What did Andario do to escape these problems that aren't really problems?"

"I showed him a place. He thought he could escape his problems by killing himself. At first it sent chills down my spine. A kid, missing out on so much just when he was fixing to be free to soar. The pain. The loss his family would feel. The way his whole school would fall into mourning. The toll that would take on the kids. The articles in the paper. The shocked readers all over town. I had to do something. Something that would show him some perspective so I took him out and showed him Piedra View. I showed him the expanse of desert. I asked him if he saw any problems out there. He didn't think before he said 'no'. I told him if he walked out there for less than a day his problems out there would be triple his problems at school. He told me he wished he could just walk out there and keep walking until he couldn't walk anymore and when he couldn't walk he'd crawl and when he couldn't crawl he'd be far enough away that there would be no finding him. And then pretty soon he'd be free. I told him he could try it. I told him if he turned around at any time he could see the rock and know the way back. I just hope he didn't try it. How far have you tracked a man before?"

"Four days. Fifteen miles. A week old trail. He was an experienced woodsman, though, not some teenage kid. Are you suggesting I check out Piedra View?"

"Couldn't hurt. You're not going out there alone are you?"

"No, I'm just one small part of a team. I usually go out with an EMT. I bet I go out with two, since we don't know what Andario's reaction is going to be. How long have you known Andario?"

"I don't claim to know him at all. He's a kid who comes in. I talked to him once and he adopted me. We'd talk for ten or fifteen minutes a day. He'll be okay, if he can just stay on track. He just doesn't see it."

Piedra View was a rocky promontory that overlooked the town one direction and desert the other. Rock climbers frequented the face of it. Lovers frequented the top. I drove out there quickly. I took the windy road up the backside of it. I stood on top looking at the vast desert below. Come sundown the top of the bluff would fill up with cars but during the day it revealed miles of waterless nothingness. It was true. If Andario walked out there, he could walk far enough to be unfindable, except by me. I followed the trail to the bottom of the bluff. Many people had walked this trail, climbed a few rocks and walked back up. I walked down, followed the base of the bluff and watched for tracks. There were too many close to the base so I widened my search making a bigger circle and still a bigger one. At last I was down to just a few sets of tracks and only one headed out into the emptiness of the Mojave Desert. I squatted down next to a good track sample and memorized the size, tread and stride. It all seemed to match a teenage boy. Tall, slightly gangly, slightly big feet, feet he would grow into. I followed his tracks out into the desert until I was convinced, then I zigzagged back to try and find a return trail. There was none.

Chapter 15

I strode purposefully into the command center and quickly took stock of the situation. Schroeder stopped what he was saying, took note of my presence and attitude. A question flickered there before he went on. It appeared they were still combing Andario's social circles for a missing link. We couldn't start a search tonight so I let him finish.

"Where have you been all afternoon?" he finally asked me.

"Following up on a hunch."

"Oh no. What happened?"

"It paid off."

"That's it? No trouble?"

"I almost had my head shaved. Does that count?"

"Why would you do that?"

"A misunderstanding. Do you want to know what I learned or not."

"I'm not sure. Anybody else I'd say fork it over."

I walked over to the white board.

"Does anybody know who Buck is?"

"No, Andario only mentioned him to one person. That person doesn't know who he is either. It was just a name that went by in a conversation. They happened to remember it so it made the list."

"I know who he is."

Schroeder cocked his head like a parrot hearing a new and interesting word for the first time.

"Every afternoon Buck goes to the coffee shop near Andario's house. He drinks Foglifters and writes outdoor adventure stories about places he's never visited. Every afternoon Andario stops at this coffee house on the way home from school and he talks to Buck there. The place makes good white chocolate mocha cappuccinos. Buck told me where to look for Andario. I checked it out and he was right. There is one trail of tracks leading off into the desert. One trail. None coming back. I can be ready to track at first light."

Schroeder wasn't going to believe me that easily. I had to go back and replay the afternoon in detail. When I finished he sat back put his head in his hands and said, "Oh lord, why me?"

The search for the first two days went surprisingly easy. Andario did exactly as Buck had said and walked off into the desert. The first day I could tell his emotions were a mess. He was driven to walk. As he grew tired his brain started thinking beyond the emotions of the moment. As he became exhausted he wasn't sure this was a good plan anymore. He stopped frequently but I wasn't convinced it was because he had to. I thought he was reconsidering. Maybe the desert wasn't such an easy way out. Maybe the problems back home were more bearable than this.

The enemy for any search is weather. Rain erodes tracks. Snow covers tracks. In our case the enemy was wind. By ten o'clock in the morning a windstorm had whipped up to make tracking miserable. Dust got whipped up into our eyes. It got in our ears. Little rocks stung when they hit.

I tracked as fast as I could. Despite the ease of the trail I knew I had but hours to find Andario. In two hours his tracks would be in the next county. I pulled up the collar on my jacket and hunkered down in. I wished I could wear sunglasses but they interfered with reading the ground. I walked quickly only verifying the tracks as I went. Time was precious when my information was blowing away one grain at a time. I could see it eroding before my eyes.

"We need air support!" I yelled over the blowing wind. "The tracks aren't going to hold out."

"Strict won't send a helicopter into this," Victor yelled back. "It's too dangerous and visibility from the air is zilch. We'll go as far as we can and turn it into a field search. At least we will pin point a direction to look in."

It didn't even do any good to call his name. Our voices came right back at us. We couldn't be heard more than three feet away. I had to lean into the wind and I was glad I brought my heavy pack.

Finally about a half hour later we managed to see a lone figure stumbling around in the desert, arms held over his eyes. The three of us hurried forward, eager to put an end to this search. The guys made better headway against the wind. A gust knocked Andario over and he pushed himself to his feet about the time Victor caught up to him. Andario stumbled back in surprise, looked for a place to run. He raised a fist and Victor blocked it just in time.

"Hold it!" he called out. "We're friends here!"

The words whipped away and I pieced them together as a few blew by at fifty miles an hour.

"...no friends," Andario said.

I caught up about then.

"Yes, you do," I said. "We found lots of friends when we tried to figure out where to look for you. We talked to lots of people who need you back."

"A girl! You jerks! What are you doing hauling a girl out here! This is hell," Andario said. At least he wasn't totally focused on his problems.

"We didn't haul her out here. She hauled us. Come on, let's get out of here. You're tired and hungry. Let's go get some grub," Victor said.

"No." Andario said, "I'm not going back. You came out here for nothing."

"We don't do searches for nothing," I said. "We do it for you. Because we know life is more precious than you would ever believe. You've got so much time going for you. Imagine all the things you could do if you'd give yourself a chance. Your highest highs are still ahead of you. You keep walking and you'll never see them. There's a big wide world out there. I've seen some of the best of it. It's awesome. And I've seen some of the worst of it and this ugly storm doesn't even come close to being the worst of it. One glimpse of awesome is worth months of darkness. Come home. Find that out for yourself."

Landon looked at me like, *"where did that little speech come from?"*

Andario waffled as we stood there in the blowing dust and desert sand. Landon jumped to the side and let a tumbleweed pass. It wasn't tumbling. It was flying. Another one hit Andario square in the back sending little branches flying around him and hitting all of us. He cried out in pain as hundreds of little stickers penetrated his clothes.

"Let's get the hell...Oh Hell! Hit the dirt! Everybody! Hit the dirt!"

We turned to see a wall of dirt bearing down on us. A massive dust cloud miles wide and hundreds of feet high. It was pure desert fury. I dropped my pack and pulled out my tent. I knew the floor of it would protect against the sand and flying rocks. I kept the bundle small until I located the door, then I stepped into it and pulled the tent around me.

"What are you doing?" Landon yelled. "Get down! Cassidy! Get down!"

A sudden gust of wind caught the door, filled the tent with air and whisked me and the tent right off the ground. I fell to the bottom of it and I felt the tent fly away like a magic carpet into the desert sky. My weight wasn't nearly enough to offset the wind. Away it sailed with me hanging onto any loose fabric I could, wondering how in the world I was going to come down and where.

I don't know how long I was in the air. All I could see was dust, dirt, little branches and leaves, anything that could be picked up by the wind. It was a brown swirling mass of confusion. I had no idea how high up I was. I couldn't move around much for fear of collapsing the tent and having it plummet from an unknown height. Everything was tan, gritty, musty smelling. I closed my eyes to protect them from the sand. Occasionally the wind would shift and the sides of the tent buckled making me worry about taking a plunge straight to the desert floor.

I came in for a very rough landing. The tent slammed into a solid object and I slammed into the side of the tent and slid to the bottom. The sides of the tent folded around me before I could get a handle on my situation. I slid to the bottom of the tent and hung there while the storm raged. There was no point finding my way out. It was safer to stay in the confines of the tent. Outside was a confusion of howling wind, the tapping of sand on the tent fabric, a flapping of nylon. I checked my cuts to make sure they were superficial and then made myself as comfortable as possible to wait out the dust storm. One thing a trouble magnet learns very quickly is when to admit that doing nothing was the best course of action. Finding my way out of the tent would accomplish nothing, but a rest would help me prepare for whatever happened next.

I woke to the motions of the tent still rattling in the wind. It flapped about me making an awful racket. I looked up. The tent had been skewered by a Joshua tree. A Joshua tree is half tree and half yucca. It has a trunk like a tree but there the resemblance ends. The top of it is like a huge yucca pant, or perhaps like Spanish dagger. It's not a pleasant place to be. My cuts on my arm and side bled and stung. I had plenty of time to analyze my situation and I didn't like the conclusions I came to. I had no pack, no food, no water, and I didn't know where I was, besides up a tree. I wasn't even sure how I'd get down. Joshua trees come in all shapes and sizes.

My thoughts wandered back to the guys. I wondered what the storm had been like for them. Then I ran through what I could remember of windstorms in this area. Seemed to me they could last all day and half the night but I usually woke to a calm morning. Sigh, so I could he here for half a day. Then I started arguing with myself whether to brave the storm or wait it out. Judging from previous experience I thought if I tried to walk around out there I'd be blown away again. I'd had to fight the wind before the big storm hit and then I was wearing my pack. I was better off here...except that the guys would be looking for me. They would radio Strict. Strict would roll his eyes and formulate a plan. But I didn't need rescuing. I just needed to be on the ground knowing what direction to head. I was sure, given those two things, I'd be in good shape.

I tried to quit thinking, to just lie in the bottom of the tent and try to sleep, to conserve energy in case it was needed later but I couldn't rest. I tried climbing to the top of the tent and looking out but I was met with a shower of dirt and the tent ripped more. I didn't want the tent to fall until I knew a little more about my situation. I was going to feel very silly if I climbed to the top of the tent and found myself close to the ground. There was a window under me so I unzipped a corner of it and looked down. Damn. This was a big Joshua tree and the storm still raged. Unzipping the window did give me a better idea how to get down, though. The screen and the tent fabric would both unzip so I could just lower myself out the window when the storm stopped. The flap of the window would get me a couple feet closer to the ground. Every little bit helped.

My stomach began growling in the middle of the afternoon. I had eaten breakfast but I'd lost my pack before lunch. One packet of oatmeal and a cup of hot chocolate was all I'd eaten that day. Seems like I could find something better, especially if it was supposed to hold me until I remembered to eat again. Or was able.

It was well after dark when the wind finally let up. Little gusts still rocked the tent but I decided it was time to assess my situation. I tried climbing the tent again but the fabric ripped alarmingly. I didn't want to be dragged down those prickly daggers. I looked out the window. Not much help there. It was dark enough that I had trouble judging how far up I was. Well, there was nothing for it but to try. I could wait until morning but then I'd be risking another dust storm, plus I was thinking the lights of the city and the highway would guide me in the right direction. I unzipped the flap of the window and looked through the screen. The lights looked a long way away. I wasn't sure which town I was seeing. It didn't matter, though, I'd walk to any close town.

Okay, Cass, time to take the plunge. I kept a firm grip on the window flap as I unzipped the screen. When I'd unzipped a slit big enough for me to slide through I put my feet through and held on tight as my body was drawn downward. I came to a quick halt as the flap ended, then the weight of the tent ripped it loose a little more lowering me another few feet. I looked down. It still looked impossibly high but I was stuck now. I let go ready to land on bent knees and roll.

The ground came much quicker than I thought possible. My knees sure bent all right, but I didn't have time to even think about rolling as I met the ground and pain shot up through my legs. My head hit the ground hard. I lay there wondering if I should just stay put and wait for help, or try to walk out on my own. The tent would be visible from the air but who knew how far it had carried me? I tried standing to find the lights I'd seen from above. I quickly sat down again. My head throbbed and my shins felt like I'd just jumped off a second story balcony. What a coincidence.

Okay, call me stupid. I wasn't going to let the guys find me sitting in the middle of the desert, helpless. If they were going to find me they were going to find me following a logical plan. I had a reputation to uphold. That reputation was stubborn determination in the face of all odds, so I gritted my teeth, stood up again and pointed myself in the direction of the lights.

The first rule of desert survival is conserve your resources and I had very little to conserve. The first thing to conserve is water. There are two forms of water. The external and the internal. You conserve your water internally by doing things in a calm manner. Don't work up a sweat. Don't exhaust yourself. External water should be used wisely, but it should be used. It bugged me to find a lost person with a full bottle of water. However, I didn't have any water with me. I had plenty in my pack but the guys had my pack.

Next is energy. The pain in my legs took a toll on my energy real fast. The more energy I used up the more water I would need and the more water I needed the less energy I would have. I was in a downward spiral as far as making it out of this fix. The only thing I had going for me was that it wouldn't get hot until the sun came up.

Time to walk, Cass, walk to keep warm, walk to the lights. One step after another I headed slowly toward the lights. I blinked back tears as I walked. When the terrain went downhill I lost sight of the lights. All I could do was hope I was walking a straight line until I found the lights again. I was glad for the little bit of moonlight I had. I could see shapes in the dark and avoided the cacti.

I heard a plane go over and I waved at it in case it was search and rescue with night vision equipment on board. I couldn't tell if I got a response.

After the frigid desert night, I was disappointed when the sun came up and all the lights of the town ahead switched off one by one. The sandstone colored buildings blended into the sand colored land around it. I had no visual cues to follow. Walking was slow and the town never appeared to get closer. I hobbled along on legs that barely supported me. I wondered if they were broken. All I knew for sure was I had no compound fractures. I could put my weight on them but I sure felt like I shouldn't.

I was glad the wind didn't kick up again. Maybe Strict would send out a chopper.

I walked. I looked to the end of the walk. I didn't think about the steps. I thought about seeing a road in the distance, flagging down a car. Seeing a house in the distance, knocking on the door, asking to use the phone. Hearing Rusty's voice on the other end. Then I'd trip and the steps looked hard again. As a tracker I knew what the trips signified. They indicated that my attention was slipping and my attention was slipping because I was running on empty. I debated which was more important, closing the gap between me and that town, or refueling.

I was just walking, trying to keep to the right direction when a rabbit dashed out from under a bush. I unclipped my 9mm and followed it until it found another hiding place. I stalked it until I could get a good aim on it. I squeezed off a shot and watched as the rabbit jerked up into the air and fell back down. I had mixed feelings. I needed the food but I hated having to shoot the rabbit. I holstered my pistol and unclipped my hunting knife. I cut brush wishing I had some real wood to cook over. These little branches would smoke like crazy, smell awful, and burn up real quick. Still, food was food. I thought I better take advantage of the chance to eat.

When I am away from town I always carry two things: my knife and magnesium stick. I dressed and skinned the rabbit using the knife. It took me over an hour to do that. Then it took me several tries with the magnesium stick before I got those green branches to catch. I had to constantly scrounge for more sticks and guard the fire. I thought the rabbit would never cook enough to eat. I didn't have anything to help me cook it properly. As the grease dripped off I caught what I could, knowing every little bit of nourishment I could get would help me. My hands were filthy with grease.

About the time I judged the rabbit cooked enough I heard a helicopter. I stood and wiped my hands on my pants. When I looked up I fell over backwards. Police. Radaring the highway? I waved, just in case they had a ride along. If they were monitoring traffic they might make several passes.

They weren't monitoring traffic. The chopper circled around. They found a piece of desert to land in and I walked stiffly their direction. Rusty jumped out and wrapped me in a crushing hug.

"Rusty, easy, I know…I'm sorry, I can't just take off. I have a fire to tend to. I'd like a few bites of this rabbit. It's the first food I've had since breakfast yesterday." I was wearily rambling. He signaled the pilot and they shut off the chopper. Rusty followed me back to the fire. I sat down and I picked up the rabbit. I began pulling pieces off the outside, eating them burnt pieces and all.

The pilot walked up. "Mitchell? My wife, Cassidy."

Mitchell Perry squatted down by the fire. He watched me pull off another piece of rabbit.

"It's good to meet you," I said. "I wish it could have been under better circumstances. Want some rabbit?"

"No thanks, actually, you just confirmed what everybody's been saying about you."

"Did you find the tent hanging in a Joshua tree?"

"Yeah."

"How far away is it?"

The guys shrugged.

"A mile or two?" Rusty said.

"That's all? Damn, I knew I was in sorry shape but I thought I got farther than that. How far to the town?"

"About eight miles," Mitchell said.

"I'd have made it."

"How'd you get all cut up?" Rusty asked.

"Landed in the Joshua tree. You know those boxes they stick a person in and then they stick swords into it? Now I know how that feels. Did the guys make it out okay?"

"Yeah, they're all fine," Rusty said. "They radioed Strict about what happened as soon as they could, but we couldn't take off until morning."

"It's okay," I answered. "I wasn't expecting a ride at all. I'm used to making my way. Do you have a shovel in that chopper?"

There's no telling what the police will haul around in their vehicles. They find the oddest things useful, so it didn't surprise me when Mitchell came back with a shovel. I took it from him and started scooping up sand to smother the fire. My legs were killing me, but mentally I was still making my way home so I did what I'd do to get home.

When the fire was sufficiently put out, I took out my 9mm, switched the safety back on, put it back in the holster, made sure I had my knife and magnesium stick and walked to the chopper. I climbed in and lay on the bench back there. Nobody else wanted it. Rusty climbed in and sat by the bench. I started to get up and make room for him but he stopped me.

"What's wrong, babe?"

"I just hurt. I'm all banged up."

"Let me tell you something that might make you feel better. Landon made a dive for the tent when it blew away. When he missed he got on the radio, still laying there in that huge dust storm. He called Strict and reported what happened. Landon was pretty well freaked out, watching you get carried away so easily. Then Andario got worried about you. As they were waiting out the storm Victor told Andario about you, how he knew you would figure out what to do, how you bounced back time and again. Andario's problems seemed small by the time Victor finished. He came back willingly."

"I wonder which story Victor pulled out of the hat to convince him."

"You can ask him when you see him."

"I thought the tent would protect me from the sand. The wind caught it before I could do anything."

"You should have had the tent on our honeymoon. It worked better than your parachute."

I gave him a tired smile.

The blades started turning so he made his way to the front seat.

"Joshua General, Mitch."

Shoot. I was such a wimp. I couldn't fool him anymore.

Doctor Ron always knew it was going to be an interesting time when he got called in because of me. He took a bed count of ICU before he made his way to ER. He was pleasantly surprised when I was semi mobile.

"What happened this time?" He asked.

"First I got body slammed by a Joshua tree, then I jumped out of it and walked a mile or two."

"I'm sure you know Joshua trees are inanimate. They don't run around body slamming people. Explain."

"I got blown away by that awful dust storm…and the Joshua tree caught me."

"Joshua trees are getting more talented all the time. Okay, let's look at this from a different point of view. Why are you here?"

"Just x-ray my legs and let me go."

"Ahh, now we're getting somewhere. What did you do to your legs?"

"I jumped out of the Joshua tree."

"But you walked in here. Usually, if you can walk, you run away from this place."

"Just x-ray my legs."

"Hurts, does it?"

"Yeah."

Rusty stood off to the side. He liked Doctor Ron. Doctor Ron could get me to do things he couldn't. He wondered how the guy did it.

Doctor Ron didn't ask questions. If I thought I needed an x-ray he took it seriously whether he could feel something or not. He had a nurse treat my cuts as he arranged for the x-rays.

"What's this?" the guy in the casting office asked. "'Cause of injury. Patient was blown into the branches of a large Joshua tree and jumped out.'"

"That's right," I said.

"That's a new one."

While I was getting a cast put on my leg, Rusty got a ride to the police station and brought the Explorer back. I crutched out of the hospital.

When I arrived home, Bertie looked like a whole new person. Her clothes were clean. She was bathed. She looked like she lost forty pounds because she only had one layer of clothes on.

"Do you always come back from your searches injured?" she asked.

"No, only about every eight weeks."

"How long are you going to be on crutches?"

"About eight weeks."

"Do I see a correlation here?"

"Most definitely," said Rusty.

Katie thought the cast was cool. She saw a gap between the cast and my leg and was sure something was hidden down there. After a few days I had little baby fingernail scratches all the way around the top of the cast.

Landon came by to visit. He almost always did after I did something to shake him up.

"What got it into your head to open up a tent with a wind like that?"

"It was survival tip I read somewhere. It said the bottom of the tent would protect a person from the dust and dirt. The idea is to wrap yourself in the tent. Had it worked, I bet I would have come out of it cleaner than any of you guys did."

"The key words being *had it worked*. It didn't."

"I'll have to remember, if I need a quick escape in a windstorm, just open my tent."

"Please don't. You never know where or how you are going to come down."

"You're telling me! Oh shoot, where's Katie? One disadvantage to being like this is she's faster than me."

I hopped in the direction I thought she'd gone. Landon went another direction.

"Got her," Landon called from the kitchen. He carried her to me and went back to the kitchen. There was a drawer open and kitchen towels all over the floor. I put Katie in her highchair, then hopped around picking up towels and folding them again. Landon checked the cookie jar. After he had a bite of cookie, he helped me pick up towels.

"Ba-bye!" Katie called to Landon making little grabbing motions in the air. He dropped a few cookie crumbs onto her tray.

"Speaking of getting away. By the time your tent sailed out of sight you were a good fifty feet off the ground. Victor was dealing with Andario. I was trying to radio Strict. There was nothing we could do."

"I know. It's okay. How's Andario?"

"Back in perspective."

"What tall tail did Victor tell him to put him back in perspective?"

"Actually, he told him about your honeymoon. Andario had fallen from the top of the heap. Victor showed him, when you're down there's only one way to go and that's up. He told about you bailing out of the flaming plane and landing in the lake with nothing but a hunting knife, making do, fighting your way back. Andario didn't believe him at first. He thought we were fools to bring a girl along. But after you got blown away he started worrying and Victor told him about the last time you had to make do in the desert and again, you had nothing to work with and made something out of nothing. Victor knew you'd come through again. And Andario was impressed when you were found and you were okay. He seemed to think if you could do it, he could do it."

"Well, at least some good came of the search. I don't want to go to the next meeting, though."

He laughed because at the meetings we always looked over our calls that needed improvement and decided what we could have done to make things more efficient.

At the meeting Lou approached me on the side.

"I'm trying to think of a way you haven't gotten in trouble yet. Can you think of one?"

"Hmm, give me a new search. I'll come up with something."

"You're the first rescuer who has been whisked off the search by a windstorm."

"Oh, I doubt that. Searchers have been blown off mountain tops many times."

"Well, the first one in our district. I've got a list."

"No you don't."

"Yes I do. Because when I go to regional meetings and other companies think they have problems…"

I thought he was kidding. I hoped he was kidding.

While I was in the cast my only real trouble was keeping up with Katie. We ended up spending a lot of time together just playing on the floor. Katie's first tooth came in. I took a picture of her grinning a one-toothed smile and emailed it to my mom.

Rusty settled into a calm I really only saw when he knew he'd come home to a peaceful house with his family home doing family things. He'd been coming home like that for a few days. Katie noticed it, too. He came in the front door on one of those days and Katie crawled for the living room as fast as she could. She stood up on her knees and reached for him and said, clear as could be, "Daddy!" I never saw the smile Rusty gave his baby girl. He dropped everything right there by the front door and scooped her up into his arms.

"You said daddy!" He exclaimed, "What a big girl! Cass! Did you hear that?"

"I sure did!" I called from the kitchen, then walked around the wall and gave him a big kiss. He raised Katie over his head and waggled her back and forth until she was a fit of giggles.

We spent a lot of time reading stories, a lot of time playing peek a boo crawling around the furniture.

After she mastered the ee sound it wasn't long before she was saying mommy, daddy, doddie, cookie. After she found out talking was a good thing nothing much held her back. I would read a book to her and point out horsies, doggies, ducks…anything short and easy to say. She recognized an amazing array of animals in stories.

"Where's the horsy, Katie? Point to the horsy."

"A da!" She'd say cheerfully as she pointed out the horse in the picture.

Life was good. I was home. Katie was happy and secure. She had her daddy wrapped around her little finger. I got to feeling like a real mommy.

Eight weeks on my cast went by slowly. Katie and I went to town ready for a long morning in doctor's offices. I stocked up the diaper bag with extra diapers, extra bottles, toys, animal crackers, little baggies of cereal. I made sure she had her patch bottle. I couldn't see why that little homemade toy continued to fascinate her, but I was willing to go along with anything that kept her entertained.

"Have you stayed off your leg?" Doctor Ron asked.

"Compared to before, yeah."

"That's not what I wanted to hear."

"You don't have an eight month old baby to chase after. If I take time to get my crutches she's long gone."

"So, the answer is no? You know, this cast isn't coming off until the break is healed. You want the cast off? Go have the cast removed. Take this to x-ray and when they let you go, come back here. If you aren't back here by the end of the day I'm calling Rusty."

He knew I'd go have the cast removed and go on my way if I had the chance. Rats. I was glad I brought a fully stuffed diaper bag.

Katie leaned toward Doctor Ron, "Pease!" she said.

He waved the stethoscope around and Katie tried to catch it.

"She's got some of the best coordination I've seen in a baby. She zeros in on her target. I bet she could catch it easily if I was one step closer." He set the stethoscope aside and reached for Kate. Within two minutes she had his watch in hand, waving it around victoriously. "I just can't get over how she does that. I watch her do it and I still can't understand it.

You know what you're supposed to do?"

"Yeah, I need to go get lost in the hospital until somebody takes pity on me and shows me where the right office is. Then I need to get lost in the hospital until someone shows me where x-ray is. Then I need to come here so you won't call Rusty. Then I go home."

"Nice try. You know. Do what you know is right, not what you want to do."

"Rats."

I hopped off the exam table and took Katie back. As I hobbled out the door he said, "Where are your crutches?"

"I can't carry a baby and use crutches at the same time. I tried putting her in a back pack and I thought she was going to bash in that tooth on the back of my head."

"You better watch it or you're going to end up with a nurse pushing you around in a wheelchair."

"You wouldn't."

"I wouldn't for most people. Of course, most of my patients aren't bent on self-destruction."

"At least I have been home, staying out of trouble. Once the cast comes off and I get a few weeks in at the gym I'll be on the trail again."

Katie was fascinated by the guy with the saw. Wow! Big kid toys! She seemed to be thinking. Noisy, dangerous-looking gadgets! Cool!

"Has your cast been itching?" the technician asked.

"No more than normal. What you see is my daughter's scratches. She thinks I've got a cell phone or TV remote hidden down there."

"That's a first."

"It won't surprise Doctor Ron."

A nurse held Katie while they x-rayed my leg. She handed her back to me and hurried off to do more important things.

"Wait!" I called after her. I took her watch and car keys away from Katie. "I think these are yours."

I brought the x-rays to Doctor Ron. He laughed at the scratches, looked at the x-rays, then sentenced me to two more weeks in a cast.

"What happened?" Rusty asked. "I thought the cast would come off today."

"It was supposed to."

"But?"

"But Doctor Ron likes to torture me."

"What you really mean is the bone is still cracked because you walk on it too much."

"I guess."

It was amazing how so little and so much could happen in two weeks. The weather warmed up. The mountains began calling to me with a vengeance. Katie learned how to stand up. She crept along the furniture. Now she could check out the sofa cushions whenever she wanted to. I knew when she was at it because the TV would suddenly come on with no warning. My caution doubled when Katie learned how to undo the kid locks on the cupboards and drawers. After creeping along the furniture came climbing. I almost had a heart attack when I caught her standing on the kitchen drawers reaching out to the cookie jar.

I ran over cast and all before she could fall and hit her head on the hard floor. Then I shared a cookie with her. Damn it, Cassidy, why'd you reward her for that? But there we were, my heart hammering away, sharing a cookie with my adventurous baby.

Chapter 16

I had a week to go in the cast when the doorbell rang. Now who could that be? Since I wasn't expecting anybody I checked the driveway. Big, old, banged up pickup truck. Looked like it caused the dust storm two months ago and still hadn't been washed. Rust decorated one long scrape along the side. Looked like it had hauled horses twenty years ago. But whose was it? The doorbell rang again. The knob jiggled. I opened the secret compartment next to the front door and took out my rifle. When you expect trouble you start preparing for it. The rifle lived by the front door now. I held the rifle behind the doorjamb as I answered the door and there stood… my grandmother! My dad's mother. Grandma Gordon.

"What kind of a welcome is that to offer your own grandma? Took you long enough to answer the door! Well, aren't you going to ask me in?"

I just stood there mouth open.

"I'm sorry, Grandma," I said as I lowered my weapon. I set the safety again and her eyes got big.

"What are you doing with that thing? You could shoot your eye out!"

"I've never shot myself before. I could shoot a bug off your ear when I was ten. Then the Marines fine-tuned my aim."

I put the gun away quickly.

"Clever!" Grandma said inspecting the doorframe, "Just what a true trouble magnet needs. Do you always let your baby play with steak knives?"

"Katie!" I turned and spotted her crawling across the floor, steak knife in hand. I snatched the knife out of her hand and took it to the kitchen. Oh man! How was I going to keep her out of the drawers?

When I got back she was checking out Grandma's pocket possibilities.

"Come in, Grandma," I said.

"I already did. I have a new family member I never met. When your time is limited like mine, I thought I better get down here. You never know. She may not be a Gordon, but she's still my own flesh and blood."

Grandma Gordon was the exact opposite of my dad, in looks. Five two, huggably plump, white hair in a neat bun, purple granny glasses perched on a pert little nose. She carried a large tote bag, and a humongous purse that could have doubled as a bowling bag except it was much too fancy. It was decorated with rhinestones and gold studs. Katie went for the purse first. I scooped her up.

Grandma headed for the couch in the living room.

"Cassidy, didn't you learn a thing about decorating?" she asked. "This room feels as stiff as a guard at Buckingham Palace."

"I know, Grandma, no matter what I do it feels that way. Come to the den. We feel more comfortable there too."

"Not yet, I got to see what kind of a place you have here. Looks like you've done well for yourself. Married into money?"

"Not exactly," I said.

"What do you mean, not exactly, didn't that mother of yours teach you how to choose a man?"

"I'm afraid I didn't have a boyfriend while I was under my parent's roof. I was too busy being a ranch hand. Besides, we're getting along fine. When you meet Rusty you'll see there are more important things than money."

"Humph," she said, working her way around the rooms.

"That's a good picture of you," she said when she got to the photos of me rescuing Mark Mireau. "They show the real you."

"Most people don't even recognize me in the pictures. They don't expect a woman to be doing those things so they assume it's not me."

"Narrow minded friends you got?"

I ignored the barb even though she didn't mean it that way.

"Why do you have an animal snare and a parachute framed up perty like?"

"Souvenirs of my honeymoon."

"I shoulda guessed."

"Can I get you something?"

"Got any sweet tea?"

"Not yet but I can make some."

"How can you get along without sweet tea?"

"Drink water?"

I put Katie in her high chair and then put on some water to heat and looked through the pantry for teabags.

"None of that fancy shmancy stuff. Plain ol' orange pekoe. Them fancy kinds is for silver tea parties. And none of that sugar substitute. You use real sugar. White. And lots of it. As much as the tea will hold."

"Yes, Grandma."

"Look at you, little one. Sitting there with that big empty tray. Are you hungry?"

"She just ate."

"Oh come on, just a little snack. You want a cookie?"

"Cookie!" said Katie enthusiastically.

"Oh my! She's talking already! Smart! Like a Gordon!" She started searching the kitchen for a cookie. I got one out of the cookie jar before

Grandma could hand Katie a whole one. I dropped a few little pieces on her tray and ate the rest of the cookie.

"You eat sweets like that and you'll balloon out until you look like me," Grandma said.

I looked at the clock, five ten. Good, Rusty would be home in a couple of hours. I better start some dinner. What in the world should I make for dinner with Grandma Gordon here? No venison, no buffalo, no elk. I wondered if she would settle for plain old beef. She probably hated plain old beef. She just drove down from a cattle ranch in Montana. Shoot.

"Cookie!" Katie said.

"Here you go sweetheart," Grandma said.

"Grandma, she can't snack whenever she wants to. She'll eat all the cookies and not eat dinner."

"Well, isn't that what Grandmas are for? Did you ever eat a decent meal when I was around?"

"Sigh, no, Grandma."

"And see? You survived."

When the water started boiling, I turned off the burner and added the tea. I dumped in sugar and stirred until it started settling on the bottom of the tea kettle. Rusty, help!

"I have an idea," I said. "It'll kill two birds with one stone. Let's go meet Rusty."

"Oh yes! Let's! Your mom says he's a real looker! Your mom knows quality when she sees it. That's why she married Wayne."

"Good! Katie, let's go see dada!"

"Daddy?"

I dumped all but four cookies in a gallon Ziploc bag, grabbed another bag from the freezer and set them where I'd remember to take them with us.

Grandma climbed into the Jeep and looked at it with distaste.

"What kind of a ranch kid are you with an itty bitty Jeep."

"I'm not a ranch kid. I'm a tracker."

"Still? I thought you'd outgrow that. What can you possibly do as a tracker?"

"Track?"

"What? Rabbits and deer?"

"And lost people. I tracked down a detective who was lost in Mexico recently. I tracked a runaway teenager, that's sort of how I broke my leg."

"Didja find your man?"

"Of course!"

"Good girl! That's the Gordon blood in you."

The station was quiet when we got there which was very unusual. I thought this was an office day for Rusty. I remembered he had several appointments on his calendar.

Grandma followed me as I headed through the door to the back.

"Hold it!" called out the woman at the desk. "I need to see an ID."

"It's okay Steph, she's with me."

"It doesn't matter, rules is rules."

"We're here to see Rusty. If he's busy we won't bother him."

"Hey, hold it again! Is that cookies I see?"

I went back and held the bag open so Stephanie could take a couple of cookies.

"You forgot the nuts," she said.

"Unplanned visit. I'll put nuts in next time."

"What kind of place is this?" Grandma asked.

"The local police station."

"You got the law on your side! Smart move, especially considering how much trouble you get into."

"I've never done anything illegal!" I exclaimed.

"Oh yeah? What do you call it when you drive off with another kid's motorbike and hide it on top of the stadium bleachers until the coach calls the poor boy's parents?"

"He deserved it, it's not illegal if they deserve it. Besides, I didn't steal it, I just moved it."

"It was a no good dirty trick and you shouldn't have done it."

"And I suppose he should have stuffed me in my locker and shut the door, because that's what he did. Hold it. First stop."

I knocked on Schroeder's door. He opened it tentatively.

"Oh no, what is it this time?"

"This man knows you too well," Grandma said. "But he's cute."

"Just a cookie delivery," I said to Schroeder. "No trouble."

"I'm married," he said looking over my shoulder at Grandma Gordon.

"It's an unplanned delivery so you'll just have to take what you want."

He took the rest of the first bag.

"I'll share," he said.

Rusty wasn't in his office, so we walked the halls looking for him. Grandma jauntily followed along, though I noticed a slight limp. It didn't seem to be a new injury. She probably got kicked by a horse or run over by a cow years ago and never sought medical attention. I tried to figure out how old she would be. Dad was close to sixty. That put Grandma Gordon in her eighties.

We found Rusty sparring in the gym. This was good for Grandma. It was bad news to me. We sat on the bottom bench of the short bleachers.

"Which one is he?" Grandma asked.

"The one in brown. Rusty almost always wears brown. He looks great in Levi's though."

"That one would look good in anything! Or nothing! Come on! Git him! Right hook!" Grandma said punching the air.

The officer further down the bench inched away.

I got up and walked over to the fight. Rusty didn't see me. Big John came at him with a flying kick and Rusty dodged knocking me staggering backwards. I flipped over a big exercise ball in the middle of the floor and my cast came down with a loud *bang* on the bench of the bleachers. The bench cracked and pinched the bottom of the officer sitting there. He jumped up with a loud, "Youch!" leaving part of his pants hanging from the crack in the wood, and I lay there looking up into the hole in his exercise pants.

"You haven't lost your touch!" Grandma exclaimed.

Katie sat in the middle of the gym crying. Big John picked her up.

"I thought you said he was the one in brown," Grandma said.

"He is. Big John is one of Katie's favorite people."

Rusty was standing over me arms folded. "Cass, you know better than to sneak up on me like that."

"I wasn't sneaking. I was thumping across the gym floor on a cast."

"That girl could sneak if she had peg legs!" Grandma said proudly.

"Rusty, we, um, have company," I said.

"Are you going to introduce us right side up or upside down?"

"Upside down might be a little more appropriate," I said as I got up.

The officer with the torn pants backed away into the locker room.

"Grandma, this is my husband, Rusty Michaels, and officer John Jankowski. Guys…Grandma Gordon."

"It's good to meet you," Big John said. "Are those cookies?"

At least I'd brought a peace offering.

"Cookie!" said Katie.

"Oh, you want a cookie!" Grandma said. "Here you go sweetie."

I grabbed Grandma's hand before she could draw it out of the bag.

"Not a whole one," I said.

"Party pooper," said Grandma.

"Cassidy, can I have a word with you?" Rusty said.

"Come on, honey," Grandma said. "Let the grown-ups talk."

As Grandma walked away with Katie in her arms Rusty asked, "What's going on?"

"I don't know! She just showed up at the door! I didn't have anything but beef for dinner."

"What, she's a vegetarian? I can't imagine a Gordon being a vegetarian."

"No, it's just that I doubt she wants beef. She lives on a cattle ranch in Montana. I can't cook anything that will measure up to what she's used to. I'm sure she's perfected every beef dish ever invented."

"How long is she staying?"

"I haven't asked. Probably until she's convinced her precious grandchild can be trusted with a trouble magnet like me."

"Well, the past five minutes didn't help."

"Neither did her arrival. We have to do something to keep Katie out of the drawers in the kitchen."

"That's really Big Wayne Gordon's mother?"

"Yeah, you'll see it after a little while."

"Great. So what's the plan?"

"First of all... dinner. We'll just ask what she wants."

Chapter 17

"A big, fat pizza pie!" Grandma said when we asked her.

"You're kidding! Dad wouldn't eat a pizza if it was the last thing in the house."

"He doesn't know what he's missing."

"Well, pizza's easy. We can do pizza."

"Hold it. We aren't going to a fancy place are we? I'm not dressed for a fancy place."

"This is the southwest. You can wear jeans and a blouse almost anywhere."

"I look like I stepped out of Hicksville."

"You did. But don't worry about it. You can wear whatever you want to Zeke's."

"Is this a kiddy place?"

"It's just a family place. They have great pizza, you'll see."

"Actually I like those kiddy places. I like to watch the kids."

Grandma was lucky. Zeke's was busy with the usual mixture of families, college kids, and single guys there for the beer. Grandma perked up when she saw little ones running about. Brenda seated us at a big booth.

"I'd like a Miller Lite. Oh hey! I'm not in Montana anymore. I can order whatever I want. When we go to bars in Montana we order Miller because our foreman's name is Miller. You won't tell anybody, will you?"

"Of course not."

"This is California, I could order something cute and fruity. I could order a Margarita! Or a cute little strawberry daiquiri. Oh, how will I ever decide?"

"How about a Zeke Zoner?" Brenda offered.

"No, Grandma, not that one," I warned her.

"And why not? You think I can't hold my liquor? I tell you I can keep up with the best of them. I'll try that."

"Do you know why it's called a Zoner? Because it makes you all zoned out," I said.

"Well, I'm not driving. Do I hear video games? Do they have one of those racecar games? I've been dying to try one of those racecar games."

Rusty didn't know if his day was getting better or worse. I think he decided to reserve judgment on that until Grandma got the Zoner in her.

Grandma went to look for the video games. Pretty soon we heard zooming and crashing noises from the other room.

"You can't jerk the wheel!" a kid yelled. "If you jerk it like that you'll crash every time. Precision. You have to use controlled steering. Not so fast! There's a curve coming up! Oh man, you're toast. I hope you don't really drive. Your driving sucks!"

"Young man! I appreciate the help, but I would also appreciate clean language. One more race."

"Okay, as long as you're paying."

"On your mark. Get set...." Schreeeeeech. And the kid...Zoooom!

"You're sunk, I'm going to skunk you. Eat my dust! What are you driving? Your Daddy's Buick?" Zoom crash, zoom, crash.

"Awe, you beat me again," Grandma said. "What's this? Shooting? California kids have got it made. I'll take you on at shooting!"

"Yeah right. Do you know how to play?"

"Aim the gun, pull the trigger."

"And reload. I'll show you how to reload. And don't shoot the good guys, only bad guys. Okay, here's how to reload. Ready?"

Bang, bang... bang, bang, bang...

"Man! How'd you learn to shoot like that?"

"Shooting rattlesnakes and coyotes. I do better with a real gun. This little pop gun would be useless."

The two came out of the room on better terms.

"Okay, so you can shoot better, but I can drive better," the kid said.

"High five!" Grandma said.

"Grandma, what kind of pizza do you want?" I asked.

"Pepperoni, sausage, mushroom, green chile, avocado, bell pepper..."

Brenda was writing as fast as she could.

"Just bring us a Zinger," I said. "Extra large."

"What's a Zinger?" Grandma said.

"A pizza with all the ingredients."

"Not those little hairy fish."

"No, that's a special order topping."

"Whew, if I'm going to eat little hairy fish I want it to be sardines."

"Sardines aren't hairy are they?"

"Nah, but two out of three ain't bad. You eat the bones and everything. If you haven't had them you probably never will now. Just thinking about eating a whole fish gives most people the heebie jeebies."

Brenda set Grandma's Zeke's Zoner in front of her. No straw. Grandma took a sip.

"Zowee!" she said, "What's in it?"

"A little bit of everything. I think you better wait until the food gets here."

"I don't want it to get all watered down."

Rusty and I were relieved when she slowly sipped at her drink until the food arrived. Every time she took a drink she screwed up her face and her eyes bugged out. Then she would settle down again, then sip again… about halfway through her drink she was telling stories I didn't think my grandpa wanted her to be telling.

"Your granddad had him a favorite cow when he was young. Wasn't a milk cow, it was the just the gentlest, motherliest cow you ever saw. It followed him around the ranch when he worked. One fall, when elk season rolled around, Grandpa lit out into the hunt like always. He knew where the herds grazed and where they bedded down because he grew up in those mountains. So he knew where to go to hunt. But so did that cow. Every time he turned around he was almost shooting his favorite cow. He'd get a bead on it, wait for antlers to show, and it'd be that crazy cow. He finally lassoed it and tied it up at camp, and again he went out loooooooking for his elk. If it weren't the cow it was a cow elk. He was out there for two weeks and he finally had to come home. The night before he was coming home, there was a noise in the night and Grandpa yelled at the cow to be quiet. He got up and looked around, saw the cow and went back to bed. In the morning he checked the camp over carefully before heading back. On his tour of the camp he saw elk tracks. Big elk tracks. And he found scratch marks against the trees that looked like antlers had scraped them. He figures the granddaddy of all elk paid him a visit just to mock him. He rode home and the cow followed but he cursed that fool of a cow, even though she remained his favorite for years to come and produced many strong calfs. He'll never forget the year he didn't get an elk."

"Is Cassidy's dad more like you or more like his dad?"

"Well, size wise he's sure like his dad. He's more like his dad in that he don't take no nonsense. One time Grandad knocked a guy flat in town just cause he thought the guy was lookin' at me," Grandma said as she fluffed her hair up. "But some of the things Wayne did was definitely something I'd do, like learning how to fly."

Brenda set down our pizza and left us to our conversation. She usually had a conversation of her own but she refrained this time.

"Dad learned how to fly?"

"No, he just tried to fly. He never got through the learning part. He jus' figured he could learn it on the fly. Wrecked a good airplane. It sure made a sight on the front page of the Maryville Gazette. It showed the plane wedged in the bridge, the one *useful* bridge in town. He wouldn't wait for help to arrive. He jumped out, landed in the river, only the river was too shallow. He nearly broke his leg and froze to death."

"Sounds like somebody else I know," Rusty said.

"This pissa is won'erful! I never get pissa on the ranch."

"You never get shnockered either," I said.

"You got it good in Calfinoria."

"Grandma, I think you've had enough."

"You can drive in them machines, like the devil, without hurting anybody. No tickets. You can shoot them games without hurting nobody. You get pissa. You get ev'ry kind of drink you want. I bet you could even fly, just like your daddy done." Or just grab a tent on a windy day, same result, except we had no use for bridges because we didn't have rivers. "And California is so *warm*," she gushed. "I could just feeeel the ice melting as I drove south. I think I'll shtay until spring comes up north."

I nearly choked. Spring? But I didn't panic.

"That's a good idea, you can go visit Dad and Mom. The ranch house is like a hotel. You'd have your own bathroom."

"I don' want a hotel. I don' wan a ranch visit. I vizit a ranch ev'ry day of my life. I wan' to shee what a normal family does. I wansh to play with Katherine."

"Kaitlyn." I said.

"An' shee how life treats a gal in the shity."

"Well, staying at my house isn't exactly like a city."

"S'okay, it'll do. For a little while."

Chapter 18

The next day, after zoning out until ten in the morning, Grandma woke up with a headache but still raring to go. She took two Tylenol and got ready to hit the road and be a real California grandma. She wanted to see a real mall, one of them ritzy ones where you can buy a pair of shoes for two hundred dollars.

"Why would you want to buy a two hundred dollar pair of shoes? You can get the same thing back home for twenty."

"I probably won't buy shoes. I just want to go to a fancy store that sells stuff like that."

She got dressed as classily as a Montana ranch grandma can, I guess. Her jeans were low riders, they were tight and she wore boots with them. Not her ranch boots, these boots were, umm, maybe alligator? Maybe snake? The heels were two inches too high for Grandma but she wore them anyway. Her sweater was fuchsia and had white rabbit fur around the edge of the hood. It barely covered the top of her jeans.

I put on jeans and a sweater so I'd look like we sort of belonged together, though, if I was a teenager I wouldn't claim to know the woman. I wasn't sure I was glad to have outgrown that stage. She looked me up and down.

"You're a California girl and you dress like that?" she asked.

"How should I dress?" I replied.

"You could blend in a little more. What do other people wear to the mall?"

"This."

"Oh, come now, people in California wear jeans and sweaters to the mall?"

"Yes."

"That's not what I see on TV."

"You want me to dress like they show on TV?"

"Yeah! Katherine, too!"

"Kaitlyn. Grandma, I don't think I can do that."

"Oh come on, it'll be fun! We'll be real California girls!"

I went back to my closet thinking, it's just clothes, it isn't that big a deal, she'll be gone in a few days, you can live with it, have patience. I didn't have any California girl clothes. I went for a Skipper style sundress. I was going to freeze and I was going to feel silly but I'd survive, right? Then, because I was wearing the Skipper dress I had to put on make-up and curl my hair. Grandma brightened right away when I stepped out.

"Now that's more like it! Do you have sunglasses to go with it?"

"No, my only sunglasses are for search and rescue. They go with a police uniform."

"Well, we can fix that. Hey baby! What about you?" she said to Katie.

I took Katie to the nursery and put her in a bright pink dress, put bright pink barrettes in her hair and put shiny white shoes on her feet. She wasn't used to shoes. She didn't like them except that they were good for entertainment. She took them off and played with the buckles.

Since Grandma wanted to go all out and be real California girls I got on the freeway and drove to Beverly Hills. This so totally went against my character I was gritting my teeth all the way. On the positive side Grandma kept Katie entertained all the way. She told animated little stories, and talked with her hands, and Katie watched and wondered who this weird lady was.

"What's this?" Grandma asked when I parked the Jeep and fed a handful of change into the parking meter.

"Rodeo Drive, shopping place of the stars," I told Grandma.

"The stars! Really?"

"I don't know. I've never been here. That's what it's famous for though. We'll see. Would you know a star if you saw one? I wouldn't."

"I'd recognize John Wayne! Your daddy's named after him!"

"We won't see John Wayne here. I think he's dead. Think younger."

"Movie stars! By golly, you've got it all here! Let's go!"

I started to put Katie in her stroller but then I saw all the stairs and figured it would be more of a pain than a help. I couldn't wear the backpack with the Skipper dress. There was no avoiding it; I'd have to carry her.

Grandma walked around staring into space. I wasn't sure if she was just taking in the scenery or star struck, but I didn't see anybody to get star struck about. I had never been to Rodeo Drive, but it had a reputation for California glitz and glamor, so I pointed her to a doorway.

"Let's look here," I said, just to get her started.

Silver dresses greeted us as we entered the shop.

"Oh my!" Grandma exclaimed. She wandered in between the racks afraid to touch anything.

A perfectly coiffed woman in a black suit asked if she could help us.

"Yes!" Grandma said. "Show me something that will get my husband's blood to boil."

"Grandma!" I said.

"What? You'll see, when you get to be eighty, you're just a young woman with wrinkles. You might have more experience and you might have more aches but hopefully you will still like to romance your husband and hopefully he'll like you to do it. Show me a dancing dress!"

I followed my grandmother through the store and browsed, determined I would not see anything I liked. Even if I did I was not going to try it on. I didn't want to be tempted. I didn't look at the price tags.

"What do you think of this?" Grandma asked holding up a sequined dancing dress. I couldn't imagine her wearing that to a square dance. Grandma's eyes suddenly flicked to the side and then got bigger and bigger. She began gasping like a fish out of water. Oh no, what had she spotted. A sexy negligee? I turned and looked for what had attracted Grandma's attention. Oh shit.

"Grandma, hide me!" I said dashing around behind her.

Grandma had put the dress on a rack and was furiously digging in her purse. "I've got to have a piece of paper somewhere in here!" she said frantically.

"What are you doing?"

"Looking for something to get an autograph on! Do you know who that *is*?"

"Yes! The one star I can recognize and we have to run into *her* here! My trouble magnet must be ultra-strong today."

Grandma tore a check out of her checkbook and grabbed a pen. Oh dang, there was no avoiding it. I braced myself.

"Grandma, you don't need to do that. Put the check away. I'll introduce you." I stood up and walked toward the woman. "Sherri! What are you doing here?" I gushed, "The only time I've ever been to Beverly Hills and I run into you! How's it going? How was Hawaii?"

"Cassidy?"

"Yeah."

"Are you sure you're Cassidy?"

"Not today. This is my grandmother. She lives in Montana and she wanted to spend a day as a California girl. Grandma Gordon, this is Sherri Champlain."

Grandma straightened herself up until she must have been five foot three. She took Sherri's hand gently but firmly and blushed furiously as she shook hands.

"What did you do to your leg?"

"I jumped out of a Joshua tree."

"How did you get into a Joshua tree? Those look painful to climb."

"Airmail. Don't ask."

"Okay, you're really Cassidy."

"Grandma would like your autograph. Do you still carry those five by sevens?"

"Yeah, but these aren't for the movie you're in. These are for the latest one. That reminds me, did you get your tickets to the premier? I sent you four."

"Not yet. When is it?"

"April first."

"There's still time. I get tickets to the premier? They might not even use the shots I was in and I get tickets?"

"You do if I send them to you."

She took a picture out of her purse and pulled out a Sharpie.

"What's your name?" Sherri asked.

"Isabel. Oh this is so exciting! Cassidy said the stars shopped here but I didn't hope to meet any!"

"So, are you coming?" Sherri asked me.

"I guess. If Rusty can get away. Four tickets? Who should I invite?"

"What about Landon?" Sherri said.

"What about me?" Grandma said.

I had trouble imagining Grandma Gordon going to a movie premier with Landon Wilson.

"You know that scene Nick shot of you climbing out of the alley?" Sherri laughed. "He ended up liking the one where you climbed up the wall instead of the ladder."

"So I did end up in it?"

"Oh yeah! Just wait till you see it!"

All this time Katie was studying Sherri. I had to keep a distance or Sherri would lose that Rolex or something from her purse. Sherri handed Grandma the photo. She'd written simply, "Isabel, it was nice meeting you on Rodeo Drive, Sherri Champlain".

"Have you heard from Brock or Spike lately?" I asked.

"No, Brock's on location in Italy. Who knows when we'll work together again. Oh well, it was fun while it lasted."

"Well, I'd love to chat but Grandma is just getting started here and we need to be home for dinner."

"Aw, do we have to?" Grandma said. "I wanted to try sushi!"

"They have the best sushi here. You've just got to try it," Sherri said.

"Shopping first. We'll think about dinner later."

"I'll see you in April," Sherri said as she walked away.

"You didn't tell me you knew any movie stars," Grandma accused.

"I didn't think it mattered who I knew."

"You know Sherri Champlain and Brock Larone and you think *it doesn't matter*?"

"Grandma, they're just friends. Mom has met Sherri and Brock. She invited them to Katie's baby shower."

"So what do you think of this dancing dress?"

"I think you better try it on. I think dancing dresses tend to pick you, not the other way around."

"You sound just like your mother. You know what phrase you aren't allowed to use, don't you?"

"Of course."

When going on a Gordon shopping trip one never said, "That looks like it was made for you." And you especially don't say it on Rodeo Drive because that phrase invokes Rule Number 642. Six hundred and forty-two says if something is made for you, and you are looking for that thing, you have to buy it. I didn't want to have to buy anything on Rodeo Drive.

Grandma tried on the dancing dress. It was supposed to be a short dress but on her it was ballet length.

"Um, no. I think you should look in the petite section."

"See if you can find one in petite."

The sales woman found one and three other styles and I found a chair and got off my leg. Grandma opened the dressing room door and walked out. She modeled the dress in front of the fancy beveled mirrors in the waiting area.

"Oh lordy, would you look at that!"

"Grandma, where would you ever wear a dress like that?"

"In the bedroom, with big band music playing softly, and dancing just the two of us."

"Does Grandpap dance? I can't imagine Grandpa dancing to big band music. He's more at home on a horse."

"Your Grandpa is a man of many talents. You of all people should know a big man doesn't have to be harsh. That man of yours could kick ass if he wanted to, but you see his eyes when he's near Katherine. He's a big teddy bear. I bet he's smooth as silk when he's dressed up and out on a date with you. Men are still men when they're eighty. They just have wrinkles. And less hair. On their heads. Seems like they have more other places though. So what do you think?"

"Try on the other ones."

She tried them on one by one. I just sat back entertaining Katie and staying off my leg as much as I could.

"Oh yes! I like this one! Look Cassidy! Isn't this just the bomb!"

She came out and stood in front of the mirror. She wiggled a little and the fabric moved and sparkled in just the right places. It was raspberry colored which I always thought of as a young person color, but hey, if Grandma wanted to wear raspberry I wasn't going to stop her.

"Oh goodness. I don't know if I can turn my back on this one! Why did you have to bring me here?"

"Because you asked for it. I suggest you leave it here and if you still hear it calling you by the end of the day you can always come back for it. Then we won't have to carry it around all afternoon."

She giggled and did a little jig, feeling the dress move about.

"It makes me feel young again! I can't leave it."

"Try on the other ones. You might like them better. And you better look at the price *before* you fall in love with it. Not after."

She tried on the other more mature looking dresses but the fun little raspberry dress still called to her.

"There's a lot of other shops," I told her. "This is just the first."

Grandma looked like she was abandoning a puppy at the humane society as she left the dress behind and walked out. She kept looking back at the shop.

"Here we go! Handbags!" I said cheerfully.

"Let's go for shoes. Maybe I can find a pair to wear with that dress."

"Okay, shoes."

As grandma was trying on some silver dancing shoes my cell phone rang.

"Hello?" I said as I struggled to hold Katie at the same time.

"Cassidy? We need your help," my mother said urgently.

"Mom? What's wrong?"

"How soon can you be up here? I'll take care of Katie for you. You have plane tickets out of Fresno, if you can make it by tomorrow afternoon."

"Hold on! What's going on? I can't just fly off to who knows where. I'm in Beverly Hills shopping. I need to call Rusty. I have company. I can't just take off. But you sound distressed. What is it you want me to do?"

"It's your grandmother! She told Grandpap she was going to visit the grandkids and she took off in the ranch truck. After four days Grandpap called Leroy to see how things were going and he said she never showed up! They've had the police out looking for the truck and driven up and down every road in western Montana and there's no sign of her! I don't know what you can do, but I know you've got the right mindset for these things. You would be a big help to them. You think like Grandma. I just know you can find her even if you don't follow her footsteps."

"Um, I don't think I'll have any trouble following her footsteps."

"But we don't even know where they are!"

"Mom, quit fretting. Grandma is fine. She came to visit me. That's the only reason I'd come to Beverly Hills shopping."

"*She's there?*"

"Yeah, she's here trying on shoes."

"You're shopping. In Beverly Hills. With your missing grandmother?"

"Yeah, on Rodeo Drive."

"You never go shopping with *me* on Rodeo Drive! Put her on."

"I'll have her call you when we're through. It'll give you time to settle down and it won't ruin her shopping trip. She's out here living like the *Little Old Lady from Pasadena*."

"Oh no. Buckle your seatbelt and hang on tight. You're in for it now. Don't send her up here! She'll want to do San Francisco, too! I can't do San Francisco with her."

"I'll talk to you later, Mom. I love you."

"I knew you could find her," Mom said as she hung up.

"Grandma?" I said innocently.

"Yes dear."

"Next time you decide to go visit grandkids tell Grandpap *which* grandkids. He thought you were going to Donna and Leroy's and he's had the police searching all of Montana for you."

"Oh, that man! I go away for a few days and he's got to keep tabs. He doesn't deserve the little dancing dress... but I still do!"

"He wouldn't call out the troops unless he really cared. So he does deserve the dancing dress. You can't be mad at him."

"Yes I can, but I guess I'm not really. Look at these shoes. Wouldn't they go perfect with the dancing dress?"

"Can you dance in heels?"

"Honey, when you're my size you *learn* to dance in heels."

"Try it, make sure you really can dance in them."

"Give me that baby. Babies love to dance."

She put Katie's arm around her shoulder and held out her hand and started a waltz. She danced around in a circle and ended with a dip that started Katie to giggling. Watching my rough old grandmother waltzing with my baby on Rodeo Drive was so incongruent it made her endearing in my eyes, and right then I *could* see her in the little raspberry dress and the silver high heeled dancing shoes, slow dancing with Grandpap in the bedroom to big band music.

"Grandma, I think it's time to invoke rule six forty-two," I said.

"You really think so?" she asked.

"Did you see how much it is?"

"No, did you?" she asked reluctantly.

"No."

"Maybe we better wait until we've seen the price," she suggested, though not very convincingly.

"How much is a dancing dress worth to you?" I asked.

"It's not the dress, it's the feeling. The feeling is priceless."

"I guess we'll see."

Back in the dress shop she sucked in her breath, "Oh lordy. I never seen a dress like this before. I never *felt* a dress like this before."

"You bought the shoes," I reminded her.

"Do you know this outfit's going to set me back nine hundred dollars?"

"It's your decision. One thing Gordons have always been good at is making money."

"But for a dress to only wear in the bedroom? A dress I'd be scared to death to have Harv Miller catch me in?"

"A dress to get Grandpap's blood to boiling?"

"Oh shut up," she snapped and I knew the dilemma she was in.

"I'm going to try on my size. I've got to see what it is about this dress that's worth seven hundred dollars."

I found my size and took it with me to the dressing room. Wow, some dressing room! It really was a room. It was even furnished. It had a loveseat and a hard backed chair and stairs so you could test out the outfits in different positions. Mirrors were on every wall. Potted plants stood in the corners. I set Katie down and undressed, then pulled the raspberry dress over my head. It slipped in place and… and there it was. I wasn't sure if I was wearing it or it was wearing me. It did feel good. The feel of the fabric on my skin gave me tiny shivers. Why did I have to curl my hair and put on make-up today? It even went with the dress. Grandma was going to go gaga over this dress. What if she said it? What would I do? I had seven hundred dollars of my own. Money Rusty didn't care about. But for a dress? A dress I might only wear once. To a movie premier? Oh hell.

"Grandma?"

"What is it dear?"

"Can you get me the blue one? Size seven."

"Don't rub it in."

"I'm not. I'm trying not to invoke rule six forty-two." I quickly got out of the raspberry one so she couldn't see me in it.

She knocked and I cracked the door and took the dress from her. I slipped the blue one on. Double hell. It brought out the blue in my eyes.

"Grandma, why do you do these things to me?" I called out. I opened the door. We stood there, red and blue bookends. Right then I could see in her face, my eyes looking back. Little laugh lines I would have someday. They weren't so bad.

"Oh dear." Grandma said. "I'm sorry! I didn't mean to! I didn't know being a California girl was so hard on the brain."

"Maybe that's why California girls are always thought of as blondes. Blondes have more fun, right? So, are we going to be real California girls or are we going to use our heads?"

"You didn't mention the rule."

"I think we better be very careful with that rule."

"Right."

"So we're just choosing whether we're going to be California girls or stuffed shirts."

"Uhh, yeah. The rule doesn't exist today."

"That's good because that dress…"

"Stop! Don't say it!" I cried. I'd been brought up on that rule. It was in the blood.

"Let's flip a coin. Heads we use our heads. Tails we buy the dresses, turn tail and run away from this place."

We both held our breath as I flipped a quarter. On Rodeo Drive I thought we ought to be flipping a dollar but I only had a quarter. I dropped the quarter. Katie grabbed it off the floor before we could read it and stuck it in her mouth.

"Ewe! Yucky coin! Yucky!" I said as I pulled it out of her mouth. I almost wiped it off on the dress. I flipped the soggy coin again. I caught it and without looking at it I flipped it over and slapped it down on the back of my hand. Heads.

"Rats," we said in unison. Then Grandma said, "You flipped it over. While it was in your hand it was tails."

"Grandma, we both wanted the coin to come up tails. Let's just call it tails."

"Can we do that?"

"The coin wasn't the deciding factor. The reaction to the coin toss was."

"Can you do that? The coin flipping police aren't going to arrest us for bending the coin flipping rules?"

"No but our husbands might."

"Tell you what, I'll buy yours for you, if you'll buy mine for me. That way we can't say, 'dear, I bought myself a dress…'"

"Good idea. But you bought your own shoes."

"I was forced to because of the dress," she said.

"Right. So, have you had enough of being a California girl?"

"I think I better, whether I want to or not. I don't think I can handle another decision like this one."

We bought the dresses, turned tail and ran.

Chapter 19

Speaking of tough decisions, sushi isn't exactly a decision-free meal. I had no idea what the menu said. It was in English but it was in Sushinese. I gave up on decision making. I asked the waitress for the most American sushi they had. Grandma wasn't finished being adventurous.

"What would you like to drink?" the waitress asked.

"Iced tea," I answered.

"What's traditional to drink with sushi?" Grandma asked.

"Ocha, or sake," she answered.

"What's that?"

"Ocha is a green tea. Sake is rice wine."

"Ocha," I said.

"Now hold on! I can order for myself. This rice wine stuff sounds interesting."

"Ocha," I said again.

"Oh for Pete's sake. All right if you want to be boring. But just for that I'm going to try something really different. Bring me the caterpillar roll."

The waitress jotted down the order, bowed slightly and left.

"Grandma, do you know what you just ordered?"

"No, but that's the fun of it. You don't know what you ordered either."

"But at least they know I'm a chicken."

When the waitress set down our food it all looked simple enough.

"Shoyu, wasabi, gari," the waitress said pointing to the condiments on our plates.

"Wasabi?" Grandma said. "I like the way that word rolls off the tongue. Wasabi. Wa'sabi. Wasabi'. Wasa'bi. Cool word. I wonder what it means. And where's the caterpillar? This doesn't look like caterpillar."

"Taste it. Maybe it tastes like caterpillar."

I took a bite of mine. Hmm, it was okay. I wondered how anybody could make a whole meal out of five little circular bites.

Grandma picked up a piece and dunked it in the wasabi. She took a bite and her eyes teared up. She looked desperately for her tea, which hadn't arrived yet. She swallowed and at first I thought she was choking, then I thought she was crying. Then the tea arrived and she gulped it down. The tea was hot so it burned, too. When her little cup was empty she grabbed my iced tea.

"Grandma! What in the world is that stuff?"

Her nose started running and she blew it on her napkin.

She couldn't talk for a while. When she got herself back under control she gasped, "Wasabi is Japanese for Warning! Warning! Wow that stuff is hot! And it goes straight to your sinuses! You don't have to put it on your food, just wave it over. Whatever you do, don't eat it."

"So did it taste like caterpillar?"

"No, it tasted like fire."

I flagged down the waitress.

"I think we're going to need more tea," I said.

"And a translation! What is this stuff?" Grandma asked.

"Shoyu is soy sauce. Wasabi is Japanese horseradish. And gari is pickled gingerroot."

"The soy sauce should be pretty safe," I said and tried a bite dipped in it.

Grandma ate her sushi with a critical eye, sniffling a lot the whole time. I think she was trying to figure out what caterpillar tasted like. When the waitress arrived with fresh tea we were down to our last bites of sushi. I had to admit it was more filling than it looked. Grandma asked, "Okay, now that I've eaten the stuff I think it's safe to ask what it was."

"You granddaughter had California Roll. It's a very mild, traditional sushi, good for beginners. The Caterpillar Roll is made with rice, nori, avocado and eel."

"Eel? I ate *eel*? You mean them electric, long, snake-like critters who live in the ocean?"

"Yes!" the waitress said brightly.

"And what's in a California Roll?"

"Rice, nori, avocado and crab."

"And what's nori?"

"It is seaweed, dried and flattened. It aids in keeping the ingredients together. You like?"

"I don't know. I did while I was eating it, except for the hell fire wasabi. Now I'm not so sure. That was really eel?"

"Yes."

"By golly, what will you Californians think of next? Squid? Octopus?"

"Would you like to try some with octopus?"

"You have octopus sushi?" she shivered.

"And sea urchin, though I don't recommend that to beginners."

"I think I've had quite enough culinary adventures for one day. I'm going to go for good old chicken fried steak for dinner. At least I know that's really chicken."

The waitress and I just looked at each other. We knew, but we weren't going to correct Grandma. At least now I knew what to do with that beef.

Chapter 20

Rusty came home from work and Katie struggled out of Grandma's arms and slid off the couch. She crawled madly for the living room saying, "dadadadadada," all the way. Rusty picked her up.

"Hey princess, can you say Daddy?" he asked.

"Dada."

"Say Daddy."

"Dada."

He kissed her on the forehead and found me in the kitchen.

"Hey beautiful. How was your day?"

"It was interesting. And surprisingly trouble free."

"That's my girl. I knew you could do it. What did you do?"

"Grandma and I went shopping."

"And nothing happened?"

"Yeah, well, no. Hmm, I hope you like it."

"I like it anytime you manage to go shopping without getting into trouble."

"Good. We'll just leave it at that then."

Grandma nodded in agreement.

"Did you buy anything?"

Grandma's head came back up.

"Yeah! We found the cutest dress."

"When do I get to see it?"

"April first. Keep that day open."

"Okay, big date?"

"Yeah, you could say that. Double date."

"A big date and a double date are not the same thing."

"Sherri sent us four tickets to the premier of Payback."

"Payback?"

"Yeah, the movie I worked on with Sherri."

"Appropriate title. Jealous extra takes revenge on successful actress, gets busted."

"That's not what the movie is about, it's just what the job was about," I told Grandma.

"What's the movie about?"

"I came on in the last two weeks of shooting so I don't really know. All I know is I play a bad guy in black grunge with red and black hair. They did several shots of me in that getup. And I was in the big final fight scene. We won't know how much of it they used until we see the movie."

"You're in the movie? I better call home so they'll go to town and see the movie!"

"You better call Mom, Dad, and Grandpap first so they know where you are. I told Mom you would call when we got home."

"Well, it might be safe now. I have something to change the subject to."

She called the ranch while I made chicken fried steak out of cow.

At dinner I warned Grandma, "Tomorrow we aren't being California girls. We're going to town and they are supposed to take my cast off. Then I am stopping by the gym to test out my leg."

"Rats, I was hoping to go to take in an amusement park."

"Grandma, do you have a list of all the things to do in California?"

"Well… yes. Let's see, I still want to go to the beach and see all the hunky surfers and girls in bikinis, I want to buy a big bag of oranges, and ride a roller coaster."

"You should have come in June or July. It's too cold at the beach to swim. If we go to the beach we'll see people in sweatshirts walking and trying not to get their feet wet. I think we can find some oranges."

"Not just any oranges. I want to buy them straight from the orange groves."

"Okay, I think we can manage that, too."

"Just drive the 126 from Valencia to Oxnard, then go to the beach in Ventura. That ought to fill up a day," Rusty said. "If it was summer Cassidy might even be out there surfing."

"You surf?"

"I'm still learning. I don't get much practice."

"Well, shoot, let's go!"

"I'd need a wet suit. It's too cold to surf now. All the surfers you see out there are going to look more like scuba divers."

"Ba-bite!" said Katie.

"What's it baby?" Grandma asked, "Are you hungry? Look at you, your tray is empty."

She cut up more tiny bites and put them on Katie's tray. Katie had decided baby food was for little kids. She still liked her bottle, but baby food was a no-no.

"Finally, some food that I can identify," Grandma said about the chicken fried steak.

"You've been walking on this cast," Doctor Ron said.

"A little bit."

"I bet your crutches aren't as worn as the cast."

"Just cut the thing off. I have to take my grandmother to an amusement park. I have to wear a fancy dress to a movie premier. I don't want a cast on my leg for either of those."

"At least you aren't invading any foreign countries."

He pulled out my old x-rays, debated.

"Okay, go have it cut. If I don't let them do it you'll probably do it yourself."

"I could do that?"

Doctor Ron realized his mistake. "You'd probably be back getting more stitches but it's just plaster and gauze. At least at the office they'll do it in a safe manner."

I walked funny out of the casting office. My foot felt too light. I went to the gym and did a little bit of light weight training. I walked half a mile. I was ready to take on Grandma's list. I went home, took Katie off Grandma's hands and shaved my legs.

I thought a drive to the beach by way of the orange groves was more what Doctor Ron would prefer so the next day we piled into the Jeep again. Grandma wanted to stop at each fruit stand we came to. She chatted with the owners comparing farming in California to ranching in Montana. She bought a few oranges at each stop to be friendly. She peeled and ate oranges as we drove along.

"Oh, these are so good. We hardly ever get oranges at the ranch. We might get a few on a trip to town but they get eaten up fast and then we're out until we get to town again. I was determined to get sick of oranges on this trip. How far to the beach?"

"Not far. When we get to the end of this road it's just a few miles."

I bundled Katie up in her little jacket with horses printed on it. Another one of mom's sales finds. We headed for the beach but it wasn't long before Grandma was running back to the Jeep. She dug around until I asked what she was looking for.

"Binoculars. A ranch kid's got to have binoculars."

"Try the glove compartment."

She popped it open and scrounged around. She pulled a small pair out.

"These rinky dink things? How can you spot cattle in the brush with these?"

"I don't look for cattle in the brush I look for deer and I spot them better without those. I keep those for Patrick. He likes to watch the birds with them."

"Birds, huh. I'm not going to watch any flitty little birds. I got better things to watch. Men."

"Then we should have gone to San Diego. You could watch Rusty's little brother. He's a surfer. Spends most of his time at Mission Beach."

"Is he as good looking as Rusty?"

"Yeah, a little younger, a little blonder."

"Hooee, you sure know how to pick 'em!"

"I didn't pick him. He picked me. I just lucked out."

Grandma staked out a spot where she could see up and down the beach and out to sea. There weren't many surfers. There were no swimmers. The wind blew and the tourists wouldn't show up for a few months. A few hardy walkers breezed past. The walkers the other direction trudged into the wind. A man dressed in spandex on a mountain bike coasted by, then quickly bogged down in the sand.

"Would you look at all that water!" Grandma said. "I only seen the ocean a few times and I always wonder at it."

I took off my shoes and walked to the water's edge. The water was frigid. There was no way I was going out there.

Grandma came up next to me and stuck her big toe in. She rolled up her pants to calf length and waded with the water up to her ankles.

"How can you do that?" I asked.

"What? This? The lakes back home are like this in the summer!"

"You're not going out there. Some officer riding patrol will decide you're trying to kill yourself and try to save you and then he'll catch pneumonia and die."

"Will he be cute?"

"If he's on patrol on a bicycle, probably. If he's in a Jeep there's no telling."

"And you won't let me go swimming. Are you going to surf?"

"No, it's too cold."

"Well… will you, at least, take my picture with your surfboard so it looks like we surfed?"

"Sure. You hold Katie and I'll get the surfboard."

I jogged over to the Jeep and unstrapped the surfboard from on top. I pulled it down and found the balance point so it would rest under one arm easily, then I jogged back and almost got blown away when the wind caught the surfboard broadside. I stood the surfboard sideways to the wind and grandma searched for the camera in her purse.

"This thing's all wet!" she said when she pulled it out.

Katie gave a mischievous smile. She reached for the camera, "Ga! Mama!"

"Did you have your purse beside Katie's car seat on the way here?"

"It was just sitting in the back seat."

"Then it's probably wet because Katie's been chewing on it."

I took a picture of Grandma standing next to the surfboard with the beach and plenty of ocean in it. Then she found a spot and trained her binoculars on the surfers.

"This is a mite disappointing. This isn't the California I see on TV."

"It's more interesting in the summer. You better keep that purse away from Katie. She's a little pickpocket. There's no telling what you might be missing now. We'll have to search the Jeep and see what she took out and dropped."

"Oh, I'm sure all I'm missing is a few pictures."

"If all you're missing is a few pictures then something is very wrong with Katie. You'll see. The back of the Jeep will be full of stuff from your purse."

On the floor and seat of the Jeep we found Grandma's glasses, out of the case; cell phone; wallet with the contents carefully picked out, examined and dropped; three pens, thankfully still capped; and a lucky rabbit's foot dyed pink.

The drive back was uneventful. Grandma had rated the fruit stands as she went and we stopped at her favorite one. She bought a twenty pound bag of oranges to take home.

"What are you going to do with twenty pounds of oranges?"

"Eat them!" she said.

We merged from the 126 to the 5 right at rush hour so we were creeping down the 5 when Grandma grabbed my arm.

"Cassidy! What on earth is that?"

"That… is Six Flags."

"Is that what it looks like?"

"It's roller coasters."

"Oh lordy."

We watched as a train of cars was lifted to the top of an immense hill, there was a tense pause at the top and then it swooped downhill and through three loops.

"Oh, Isabel, what did you get yourself into?" she said to herself. "I never seen one like that before! I told myself I was going to ride a big, fast roller coaster! I pictured the kind at the fair! I never imagined a monster one like that!"

Chapter 21

"Is this your weekend off?" I asked Rusty after dinner.

"Yeah, unless something comes up to change things."

"How would you like to go to Six Flags tomorrow? Grandma has a roller coaster death wish and she saw the park off the 5 on the way home. Katie can't ride the rides but she'd enjoy going."

"You think you can get me on one of those roller coasters?"

"Oh, come on, if a group of guys got on one you'd be right there with them."

"That's different."

"I don't want Grandma to have to ride the rides all by herself. You can watch Katie. I'll go on the roller coasters. You can take her to the kiddy rides. She likes anything that moves. Show her the characters that walk around in costume. She'll think they are all doggies, but that's okay."

Grandma looked like she was being marched to her death as we approached the ticket booth.

"Welcome to Six Flags Magic Mountain!" the teller said. She was in uniform and was tired of smiling but she did it anyway.

"Three adults and one infant," Rusty said.

"Children two and under are free," she said still smiling.

"I can't believe I'm actually paying for this," Grandma grumbled. I thought it was going to be worth it just to see her reaction to a real roller coaster. "This is craziness. I'm gonna make a fool out of myself. I just know it. I'm going to shit my britches. Cassidy, we don't have to do this."

"What's the matter, Grandma? Are you getting cold feet?"

"Nah, my feet are warm. They warmed up about the time I crossed over into Nevada. Now they're sweating bullets. Look at these things! It's like riding a fighter jet! It's craziness, sheer craziness."

"I thought you wanted to see how Californians live."

"You sure this isn't how they *die*? I want to see how they live, not how they meet their maker."

"People come from all over the world to do this. In the summer there's an hour long wait for each ride. We'll start you off easy and work our way up."

"Easy huh? What exactly do you consider easy here?"

"Here we go. A mine train. This is a good one to start on."

"This is an easy one is it?"

"Yes, I bet even Rusty will go on this one. What do you say, Rusty?"

"You want to ride this one. I know it," he said. "If she wants to go again I'll go for the second ride."

He was right. I did want to ride the first one. I wanted to see Grandma's face. I wanted to be able to tell my mom about it later.

"Now Grandma, the secret to riding roller coasters is just to sit back and relax," I advised her as we stood in line. "If you tense up you're going to be miserable. If you get scared just sit back and tell yourself it's less than five minutes. In five minutes or less it'll all be over. And relax. Make yourself relax."

"Easy for you to say."

"And don't close your eyes. If you don't want to look down, look to the side."

"What if I look to the side and all I see is clear blue sky?"

"It's still better than closing your eyes. If you close your eyes you don't know what's going on and you tense up."

"Let's go take Katie to Bugs Bunny World."

"We're almost there. Look, only about four more trains to go."

I thought she was going to turn green and run off even before we got to the front of the line.

"Grandma, if you survive this and actually like it ask to go again. I want to see Rusty get on this ride."

"Why?"

"Because he's a roller coaster coward. He'll only get on one to prove a point."

"That big tough guy won't get on a ride like this? Ha, we'll show him, won't we?"

I should have thought of that sooner. She'd do anything to come out the winner. I bet she'd even outride me if I pushed it.

The clanking and clattering of the trains going overhead made her jump and look around. She kept looking for a quick exit, calculating whether being considered a chicken was worth getting out of the ride. A half second before she could make her last decision the turnstile turned over and she was pointed to a yellow line on the timber floor.

"Cassidy? You're sure about this?"

"Sure, Grandma, this ride is nothing compared to the big ones. If you like roller coasters this is a good start."

"If. What if I don't know yet?"

"Here's the train, just scoot all the way to the far side and I'll sit with you."

The train came clattering into the station and ground to a halt before us.

Grandma swallowed big, and looked longingly at the exit. I silently laughed. I thought her knees looked a little shaky as the riders exited across the station from us and we stepped into the train. Why did they have to put us in the first car? I thought, she'll be staring down that hill. Oh well, she asked for it.

"Cassidy, if I die of a heart attack, don't let me fall out."

"You're not going to die, Grandma. Just relax."

The bar snapped down and she jumped again. Her knuckles turned white as the train rumbled out of the station. I patted her hands. "Relax. Don't lean forward. Just sit back. Look, feet out, hands on the bar, lean back, relax."

"I'm'a trying. It isn't working."

The train lurched and bumped uphill and Grandma was hyperventilating already. She knew what this lift meant. It meant downhill was next. When she felt the machinery release the car I could have sworn she was a six year old riding her first scary ride all over again. The train was released and it coasted down a short hill and into a curve and Grandma heaved a sigh of relief.

"That was a dirty rotten no good trick," she said. The train sped up as it twisted and turned its way through a maze of track. She held on tight, whooping and hollering, "Yahooooo! Yeehaw!" and "Oopsie daisy," like some hick rancher woman. Once she got to hollering, though, she was able to relax until we reached the big drop. She stared at the hill dreading the sound of the machinery disengaging.

"Don't close your eyes!" I warned.

"Drop it, you mean old tormentors you! Don't keep me a'hanging here."

"It's only a few seconds. You're stretching them by getting all nervous."

Clack, release, sliiide.

"Yaaaahhhhoooo!" she yelled as we went down the hill, "Oh there goes my bun."

As she felt the brakes grab and the train slow she heaved a sigh of relief. She'd survived.

"Whew," she said. "Now that I got through the first run, let's ride it for fun."

"Rusty has to go this time."

"Can I pretend I'm scared and hold onto him?"

"I'm afraid it won't work. He's going to be more scared than you. He just won't admit it."

"Ha, ha, I'll show him."

But when we got back to the stroller Rusty was nowhere to be seen. We waited but he didn't show. I pictured him standing out of sight waiting for us to move on.

"Well… we can wait all day for Rusty to make an appearance, we can ride this one again, or we can go on to the next ride. You ready for one just a bit different?"

"Let me put my hair up again. It got all wind-blown on that ride."

"It's no use, Grandma, every ride is going to be faster. You might as well just brush it down and hope for the best. Do you see any California Grandmas with their hair up?"

She looked around, shrugged and we kept going.

"Did you like that one?" I asked.

"I wouldn't go so far as to say *like*. I could get used to it."

"Good, the next one should help. It's smoother. The train hangs from the track."

"That's supposed to encourage me? I don't like the sound of that."

"You'll like it. It's smoother and faster but it isn't real high."

We got in line for the Ninja. Grandma wasn't quite as scared. She watched the goings on with big wide eyes.

"This time just relax from the very start," I told her. "When the train swings out go with the feel of it, look straight ahead. If you look into the curve the wind gets you and if you look out the scenery passes so fast it'll startle you. On this one go for the feel."

"Right, go for the feel."

She gave herself a little pep talk until the train came to a stop and then she looked like she was saying a little prayer before she stepped into the car.

Her reaction was improving. This time she yelled, "Wooohoo! I am the swinging Grandma! Eighty years and I am swiiiiinging high! Luther you don't know what you're missing!"

This time when we got off Rusty was standing there with a sleeping Katie.

"She conked out on me," he said.

"Come on, Rusty, you've got to try this thing," Grandma said dragging the poor guy off to stand in line.

"Mrs. Gordon, I..."

He never had a chance.

I pushed Katie around in the stroller while she napped. I looked through a gift shop and bought Grandma a postcard of the roller coaster she'd gone on so she could show the folks back home. And I stayed just out of sight as I watched Grandma and Rusty exit the ride, Rusty white as a sheet and Grandma tugging on his arm saying, "Okay, I'm all prepped now. Where's that big three looper job I saw from the freeway?"

Rusty turned whiter and looked around for me frantically. He pulled out his cell phone and in just a second mine rang in my pocket. I fished it out but let him stew for a few rings before I answered it.

"Hi! How'd it go?" I said cheerily.

"Get over here!" he said. "You've created a monster!"

"Aw, it wasn't that bad, was it?"

"If I have to go on this three looper job…"

"Thousands of people go on Viper every summer."

"Yeah and you might notice I'm never one of them."

I laughed, "Don't worry, I'll save you."

"Katie likes the tea cup ride."

"Okay, I'll catch up with you after we do that," I joked.

"Cass…"

I let Grandma lead him into the line and get settled. He wasn't much interested in the little TVs they had for people to watch while they were waiting. Nope, he was watching for one thing, a way out. My big, strong detective would lead a standoff, would take a bullet for me, but he wouldn't ride a roller coaster. It was mean of me to let him stew so I waved him out of line.

"What have you done?" he said. "She's determined to ride them all."

"It's okay. You don't mind watching Katie?"

"No, she's actually a lot of fun when she's awake. I've had to frisk her a few times, if she lifts a flash pass off somebody do you want it?"

"No, the lines aren't too bad this time of year."

"You're really going to get on this?"

"Sure, I bet Grandma wears out before she rides them all. She's eighty years old."

"Could have fooled me."

"Just wait until Katie is tall enough to get on a roller coaster. She loves anything fast. She'll want to ride them all, too."

"I'm glad she's got you then."

"I better go find Grandma."

I found Grandma talking to a kid in line.

"The biggest loop is a hundred feet tall! And there's a corkscrew."

"A corkscrew? What's that?" Grandma asked.

"You know, like they use to open wine bottles," the thirteen year old girl said. She made a corkscrew motion in the air.

"Now what would a young thing like you know about wine?"

"Huh! Where are *you* from? This is California. Everybody my age knows about wine. It's what we buy when we're broke."

"Cassidy," Grandma said. "What's a corkscrew?"

"She just told you. The train goes a round and around like a sideways corkscrew."

"Oh golly, what will they think of next?"

"How did Rusty do on the Ninja?"

"He faked it all the way. Tell that man women can read him like a book."

I laughed. It was true. Off the job, he was a romance novel. Sexy, strong, readable, and unputdownable.

"I think after Katie wakes up we should ride something we can all go on."

She whooped and hollered all the way through Viper. She held her breath waiting for the drop into the huge loop, counting the seconds, then gasping for breath as the seconds whisked behind us on a wild rush down the hill, the weightless feeling at the top of the loop, another rush down.

"Casssssiddddyyy! What did you get me on! Oh dear. Oh no, not the corkscrew, I can't look. I just can't look."

"Grandma, it's over, you can look now."

The girl was impressed with Grandma's fortitude. "Hey granny! Way to go!" she said with a thumbs up.

We found Rusty sharing a hotdog with Katie.

"Ga-mama! Ba bite!" Katie said holding up a piece of bun.

"That's a good idea," Grandma said. Pretty soon we had hotdogs all around. I could only eat one but Rusty ate three.

"You forgot to frisk Katie at the hotdog stand," I said pulling a greasy towel and a pair of tongs from the stroller.

After we finished off the hotdogs and cleaned all the ketchup off Katie we returned the tongs and towel to the hotdog man and headed for Roaring Rapids.

"You pore Californians. You got to manufacture a river for a good raft ride," Grandma said.

I held Katie and Rusty watched her try and catch splashes of water.

"Katie, water, can you say water?"

She was too busy trying to catch it.

Rusty soaked up the family time. That peaceful look came over him as he watched me play with Katie. Minutes of peace. That's what Rusty valued the most. His family safe and happy together.

Grandma and I went on several more roller coasters. But what I really liked that day was watching Rusty and Katie. Katie loved motion of any kind and, sitting in Rusty's lap on the rides, her baby giggles echoed over the park. Her smiley eyes shined from the windows of the cars. She bobbed up and down and tried to say, "choo, choo," on the train ride.

"Say choo, choo, Katie, say choo, choo for Daddy," I said.

"Daddy! Choo, choo chain!"

"That's right!" Rusty beamed. "My princess rode the choo choo train. What a big girl!"

One new word and it was celebration time. It took so little. A little peace, a little progress, a big smile. If only I could keep that up. Katie would hold up her end of the deal if I could just keep the peace.

Peace reigned in the Michaels house after the trip to Six Flags. Grandma was satisfied with normal visiting. We took trips to town. She wanted to see the western wear stores and bought new clothes for Grandpap and found souvenirs for the hands and Leroy and Donna as a kind of peace offering. She even debated bringing something back for Grady Clark, their sheriff friend who probably led the search operations for Grandma. One thing Grandma was determined to do was attend that movie premier. She knew she should really get back but getting all gussied up for a night on the town with movie stars was just too tempting. It was California, just like on TV.

One day Big John let Grandma ride along as he did patrol. Fortunately, she came back disappointed.

"It was boring," she said. "Driving around and around, he didn't even give out but maybe four tickets all day. There were no bank robberies, no shoot 'em ups. I got to see no action at all."

"Sorry, Grandma," I said. "Next time I'll go to the bank and maybe that will help."

"Oh, no you don't," Rusty said.

"The mall?"

"Not unless you really have a reason to go."

"For most women a reason to go is to get out and walk around."

"The chances of the car your grandmother is in being called to a robbery is zilch. Big John probably let her ride along so he'd have a peaceful day."

Chapter 22

Grandma got her share of action a few days later. We were driving to the grocery store when we passed a car stopped on the side of the road, engine running. The driver was bent over talking to a couple of kids on the sidewalk.

"Oh, no, kiddies, don't even go there!" Grandma said.

I agreed with her. This spelled trouble.

"Circle the block, Cassidy. You got that little popgun along?"

"No, I'll circle the block but you are not using the pistol, no matter what happens."

"Why? You know I can use it right."

"I know. I also know you use it a little too freely."

I hung a right and another right and went back several blocks so I was coming up on the car from behind. Two more rights and I was on the street we saw the car on.

"Grandma, take down the license plate number," I said.

I pulled up behind the car far enough back that he wouldn't be suspicious of me. Grandma took out pen and a pad of paper. I guess after nearly missing an autograph opportunity she was prepared now.

The older kid stood back away from the car shaking her head "no" but the little kid began stepping closer to the car. The big kid took the little one's hand and started walking away but she walked the same way the car was pointed. No! Not that way! I thought, he'll just follow you. It was every parent's worst nightmare. The car pulled forward. The man got out.

I got out my cell phone and called 911. It was obvious this wasn't Uncle Tony stopping to give his nieces a lift.

"911 Emergency Dispatch," a woman said.

"This is Cassidy Michaels. I'm parked in the six hundred block of Sage and I'm watching a man try to pick up two kids."

"Cassidy?"

"Yeah, Denise?"

"Yeah, don't get out of your car."

"License plate XXX-000, white Lincoln. Big car. North bound side."

The man was offering the kids something. Showing them the contents of a bag. It wasn't working. Way to go kids!

As soon as the man edged close enough to show the kids the bag his arm darted out and he had the older one. The little one jumped back crying. The older one got stuffed into the car.

"Aw shit," I told Denise. "Where's that car?"

Once he had the older kid the younger one was an easy catch. She looked like she was ready to run but she was worried about the other girl. Run, kid, run!

"I'm going to have to follow them. Can you put me in contact with the responding officer? I can't talk and shift so I may have to hand you over to my grandmother."

Grandma was frantically looking around the Jeep. She wasn't finding what she was looking for and I was glad. I didn't think she could get her hands on my 9mm.

The man ran around to the driver's side and peeled away from the curb. I pulled out and hit the gas to stay in sight of him. I handed the phone to Grandma, hoping it would slow down her search for my gun.

"Grandma, keep the police updated. I need to drive."

"Hello?" Grandma said. "No this isn't Cassidy, this is Isabel. Cassidy's driving. Come on Cass! Hit the gas!"

"I don't want to catch up. I just want to stay on his tail. Find out the officer's name."

"He can hear you. It's Thompson."

"Good, Jayce, we're north bound on Sage Street. Just past Arroyo Road."

There was a pause as I focused on positioning myself in traffic. I didn't want the driver to know he was being followed so I wanted to stay close, but not close enough to be suspicious.

"Atta girl Cass! We got him now," Grandma said. She was still looking for the gun.

Shoot, she dragged out a small toolbox. It wasn't a toolbox, though. It was a gun box, well, it also had a couple of handy tools but I mainly hid a gun there. It was locked. Ha, ha, Grandma, you can't just use a gun any time you want to.

"East on Canyon!" I called out to Jayce.

"Did you get that?" Grandma asked him as she pulled out a hairpin from her bun. She bent it a little and fiddled with the toolbox.

The lid popped open!

"Is this thing loaded?" she asked.

Oh hell. "Yes! Don't point it at anybody! Grandma, put that gun back!" I yelled more for Jayce's information than anything else. I knew she wouldn't put it back.

"Get closer!" Grandma said.

"Grandma! Put that gun down! Jayce, she's better with it than you think. She's used to shooting rattlesnakes."

Grandma laughed, "He wants to know if I'm better than Victor," then to

Jayce she said, "Hell yeah."

I didn't know that little story got circulated, about Victor trying to shoot a rattlesnake at my feet and taking off the end of my toe instead. I didn't have time to reminisce. Where was that car?

"South of Sheffield!" I called to Jayce. This was bad news. He was headed into a residential area and he'd figure out real quick he had someone on his tail.

Three turns and he was checking his rear view mirror. I saw a scowl and the Lincoln took off going forty in the twenty-five zone.

"Okay, we got him running. I don't know how long I can keep up now."

"He says you sure know how to turn a guy around," Grandma said of Jayce Thompson.

"Me? I'm just following!"

Katie slept though the gentle stuff but when I picked up speed and the Jeep rocked more she woke up. Like usual, when she woke up, she was hungry and wet.

Just what I needed a gun toting grandmother and a fussy baby.

The car headed for a major street and made a beeline out of town. We passed cars left and right with Grandma relaying street names as they passed. As the houses thinned and the roads narrowed Grandma shifted rolls. She rolled her window down and leaned out.

"Grandma! No! There's kids in the car!" I yelled.

"Get closer, Cass! I can get his tires!"

"No, you'll cause an accident and I won't put the kids through that. Get back in here and let the police handle it."

"Waaaaahhhhh," went Katie.

"Get closer, this pistol is useless from a distance!"

"I'm not going to get close enough for you to use that thing so you might as well put it down!"

"Insolent kids these days! Who taught you to obey your elders?"

"My dad! But he wasn't talking about armed grandmas who could hit a helpless kid in the back of a getaway car! Tell me to clean my room! I'll do that!"

"Officer Thompson is laughing at you."

"Tell him to laugh with a lead foot!"

"He wants to know if the suspect is armed."

"I didn't see any weapon. That doesn't mean there isn't one."

A dust cloud flew up ahead when he dropped a wheel off the pavement. I prayed he maintained control as he pulled back onto the pavement but he didn't. He pulled off and took off running for a house. Yes! And no! I was glad he was fleeing and leaving the kids behind but now I had to follow him on foot and I didn't know who might be in that house. I pulled to a stop behind the Lincoln.

"Grandma, take care of the kids. Give me the gun. And the phone. Don't go near the house! Your job is to keep the kids away from the house."

"What are you doing telling me what to do? I've got the gun! I think I should go to the house."

"Grandma! When you go to police academy and they hand you your fancy little badge, then you can go investigate the house. In the meantime, hand it over!"

She pouted as she handed me the gun, then the phone.

"Jayce? I'm trying to get a house number. I think the kids are okay."

"That was really your grandmother?"

"Yeah. I don't see a house number. We're way out on Mojave Road. You'll see my tan Jeep and the white Lincoln parked in front of a green house that is off a ways from the road. You should have backup."

"What are you doing?"

"Tracking. This guy is scared. He's probably holing up in here. I just hope he isn't armed."

"Just back off and wait."

"You guys had problems with pedophiles before?"

"There's always a few kooks out there."

The house appeared to be empty. I wondered if the guy knew it would be. I wondered if he passed up his first destination because it was too public. I followed his tracks staying out of sight of the house and the direction the tracks were leading. I thought he'd find a back way into the house but as I followed his tracks I realized he was fleeing out the backside of the property.

"Don't bust into the house," I told Jayce. "He's not in there."

"I never thought I'd be relieved to find out you had the gun."

"Gee thanks."

"I thought your grandmother was going to shoot up the Lincoln."

"Me, too. If I'd gotten a little closer I bet she would have. If it had been a rifle or I'd given her a good shot she would have tried for the tires."

I couldn't figure out what this guy thought he was doing running off into the desert. Guess he didn't expect to get followed by a tracker. He thought he had time on his side while the cops caught up. But even then, they would just send out a helicopter that would spot him on the open expanse easily.

"Cassidy, we're at the house. Wait for back up."

"He's running, Jayce. He's easy to track."

"Then we'll catch up with him but you need backup before you catch him."

"Is Katie okay?"

"Your Grandma's giving her a bottle and telling the girls stories about you."

"Oh great."

"They don't know it's real."

"I hope she picked one with a happy outcome."

"What's your twenty?"

"I'm about a quarter mile behind the house. I'm following but I don't think I'm closing in. I'm leaving a good trail for you. It should be easy."

"Should be. Yeah right, I'll call Chase."

"Very funny," I said

I heard a shot and hit the dirt. Sand and rocks jumped around to my right. "Okay, he's armed," I reported.

"Cassidy, just stop."

"I am stopped. Where are you, you creep? If you can see me, I can see you too." I scanned the desert in the direction the tracks led.

"Stay put."

"Don't follow me," I told Jayce. "If he can see me he can certainly spot a team of officers."

I found the only possible cover he could be hiding in and crawled along the tracks, staying low, keeping that hiding place in view, trying to catch a glimpse of a figure hidden behind it. When the tracks turned toward the Joshua tree I'd been watching I quit tracking. I found denser cover and stuck to that. I dropped down into a shallow fold in the earth and quickly crawled up it, always keeping that Joshua tree in sight. When I came up beside it I could see the man, crouched behind it, watching the direction of the house, glancing back to the place he'd last seen me. Rusty would kill me if I got closer than this. But I had to get within hailing distance. I mentally practiced my authoritative voice. The one that backfired most of the time. The one that sounded like kids playing cops and robbers. Then, since I wasn't a cop today, I thought I ought to go with my dad's version, so I crept in from the side as the guy watched the house.

The man got tired of waiting for pursuit. He wasn't sure what was going on but something felt wrong about his situation. He'd heard the sirens. Where were the cops? His unease finally shifted to action. He backed away from the Joshua tree, preparing to flee.

"I wouldn't do that if I were you," I said in my best imitation of my dad.

He froze, scanning the desert around him.

"I've got a gun, and I know how to use it," I warned him. "Throw down your weapon."

"Where are you? Prove it."

"Name a body part." I said.

"That rock," the guy said shaking.

"You've got rocks in your head. I'll go for that. I'm not falling for that trick. If I fire at the rock you'll know where I am and you'll shoot while I'm setting up for my next shot. It would be wiser for you to just give up and walk quietly back to the house. I've got some friends there who want to show you a good time."

I heard snickering from the phone in my hand. Tense snickering.

"Jayce?" I said. "I think it's safe to close in now. If he so much as raises his gun I'll take his hand off. He won't touch another kid again."

I got up and showed him what he was dealing with. When he saw me he rolled his eyes. There wasn't a guy around who liked being brought in by a little blonde woman. I don't know what it was. They just never seemed happy about it.

"Drop your gun. Put your hands on top of your head."

He didn't do it.

I could see a group of guys heading out from the house at a jog.

He saw them, too.

"Drop the gun, or I'll *make* you drop the gun."

"Yeah right. Just because your dad keeps a gun in the car doesn't mean you know how to use it."

"It's mine and I use it at work. I practice weekly, but I don't like using force."

"Use the force, Cass," I heard from my cell phone, which was no longer up to my ear. Jayce was still listening in.

As the guys neared, the kidnapper began looking around himself wildly. I recognized the frantic thinking that goes before a run. Something was going to happen in those next few seconds. I had to be ready for either or both.

He raised his hand. I raised my gun. He pointed his gun toward the guys. I aimed, followed the movements of his hand, pulled the trigger.

His gun jumped from his hand and he jerked his hand back like it had been snake bit. He turned to run. I had a head start over the guys. I could at least bring him down until the guys could take over, so I took off after him. I didn't have time to put things away, so gun in one hand and cell phone in the other I chased him down until I could tackle him. He turned and put a fist into my face and I returned the hit with one of my own, gun in hand. Oh man! That hurt! Both of us. He was lucky I didn't shoot him in the head the way my fist came up automatically. As it was the barrel of the pistol caught him in the eye. After the barrel hit him my hand continued forward crushing my knuckles between his head and the grip. I nearly dropped the gun, but I still had a very mad kidnapper on my hands. He scrambled and punched awkwardly at me until the guys finally caught up and pulled him off. The way

Jayce did it I thought I was under arrest, too. Two officers cuffed the guy. Jayce hauled me up by the arms, and shoved me towards the cars. I shrugged loose but he roughly pointed me back at the cars and kept me walking. I wished I could get behind him. Something was eating at him and I would feel better trying to read it in his tracks than looking into that scowl on his face. When we got to the squad cars I headed for Katie.

"Not yet," he snapped. "What made you think you should take that guy on by yourself?"

"If I was on duty you wouldn't ask that. You'd know. The guy needed stopping. I was the only one on hand who could do it."

"No you weren't!" Grandma said. "I would have, but you stuck me with the kids. One shot and we would have saved the glorious state of California a fist full of dollars. Now I bet there's a big trial and he'll get put up in a fancy jail for years. He's a skunk. He should have…"

"Any more questions?" I asked Jayce.

He opened his trunk, took out the first aid kit, got out a cold pack and handed it to me with a sigh of resignation. I pocketed my gun and cell phone and put the ice pack to my hand. He got another one and put it to my eye.

Grandma took a closer look. "Hooboy! You got a shiner! It's going to clash with your dress."

My dress! Oh man, how long was it until the movie premier?

"It's okay," Grandma continued. "You said you were a bad guy stunt man. The black eye will go with your character."

"What's she talking about?" Jayce asked.

"The premier for Payback is coming up. I've got tickets. Rusty, Grandma and I are supposed to go to it April first."

I took the cold pack and put it over my eye willing the bruise to fade.

"Payback? That job you had with Sherri Champlain?"

"Yeah."

His attitude changed remarkably.

"And you're in it?"

"Yeah. Maybe. A little?"

"I've got to see this."

"You won't recognize me."

"Why? I've known you for years."

"You still won't recognize me. I didn't even recognize myself."

"Go to the station," he said. "Fill in your report while it's still fresh in your mind."

"Rusty will see me."

"Good. Maybe he'll talk some sense into you."

"You should have let me shoot out his tires" Grandma said as we drove back into town. "It would have saved you a black eye."

"Maybe. Might have given the girls more than a black eye. Sorry Grandma."

"You're turning into a sissified, stay-at-home mom."

"Yeah, but I think we did better with the black eye method."

"What about the premier?"

"It'll fade by then."

"Where're we going?"

"The station to file my report. I want to make sure I don't forget anything. You should fill one out too. The more witnesses we have the easier it will be to convict him."

The woman at the front desk didn't ask any questions as I led Grandma to the back of the station. The black eye, the dust and dirt kind of spoke for itself. I led Grandma to the desk where I picked up the right forms, then, despite my reservations, I led her to Rusty's office. I glanced in his little window and knocked lightly. He was deep in his work. A frown creased his brow as he bent over his desk. He waved me in. I opened the door a little, "You're busy. We'll find an empty meeting room. We just need a flat surface for a little while."

I knew he was tense and busy when he just let us go. We found a meeting room that wasn't being used. Grandma held Katie as I led her through her form. Then I puzzled over my own version of the story. It was the same as Grandma's except that I had to explain why I fired my weapon and what the results were. When I was just about finished Rusty wandered in. He was weary. He walked slow and sat down heavily. He ran his hands through his hair. He held out his arms for Katie and Grandma handed her over.

"What brings you here?" he asked.

"I tried to go shopping."

He stilled himself, another thing that tipped me off that work was tense. The phrase wasn't all that uncommon between us. He knew what it meant. It meant I tried to go shopping but trouble prevented me from doing it. And the fact that I was at the station filling out reports told him more. I just handed him my finished report and let it do the talking.

"You should have waited for the guys to take care of it," he finally said.

"If I'd have waited, I still would have had to track him down, and it would have taken longer. It would have been even more complicated. It probably would have involved air support. It worked out this way. It's all taken care of."

"Maybe *it* is. What about you?" he said fingering the bruise on my cheek. "What does the rest of you look like?"

"This is the worst of it. It's the only good solid hit he got in."

"I thought you quit doing apprehensions."

"Rusty, I wasn't going to just let him go. He had two kids in the car! Grandma was along to watch Katie. I was armed."

"Why do you keep your gun locked up in a box? You need it where you can get to it!" Grandma said.

"Because I don't want Katie to get hold of it. Or you either for that matter. How did you learn to pick locks?"

"Toolboxes are easy. Grandpap don't trust anybody. He's always locking up his tools, making it impossible for anybody else to use them. He should know the ranch hands have to use them but he's got to lock up everything. I learned early on that if I wanted to use a tool I had to search out the key... or pick the lock, so I learned right quick how to pick locks."

"Should have known."

We were lying in bed, both tense. Katie was finally asleep. Grandma might have been. Rusty wasn't going to get to sleep soon in spite of what he told Grandma. I think he just wanted some one on one time.

"Do you know how close that was today?" he asked. "If the guy had taken the time to aim better... It was too close."

"Yeah, there wasn't much I could do about it though. All I could do was get close enough to surprise him."

"No, you could have stayed out of it."

"Maybe somebody else could. But I couldn't. If you had seen him take those two kids you would have gone after him, too. Even if Katie and I were along. You would have done what I did, get on the phone, call 911, get the responding officer online and feed him information."

"I guess I was just wishing peace was here to stay. It's been weeks. I was just getting settled in, thinking trouble was giving up on us."

This little reminder had scared him more than he wanted to admit. The hard day at work didn't help.

He kissed my black eye. "Never again," he said quietly. "I read the report and all I saw was my world coming so close to crumbling again. He might have missed but from where he stood it was by just a few degrees."

"You can't think like that. It's over. He missed. You can't look at life in degrees."

"Okay minutes," he said so seriously I doubted he even saw the pun. I caught it but I couldn't laugh. He was so serious.

"Rusty, our minutes have turned into years."

"I don't know. It doesn't feel like years. It feels like a week here and a month there. When you're hurt time stops. When you're getting back on your feet it slows. When you're well and we're finally at peace it feels like it speeds up. Weeks go by so fast. One day Katie's breathing her first breath laying in my hands. Then seems like I take a breath and she's crawling. She says mommy and daddy and choo choo train and cookie. Another breath and she'll be walking but where will we be? Will you see it happen? Please be here to share it with me."

"Rusty, you're working yourself up. You need to do something to relax."

"I don't want to relax. I want to know."

"Know I love you. I'll be here."

I worried about Rusty. Whenever we were together he was teaching Katie to walk. I worried that she would walk when he was at work. If she did I wouldn't tell him. He wanted to share that moment. He seemed obsessed with the idea that I had to be there with him when Katie walked, like it would prove to him that I'd be there for the next milestone and maybe the next.

Chapter 23

April first was on us before I could think. I'd been focusing on Rusty and Katie. Grandma had decided she'd seen enough action for a while so she found a hobby and crocheted Katie a baby blanket. I realized with a start that I hadn't invited Landon to the premier. I needed to line up a babysitter, too.

The phone rang several times before Landon answered it. "Hello?"

"Landon, it's Cassidy."

"Hi! Long time no see."

"Tourist season is coming up. I'm sure the first search of the tourist season isn't too far off."

"I know you didn't call to chat."

"No, actually I'm calling on behalf of Sherri again."

He didn't say anything but I could picture raised eyebrows.

"I have four tickets to the premier of Payback. My Grandma was with me when Sherri told us about them and she asked to go, so I couldn't say no. I have one ticket left and Sherri suggested I invite you. April first. Seven PM. Hollywood. Red carpet. Hundreds of adoring fans. Of course they're there to see Sherri and Brock but still..."

"April first? You're kidding."

"No."

"I can't. I have a previous commitment."

"You have a date?"

"Okay, yes, I have a date."

"That's great! I mean, I wish you could go, but I'm glad you've got a date."

"You are?"

"You'll have a great time."

"I suppose."

Rats, so who else could I invite? The two people I could think of I wasn't sure I wanted along. I wasn't sure Bailee was even allowed to see the movie and I wasn't sure what her reaction would be. The other option was Lawanda. I knew Lawanda would do anything to go. The problem was, Lawanda would do *anything* to go. And I wasn't sure I could count on her to act like a responsible adult if she got to. She was one of those people who bought tabloids, *Soap Opera Digest*, *People*, anything to stay on top of what the stars were up to. I also wasn't sure I wanted to listen Grandma and Lawanda feed off each other's excitement until they were both acting like small children.

"What did you say we were doing in town?" Grandma asked.

"Lining up a babysitter for Premier night and feeling out a friend to see if we want to invite her along."

"Why does she need feeling out?"

"Because she's like a kid in a candy store when it comes to all things Hollywood and she might be embarrassingly over emotional at a movie premier, surrounded by actors, actresses, directors and the like. She might just make a fool out of herself. We don't want to admit we have a ticket unless we're sure we're going to invite her."

"Why don't you just call these people?"

"Bertie doesn't have a telephone. And Lawanda is at work. It's the only place I know how to get a hold of her. And don't gawk at Bertie. She is who she is just like you, got it?"

"Got it. Why would I gawk? She doesn't have three eyes or anything, does she?"

"No, she just isn't what you'd expect in a babysitter."

Grandma really wondered what we were up to when I pulled into a parking place at the local library.

"This is the first place I always look for Bertie. If I don't find her here I have to go to the police station and get a Bertie report. The officers all know her comings and goings."

"You hire a babysitter that the police keep tabs on? Well, at least she reads. That's a good sign."

I led Grandma to the back corner of the first floor and after shushing Katie whenever she saw a purse, tote bag, uniform or suit, we found Bertie sitting in a big reading chair with the morning's paper open before her.

"Imagine, some guy trying to make off with two young girls. What's this world coming to?" she mumbled to herself.

"Don't even talk about it," I warned Grandma. "Hi Bertie!"

"Ga-mama!" Katie said struggling to get down. I set her down and she made a beeline for Bertie's bags.

"Hey! I'm the ga-mama," said Grandma.

"Katie, there's my baby!" said Bertie enthusiastically.

She folded up her newspaper and set it aside, then pulled Katie up into her lap. Katie had her hands in Bertie's pockets before I could blink. She came up with a package of Oreos.

"Nope, you can't have that!" Bertie said. "That's my jackpot of the week! Who would throw away a good package of Oreos? I bet they didn't know they were doing it. What's up girls?"

"Bertie, this is my grandmother, Isabel Gordon. Grandma, this is Bertie, Katie's baby sitter."

"You've got a grandma in town and you need a baby sitter?"

"Grandma's here visiting from Montana and we have to go to an event in LA on April first. It's going to be a long evening. Katie should sleep through most of it so you will have plenty of free time."

"Do I get to use the sexy shower?"

"You can use whatever you like, just be out of the sexy shower before Rusty walks in. Rusty can bring you home from work that day."

"Do I have to ride in the squad car? It never makes a good impression for me to get picked up by a squad car. Makes people think that homeless people aren't law abiding citizens."

"He doesn't drive a squad car. He drives an Explorer."

"Okay, then, April first? Early evening? Tell him I'll be on the bench in front of the station."

"Will do. Thanks Bertie."

"Why her?" Grandma asked as we climbed into the Jeep again.

"She's capable, it helps her and it helps me. In return for baby-sitting she washes her clothes and gets in a good shower and I pay her enough to splurge for a week. It's a good set up. She only has commitments every other Friday, so if I have a search she can stay for days if need be. Katie loves her. What's wrong with that?"

"Now where to?"

"The cop shop. Let me do the talking."

"What's a cop shop? Is that where the city gets their officers from?"

"No, it's where cops shop for their uniforms and gun belts and patches and stuff."

"Can I shop there, too?"

"It depends on what you want to buy."

"Rats."

Lawanda came out of the back room when the bell on the door tinkled.

"Cassidy! What can I do for you?"

"I just have a few questions. I was wondering if you were working April first."

"Of course I am. April Fool's Day isn't holiday enough to close down the cop shop."

"When do you get off?"

"Depends. If Robin wants to work I could get off. Why? You got another one of those star studded parties going on at your place?"

"Not exactly. But if I did would you come?"

"You're planning something! I can see it in your eye! You got something up your sleeve! Does Rusty know?"

"Of course he knows."

"What is it? If Rusty knows and you're planning it it's got to be safe."

"Yeah, it's safe, so far." I'm just not sure if it will be if you go ballistic on me.

"Is Sherri going to be there?"

"Yup, Sherri will be there."

"Brock?"

"Yeah, Brock will be there, too."

"Oh man! To think I have a friend who is friends with Sherri Champlain and Brock Larone! I get hot flashes just thinking about it."

"I wouldn't exactly call them friends. Just because I worked with them once doesn't mean we're friends. We just worked together and we get along."

"If I worked with someone and we got along I'd sure call them *my* friends! So… what's going down? Tell me."

"Remember when you sold me a bodyguard uniform so I could work for Sherri Champlain and I got recruited as a stunt man?"

"Of course!"

"Well the movie comes out in early April and a group of us wanted to go to the movie together."

"That sounds like fun. I thought you said Sherri and Brock would be there."

Grandma was strolling around the cop shop looking at all the paraphernalia involved in police work. "Quit beating around the bush," she said.

"The movie opens April first. In Hollywood. Rusty and Grandma and I are going. I have one more ticket."

"You're still beating around the bush."

So far Lawanda was acting pretty calm. Maybe it would be fine.

"The movie in Hollywood that is April first is the movie premier. Have you ever been to a movie premier?"

Realization was dawning, "Ohhhh, you mean…? Like the red carpet? And the stars all walking down it to go to the movie for the very first time. Where all the fans stand there and ask for autographs and the stars stop and sign autographs on the way in?"

"Yeah, like that."

"Sure, I been to one of those. I got Taylor Avenue's autograph that way. It's hard to get a spot close to the red carpet. You have to get there really early, like camp out or something to get a spot next to the red carpet."

"How would you like to be *on* the red carpet?"

"Oh, they don't let you get on the red carpet. If you even lean too far out some hunky security guard makes you get back. If I can get close to the carpet I try to lean out a lot."

"Not if you have a ticket."

"A ticket."

"Yeah, to the premier. If you have a ticket you can walk right up the red carpet and go to the movie with the stars."

"Do you know how hard those tickets are to get? And April first? Ain't no way. No way on God's green earth you're going to get a ticket."

"Lawanda, I'm trying to tell you I have one last ticket to the premier of Payback. Rusty and Grandma and I are going. I have four tickets, so that means I have one left over."

"Ohhhhh…OHHHHH, you don't mean it. You couldn't mean it."

"Would I come all the way into town if I didn't mean it?"

"You really have an extra ticket, to a real movie premier, April first, in Hollywood, to walk down the red carpet, and see Payback with the stars."

"Yeah."

Lawanda fainted. She was lucky she fell into a rack of clothes because I didn't have time to catch her. I pulled the rack out of the way and knelt beside her.

"What'd she do that for?" Grandma said as she looked down at Lawanda.

"I don't know," I said, slightly disgusted.

"Is there something wrong with her?"

"No, I don't think so but if she faints at the thought of premier tickets I wonder what she is going to do when she's surrounded by all those movie stars."

Suddenly the front door to the cop shop slammed open, turning the little copper bell inside out and six officers stormed in rifles at the ready.

"Freeze right where you are and put your hands over your head!" Kent Jacobsen barked.

Sigh. I put my hands over my head. Grandma's eyes were real big. Her hands had shot up real fast at the sight of all that firepower and the sheer officialness of the orders.

"Okay, stand up slowly and turn around. Keep your hands over your head."

I stood up and turned around. They all backed off a few inches and there were smirks from most.

"What are you guys doing here?" I asked.

"Security cameras caught Lawanda going down. Nobody recognized you. We thought the place was being robbed," Kent Jacobsen said.

"Who would rob the cop shop? That would be pretty dumb," I said. "Can I put my hands down now?"

"What happened to Lawanda?" Ben Tomlin asked.

"I invited her to the movies," I said.

Kent nodded at me and I lowered my hands. Grandma cued off of me and lowered her hands, too.

"I'm glad I found out she reacts to movie invitations this way," said Mike Townsend. "I'd been thinking of asking her out."

"Huh?" said Lawanda.

"I think it's safe to ask her out," I told him.

"Brock Larone..." Lawanda mumbled.

"Anybody got any smelling salts? That ought to bring her around," Ben said.

An ambulance pulled up outside and two paramedics got out with that calm assurance that always amazed me. They opened a back door, grabbed their box and looked in the front door. They'd heard the report but not much was matching up. They did however locate their patient. By this time Lawanda was brushing herself off and getting to her feet. She was embarrassed and I didn't blame her. "Turn my back on the store for a minute and business is booming," she said. "Come on, guys, I'm fine. Can't a woman faint in private? I appreciate the concern but you all can go back to your jobs."

"You aren't going to faint at the premier, are you?" Grandma asked.

"Of course not! I never faint. I wouldn't embarrass myself like that in front of all those important people. I'll be cool, calm."

"Premier? What premier?" Kent Jacobsen asked.

"It's the movie premier of Payback!" Grandma said excitedly. "Cassidy's in it!"

"Grandma, you don't even know that. We won't know until we see it."

"Yes, you are, at least once. Sherri said you were."

"Sherri doesn't know what the final cut looks like."

"Well, you *are* in it somewhere."

The guys all looked at each other.

"What do you say? After shift on Wednesday?" Mike Townsend said.

"I'll see what the wife says," said Kent.

There were nods all around. Oh great, I thought sarcastically.

"You better describe yourself so they'll recognize you when they see you!" said Grandma.

"There were a lot of characters who looked like me."

"Tell 'em what you looked like and what you did so if it comes up they'll know."

"Okay, black leather jacket, tight pants, biker boots, short red and black hair, I don't know what gender or race I was supposed to be. I was pregnant so I'll look fat."

Kent Jacobsen rocked back on his heels and folded his arms over his chest. He cocked his head and said, "You're right. I'll never recognize you."

"I think the alley scene is the one most likely one to identify me. They stuck me in an alley and told me to climb up to the roof. You'll see there's a ladder but the first time they shot it I climbed the wall just like I did as a kid and didn't even see the ladder. They made me go back and do it using the ladder but I heard they liked the other one better. I guess it was kind of unexpected."

"Imagine that, Cassidy doing something unexpected."

"Are you guys through investigating the robbery?"

"Yeah, I guess so."

The paramedics insisted on checking Lawanda over but she passed their inspection so they went on their way, too.

As soon as the guys all cleared out Lawanda pounced on me.

"You really have a ticket to the Payback premier?"

"Yeah, you want to go?"

"Hell yeah! I wouldn't miss it for anything! The chance to see all them stars dressed up. Uh oh, dressed up. What'll I wear? What are you wearing?"

Grandma and I looked at each other. There was no way Lawanda was going to go shopping for a Rodeo Drive dress.

"Just wear something that makes you feel good and is dressy," I said. "We don't care what you wear."

"But the fans do! Oh, they looook and they take notes. What if they see me in my old dress and think it's all the rage and then they all go out looking for it and find it in a thrift store. I'd just die. What are you wearing?"

"We…bought dresses to wear," I said vaguely.

"What's Rusty wearing?"

"Guess."

"Really? I never would have taken him for a Guess man. I bet the fans all think he's a movie star."

"Lawanda, I meant guess what he's wearing. The same thing he always wears; an old, scruffy, brown suit."

"*Humph*, the fans will still think he's a movie star."

Chapter 24

Lawanda arrived at my house in the early afternoon carrying a dress that she'd just bought at the mall.

"Can I change here? If I run home and back it'll take an hour."

"Sure, the guest room is Grandma's right now. Use Rusty's office."

She went in and closed the door but she shouted out through the closed door, "I took the whole day off. I had to find something to wear! I spent hours trying on dress after dress. I couldn't find anything! I was looking for one that fit just so…"

"I have better luck letting dresses pick me. Grandma and I had real good luck. These dresses just begged to be bought."

"Yeah, they had to, too! Golly, I can't believe we did that. It was fun but I'll never do that again. It was the funnest torture. That's always the kind husbands get mad at."

"Did Grandpap get mad at you?"

"He don't know yet. Hopefully he won't notice."

Lawanda opened the office door and stepped out.

"Ta-da! What do you think? Do I look like a movie star?"

Hmm, well, she looked about as much like a movie star as I thought she could. "Wow! You look stunning!" I said. "You'll be the hit of the night."

"Wait'll I get my make-up on!" she said enthusiastically.

Her dress was an emerald green, sequin-studded evening gown and she went to the bathroom and started putting on make-up. I was afraid to look.

Katie crawled down the hall calling out, "Ga-mama!"

"In here sweetie," said Grandma.

"Ga-mama cookie!"

"Are you hungry baby? Let's go find you a cookie," she said.

"She's not hungry and she doesn't need a cookie," I called out. "I gave all the cookies to the guys at the station."

The activity in the bathroom was starting to draw our attention. How could someone put that much effort into a little make-up?

"Go ahead, put your dress on, too. I want to see Rusty's reaction when he sees you. He probably hasn't seen you in a dress since Christmas."

"Okay, but if Katie spits up on it I'll be back to the Skipper dress."

I started with hair and make-up. My hair was always barely shoulder length in the back. I'd tried to grow it out in my teen years up but as soon as it got longer than my shoulders it went limp. So I kept it short which made me look even more like Skipper, especially when I curled it and fluffed it out a little. I was hoping my figure would mature a little through the years and I guess Katie had helped a little in that department. My hips were a little wider. Maybe I was just a tad curvier.

One thing working with Sherri had taught me was how to apply make-up. Every time I showed up and they wanted to shoot I had to get all made up, head to toe. And each time I learned a little more about the process, which was different than I had learned being Jesse's victim as kids. She always insisted boys were not going to look at me until I put some effort into attracting them. The fact was I wasn't going to attract boys because I was too much like them. Make-up or not, I was more boy than girl. Until Rusty came into the picture. Since then the feminine side of me had grown. Now I could actually wear a dress without wanting to hide. My aim when I was young was to be invisible but since I'd met Rusty there had been times when I didn't want to be invisible. I wanted *that look*. It was amazing the different ways I could get it. Sometimes it only took a suggestion. I often saw it after a bout of trouble. After the sad, concerned look came the "I need you" look. Sometimes I saw it when we'd had a fun day and he just wanted it to last. It was odd that *the look* was different. Sometimes his eyes laughed and he leaned against the doorjamb. Sometimes it was mischievous and naughty. Sometimes it held so much longing it hurt.

I worked on my make-up carefully, not wanting to go too far. Too far was worse than none at all. I curled my hair into romantic fullness, careful around my face to not let it look too young. When I finished I felt as foreign as I had as a bad guy in black leather and fire engine red hair. I was hoping it was a good way to feel.

Lawanda came out of the bathroom with a flourish. And she looked. Well, she looked like a jazz singer. She looked like she was fixing to step up to an oversized microphone and sing her heart out. Her eyes were brighter than her dress and her dress was plenty flashy on its own.

"Whoa, Cassidy!" she said. "I never seen you like this before! Why don't you do this more often? You go girl! Put your dress on! I want to see it."

I went to the bedroom and closed the door. I put on the slip and pantyhose. I slipped the dress over my head and it settled into place like it knew what it was doing. It had a totally different look on me than Grandma's did on her. It was quiet suggestiveness. It was flirty and innocent at the same time. It was tempting and elusive. I searched out shoes and slipped them on. About that time I heard activity in the living room and "Dadada..." going down the hall. Rusty was home. There was scurrying down the hall.

"Wait! Rusty, you can't go in there yet!" Lawanda said.

"Why? It's my house and my wife."

"Trust me, you want to wait."

"And what am I waiting for?"

I opened the door to tell them they could let him go and there was a collective intake of breath. I turned around to see what was behind me. All eyes turned to Rusty and he handed Katie over to Bertie. He walked up to me and hugged me on his way into the bedroom. He closed the door quietly behind us.

"Isabel, you want to spend the night at my place?" Lawanda said.

"Looks like I better."

"Cassidy…I don't know what to say. My girl," his hands brushed up and down my arms gripping gently, urgently. "I see that girl in you and pray you'll see her too. Then you do something like this and I just want to celebrate. I want to hold you close and never let go. I want to be part of you and feel that loveliness wrapped around me. And you expect me to sit through a movie with you sitting next to me like this?"

"Rusty, it's just a dress."

"It's not the dress, babe, it's you. It's you."

He turned me around, watching me move.

"What made you choose this?"

"Rule six forty-two."

"No, really."

"It felt right."

"It did?"

"Yeah, it did."

He wrapped his arms around me and put his chin on top of my head.

"I'm so glad it did," he said. "A movie. Okay, we'll do the premier first."

"First?"

"It's going to be a long night," he said as he stripped off his suit coat and shirt, but he winked as he said it. He pulled the tie out of his pocket and hung it up. He went to the closet and got out his sexier black suit. Oh man, it *was* going to be a long, long night. My hands were itching for him already.

I had company. I had a baby out there. I had six pairs of ears to the door. Okay back to business.

Chapter 25

"Bertie! Thanks so much for baby-sitting. Katie's been pretty good today."

"I feel grungy next to you gals. Look at you!"

"It's okay, we're just going to a dressy event. If we weren't given tickets we'd go to the local theater in jeans and t-shirts. Remember, make yourself at home. Keep Katie out of the kitchen drawers. Don't keep things in your pockets. If you want to sleep after Katie falls asleep put her in her crib. She can climb out of anything else. We'll be back late tonight."

"Well, are we ready?" I asked when we were all standing around looking for something to talk about.

"Not quite," Grandma said.

"What do you need to do?"

"Our ride isn't here yet."

"Your ride?"

"*Our* ride. Lawanda and I want to arrive at the premier in a limousine!"

"How will we get home? All the limos will be booked when this thing gets out."

"No they won't, we split the cost to have it for the whole evening. It was the least we could do since you offered to take us along. We'd never ever get to attend something like this without you."

"He should be here any time now," Lawanda said.

Grandma looked elegant standing there so poised. The raspberry dress gave color to her cheeks. She wore strings of pearls and put her hair up loosely with little wisps around her face. She felt elegant, too. She stood tall and proud in her silver high heeled shoes.

"Are you sure it's okay to wear the same dress to a red carpet event?" Lawanda asked.

"It doesn't matter. You can hardly tell it's the same dress. And, besides, we don't care if it's okay or not," I said.

"Some people would be horrified to have someone else wear the same dress as them."

"We're not some people."

"At these events don't they have fashion police lined up and ready?"

"Fashion commentators, maybe, but not fashion police."

"So, what if they commentate about your dresses and the rest of society, who does have some fashion sense, knows you made this huge fashion faux pas."

"After stumbling into this movie in the first place I doubt I can make any bigger mistakes," I said.

The doorbell rang and Lawanda and Grandma rushed to answer it. Rusty and I gave Katie bye-bye hugs; made sure Bertie was settled, and followed Grandma and Lawanda out the door.

"Good evening, ladies and gentleman, I'm Curtis. I'll be your driver for the evening."

Grandma just blushed. She didn't know what you were supposed to say to a limo driver.

"Thank you Curtis," said Rusty, taking matters into his own hands. He handed Curtis the tickets and the driver gave a nod. He opened the door and Grandma got in first. She bounced on the seat and felt the fabric. Lawanda got in next to her.

"I'll slide through," Rusty said saving me from trying to do it in a dress.

I sat down next to him. Curtis bowed, closed the door and hurried around to the driver's door. The long, black car backed into the road and drove smoothly down the rough, rural street to the road that snaked through the foothills, then finally to the freeway.

"Welcome to Desert Star Limousines. If you have any questions or requests you may open the window and speak with me directly or push the button overhead. Barring any unforeseen traffic problems we should reach your destination in a little over one hour."

"Thanks, Curtis," said Rusty.

Grandma and Lawanda were having a great time. They pushed buttons and sometimes quickly unpushed buttons. They discovered a cigarette lighter, music system, and television.

"Isn't this cool!" Lawanda said flipping through the channels. "I bet you can even stream to it." They were like little kids in a toy store.

"What's this? Harmony in Hollywood. Maybe it's a musical. Maybe it'll get us in the mood for a movie premier," said Grandma.

They turned on the show and a stereotypical blonde, California valley girl came on wearing a white string bikini. She'd had a boob job. I guess Grandma had never seen a woman quite like Harmony.

"Hi! I'm Harmony! I don't know how *you* do Hollywood, but it's like the most awesome place on the west coast. I'm here to show you a good time in the city of the stars! Sit back, relax, grab your partner and get ready for the ride of your life."

The picture changed to Harmony striding down Sunset Strip wearing a very short miniskirt. The skirt flipped up with each step revealing everything and nothing underneath. Grandma's eyes got bigger. She turned off the TV.

"Now I really believe it. You Californians really do have everything. Hoowee! Sometimes that might not be a good thing."

"Aw, it didn't even get to the fun stuff," said Lawanda.

"Have you seen it before?" Grandma said, shocked.

"No, but I know what's coming. They're all the same."

Rusty just sat observing and trying not to laugh at Grandma. He put an arm around me. He traced little suggestive circles on my arm.

"Anybody care if I talk to Curtis?" Lawanda asked.

Rusty and I shrugged. We were just along for the ride. It was Lawanda's and Grandma's nickel. She pushed the button.

"Yes, ma'am?" Curtis said.

"Can you talk and drive at the same time?" Lawanda asked.

"Certainly," he answered.

"Hmm, do you mind me asking you something?"

"Shoot," he said.

"Do you ever drive famous people around?"

"A common question. In Joshua Hills? Rarely. But I have had a few famous people in my car. Joshua Hills is a popular area for filming movies. In fact the movie you are attending tonight was partially filmed in this area. I had the opportunity to drive the director of that movie to dinner in town."

"Nickolai Danti," I said.

"Yes," Curtis said. "A most interesting man. In that same time frame I drove Alonso Marcos down below and back."

From Joshua Hills anything in the LA area was "down below." We were in the high desert so anything in the LA basin was considered down from where we were. Down in elevation, down south. It was all "down below."

"So, tell me about this director. I've never met a director. What's he like?" said Lawanda.

"I'm afraid I'm not allowed to speak freely about the guests in my car. It would be an infringement of their privacy."

"I worked with Nickolai a little bit," I admitted. "He's a nice guy. He's the one that put me in as a stunt man."

"Ooo, tell me about it!" Lawanda said.

"You'll see him at the movie," I said. "And you'll see him briefly in the movie. He plays a hotdog vendor. He had a few people try this bit part and when he showed them how he wanted it done they filmed that too and he ended up liking his part the best. He's very patient when it comes to directing. He had to be to work with me. I'd never acted in my life. I still don't think I have. I was just doing typical tracking, police type things. Things I had to do to get through academy. It was simple. Climb a chain link fence. Run through the woods with a rifle in hand. Climb out of an alley. No problem. The tough part was the fight scenes. I kept remembering real fights I'd been in. I bloodied one guy's nose because I slipped into fight mode. Nickolai wasn't there for that, though. That was in practice."

"You? I can't imagine you actually hitting someone," Lawanda said.

"Thanks," I said. "I wish I hadn't...I hope Spike is there. He should be if Brock is there. Spike is Brock's bodyguard. He's three hundred pounds of mean muscle who is scared of spiders and snakes, but don't mention that to him. I'm sure he won't admit it."

"Brock Larone is going to be there and you're more interested in his body guard?"

"Brock is a nice guy, too. He's just...an actor. I talked to Spike more because Brock thought I needed babysitting. He told Spike to keep an eye on me."

"And I'm glad he did, too," said Rusty. "If it weren't for Spike you and Katie might not be here today."

The stories went round and round. Curtis drove and I'm sure he was taking notes. He seemed to take it all in stride and I wondered what other stories he heard just because people were talking in his car and forgot he could hear them. I didn't care if he listened in.

Since we were all talking freely Curtis cut in, "Okay, now I'm curious. How do you all fit into the picture?"

"The picture?" I asked.

"Yeah, you have obviously been working with Nickolai and Larone. I'm trying to piece this all together."

"It's kind of complicated," I said. "I was originally employed as Sherri Champlain's bodyguard. But then Sherri wanted me working behind the scenes so she tried to get Nickolai use me as an extra and I ended up being recruited as a stuntman."

"You. A stuntman?"

"Yeah, to add more humor to the story I was four or five months pregnant at the time."

"Okay... so you were a stuntman. Not a stand in? Not a stunt*woman*?"

"We'll find out when we see the movie. I couldn't really tell at the time. I was dressed more like a guy, but since I was pregnant I thought there was no way they could make me into a man. But we'll see. It wouldn't surprise me at all if I look like a man."

"I'd like to see the house Larone lives in!" Lawanda said. "I've heard it's like a mansion and he has a pool and a sauna and maids and butlers."

"Do you think his house is on that tour of the star's homes?" Grandma asked.

"These days the stars don't even live in LA." Lawanda said.

"Maybe the old stars did, though. I wonder which stars are on the tour."

"Oh, lots of them. Back in the days when it wasn't common to fly, they all lived down there."

I could see the wheels turning in Grandma's mind. She was scheming. I wondered if I looked like that when I schemed.

"Oh no," Rusty said. "She's got that look."

Guess that answered my question.

"I wonder what Brock Larone eats for breakfast," Lawanda said.

I was beginning to worry about Lawanda meeting up with Brock at the premier. Would she faint? Would she ask endless embarrassing questions?

"He eats the same thing everybody else eats for breakfast," Grandma said. "And I bet he puts his pants on one leg at a time."

"I don't know, I bet he likes exotic things. Escargot and calamari and sushi and caviar."

"For breakfast?" Grandma asked. "Who eats fancy stuff for breakfast? I say he eats bacon and eggs or pancakes or cereal just like ninety-nine percent of the population."

"You're no fun," Lawanda said. "I bet he eats fresh fruit by the poolside."

"I think you're over glamorizing the whole job," I said. "What I saw was actors living in trailers on location, stuck there unless they wanted to draw a bunch of photographers along with them wherever they went. It seemed like it was more work than glamour. I think the glamorous part of the job is what we will see tonight. But I don't think their life is one big party. It's a lot of hard work."

"Oh yeah?" Lawanda said with mock antagonism, "Well, I don't like you unglamorizing my glamorizations! What's a girl to daydream about if not on the rich and glamorous?"

"Well, if you ask Brock what he had for breakfast don't be surprised if he says Wheaties."

"I'm not talking to Brock. I promised you I wouldn't faint tonight."

"You wouldn't faint just from talking to Brock. Would you?"

"I'm not taking any chances."

"Talking to Brock is just like talking to any other person, except that you have to wear sunglasses. The sun glaring off his teeth is a little bright."

"You've talked to Brock Larone?" Lawanda asked fanning herself.

"Of course. It's hard to avoid it when you're on the set with him."

Lawanda fanned harder. Lawanda was a lost cause. Grandma and Lawanda speculated about Brock Larone all the way to Hollywood, then when Curtis turned off the freeway they plastered their faces to the windows. I wondered if Curtis would spend the movie time wiping nose and fingerprints off the windows of his limo.

Rusty and I speculated silently about…later. A gentle touch filled with suggestion. A quiet shiver of anticipation. An inching closer. A glimpse of leg. A shifting just a little bit closer.

Curtis got in line in front of the theater. I wanted to get out a block away and walk in but I knew that just wasn't done. Each time there was a stop there was a flurry of flashbulbs ahead. As we got close Lawanda started getting nervous.

"Oh gosh!" she said. "Are they going to take pictures of *everybody*?"

She got out a compact to make sure she was still as colorful as possible. She decided she needed more lipstick. Rusty just shook his head. He'd known Lawanda for years from the cop shop but he'd never seen *this* side of Lawanda.

"They just assume anybody who gets out of a limo is famous. Guess we'll teach them a lesson," Grandma said. "They'll get those pictures back and say 'who's that?' Sorry folks, just an old ranch grandma, a store clerk, a tracker, and a detective going to the movies."

"Remember to smile!" Lawanda said. "If we're going to be in pictures we better look like we belong there."

Curtis pulled up, put the car in park and strutted around to open the doors. Lawanda stuck one high heeled, emerald green shoe out and allowed a considerable amount of leg to show, then followed it gracefully out. I think she'd been practicing. Camera flashes filled the night. Grandma got out next feeling glamorous in her dancing dress amid all the glitz of the red carpet and all the fans. There were considerably fewer flashes. I followed Grandma out, relieved the cameras had settled down to the few people who truly didn't know any better. When Rusty leaned out of the limo the cameras started up again with great enthusiasm. If the moment didn't get me to smiling that did. Rusty really did look like a movie star.

"Have a wonderful evening," said Curtis. Rusty slipped him a tip and Curtis gave the tickets to a man at a podium next to the carpet.

"Stick to Cassidy," Grandma said to Lawanda. "If anything exciting is going to happen it will happen to her."

"Right."

The cameras were disorienting to me so I looked into the crowd. Smiling and waving next to a fiery redhead was Landon Wilson. He put his hand on her shoulder and pointed. She turned and said something to him then she turned to the next limo and excitedly pointed behind us. Hoping Rusty didn't notice, I took his arm and we walked the red carpet into a bustling foyer.

"Cassidy! You're blonde again!" said a bouffant blonde woman.

Lawanda fanned a little faster even though she didn't know who this was. It was movie people, that was enough for her.

"Um, Gloria, right?" I said, embarrassed. I was just guessing she was the woman who had done my hair and I only guessed that because…well, *the hair*.

"Right! It's so good to see you back to yourself again! And skinnier, too! So what was it? A boy or a girl?"

"A girl. Her name is Kaitlyn. This is my husband, Rusty, my grandmother, Isabel and Lawanda, my friend from work."

Lawanda fanned harder.

"Gloria works in Hair," I explained.

"Yep, I'm the one who turned Cassidy from a cute blonde into a black and red haired bad guy. Theo! Theo! Over here! I told you it was a girl and here's Cassidy to prove it."

"Theo works in make-up," I warned them.

The more people talked the more Lawanda fanned. I thought she'd fanned fast enough to take off like a helicopter, but at least she wasn't fainting. Gloria and Theo had started the mingling and so we made our way from group to group. I introduced them to Andrew and Donnal, the men I had done fight scenes with, and Ramon the choreographer. Rusty put an arm around my shoulder and pointed. It was Spike. I nodded and we mingled that direction. When we finally reached Spike, Rusty extended his hand. I was touched at the look in his eyes. He still felt thankful to Spike. Spike had knocked me out of the way when a car was bearing down on me in a bout of trouble on the set.

"Spike! It's so good to see you!" I said.

"Cassidy? I never expected you to be here," he said. "Brock, our little tracker's back."

Brock Larone strolled over. "Well, well, you survived despite your propensity for trouble." He looked me up and down. "And I'd say you survived pretty good. You've changed a lot. What have you been up to lately? Don't tell me, tracking down wayward movie stars?"

"Tracking down a wayward border patrol agent in Mexico and a wayward teenager in a dust storm."

"Did you find your man?" Brock asked.

"Of course."

He smiled and Lawanda fanned like mad and tugged on my dress.

"I have a few people who would like to meet you two. This is Isabel Gordon, my grandmother and the originator of the trouble gene. And this is Lawanda, she supplies the officers in our town with uniforms and gun belts and such."

"So if we need props we know where to come, right?" Brock said.

"Oh, yeah, right!" Lawanda said flustered almost to speechlessness. "What did you have for breakfast?"

Brock looked at me and I shook my head with feigned embarrassment.

"Cold pizza," he answered.

Lawanda fanned a little slower. Okay, maybe this guy was a real person after all.

"I'm not the originator of the trouble gene, though," Grandma said. "My great grandfather stowed away on a pirate ship and got tossed overboard in the South Pacific. He washed ashore on some half deserted island and survived until a boat wandered by. It was bound for Florida. Of course it wasn't Florida then. He didn't speak a word of English. He found jobs where he could. Robbed a few plantation owners to feed himself. Eventually, he made his way west. He had adventures that would give me nightmares. He founded the ranch I live on, probably from rustled cattle. Can I have your autograph?"

"Oo, oo, me too!" Lawanda put in hastily.

"So you come by that trouble gene honestly," Brock observed as he signed two pictures and handed them over.

"Thanks for taking a break from shooting in Italy. It's good to see you again."

"Likewise," he said. Then he went on mingling another direction. He and Spike exchanged glances and we went on our way but I noticed Spike wasn't mingling with Brock. He was fading into the crowd, slipping into stealth mode. How Spike managed to disappear was a mystery. As big as he was I thought he'd stand out anywhere, but, like me, he had a talent for fading into the background.

Grandma stood on her tiptoes trying to see over the crowd. It was getting close to time for the movie to start and I thought she was searching for Sherri. We needed a lookout.

"Rusty, do you see Sherri anywhere?"

He pointed into the theater. "But there's no getting close to her. She's surrounded."

"Ladies and gentlemen, the show will be starting momentarily. If you could please find your seats."

The crowd began shuffling toward two sets of double doors. We stayed together and followed the press of people in. Rusty pulled me into a row of seats. People filed in from the other side and we met in the middle and sat down.

"We need to set up a signal," Lawanda whispered loudly. "How will we know when it's you on the screen if you're all made up?"

"Can't you just watch the movie for what it is?" I asked.

"Sure…but we should still set up a signal."

"If I notice myself I'll point to the screen but it's up to you to figure out which one is me."

"Fair enough."

The row in front of us settled in. Oh great. I was right behind Spike. How was I going to see? I scrunched to one side looking around him.

"Do you want to trade places?" Rusty offered.

"No, Lawanda wants me to tell her when I'm on the screen. I can't do that if I'm on the other side of you."

Not having seen a script or a review or a preview I had no way of knowing what the movie was about or how it would affect Rusty. It didn't take long to identify me or figure that out. The movie began with a dark figure running through the woods. It was me. The only way I knew it was me was because I remembered running the scene so many times. I signaled Lawanda. I didn't need to signal to Rusty. He knew. His hand on my shoulder tensed. The scene changed to show who was after me and his grip tightened. It was really quite clever how they had clipped apart my failed attempts and melded them with the successful run. While my mind was dissecting the movie all Rusty saw was somebody pursuing me. I stumbled, got up and ran some more. The camera caught my eyes and Rusty looked away. I ran off into the woods and the scene switched to a messenger, seen from the back, relaying a message to the big bad guy. No wonder they had dyed my hair black and red. It matched my double. Or maybe I was *his* double.

Lawanda looooked at me. "That was *you?*" her expression said.

The good guys were introduced and the plot began. While it was playing Rusty sat back and watched. It was a typical action flick. But when the action got going little pieces of action that I had done got tossed in and each time all he could see was me, in danger. I had never seen the things that were after me. When I ran down a dirt road and scrambled over a six-foot chain link fence I didn't know four armed men would follow. I didn't know they fired shots at me or that the bullets striking would be added later by computer animation.

Each time I came on the screen Rusty tensed up and pulled me close. The movements of his hand on my shoulder were a line directly to his heart and when he saw me in the line of fire his protective nature wanted to step in, to stop it, but he couldn't. All he could do was watch. It only took him a split second to recognize my movements whether my face was seen or not and then he braced for the emotional roller coaster the scene forced him into.

After a while I didn't need to signal Lawanda anymore but I longed to drag Rusty out of there. If I'd known the movie would affect him this way I wouldn't have asked him to come.

Brock and Sherri played the perfect action couple. There was tense action, romance, and humor, with an evil figure in the background making a mess of things for them.

My character worked for the bad guy. The good guys were going to win. The good guys always win. So that meant, sooner or later, I was going to lose.

The alley scene came up. They had pieced together other running scenes and it showed me sprinting down a street. Men were running behind me. Shots were fired ricocheting off the walls around me. I turned and dashed down the alley.

It had been the fourth time through the shot. I was pregnant, tired, and it was showing in my face. I ran to the end of the alley and turned around. I was trapped! I was trapped and a gang of pursuers was going to turn the corner and I'd be dead. I searched the walls, scrambled up the meters and fell. Whoa! I thought, I did not fall! I scrambled to the top, no problem. Nickolai had been amazed that I could do it at all. I reasoned out that they had taken footage of when I climbed one of the fences and dropped over the side. Then they had taken me out of one scene and put me into the alley. What would they think of next? When I fell off the meters Rusty's grip tightened again. My character looked again at the wall; my foes rounded the corner. Shots were fired, some hitting within inches of my head.

I knew exactly where Rusty's thoughts were. They were far away in San Diego where I really had stood in an alley with four gang members ready to gun me down. Rusty had rounded the corner just in time to see the shots fired. He didn't know I was wearing a bulletproof vest at the time. He only saw me go down and the gang members flee. He ran down the alley, took me in his arms and I wasn't breathing. When he picked me up he'd felt the vest but he was scared…and now he thought he was going to have to watch it all over again, only this time I wouldn't get up. I wouldn't be okay. Even if it was just fiction it cut him. Oh, but it hurt him to watch as the good guys closed in and this one bad guy, his little wife, stood in an alley. I vaulted up onto the wall and climbed to the top, shots echoing off the wall around me.

I patted his hand so he'd ease up. His other hand came up. If he could touch me he'd know. I was right here.

If we were watching this at home, I'd have turned it off long ago. I would have made love to him to show him that all was well. I was alive and whole and enjoying every minute of my life with him. But we weren't home. We were trapped in a big theater with a couple hundred other cast members who didn't understand at all that this could affect us the way it did. Not even Lawanda and Grandma could understand the depth of the hurt Rusty was feeling.

When I was not worrying about Rusty, I was dissecting the movie, wondering how they took my ten hours of real work and condensed it into the scenes before me. I was amazed at the talent behind it, certainly not mine. I admit, my movements were such that I came across as a very bad guy, but it took an eye for action to take it apart and put it back together into what I saw on the screen.

As the movie progressed Spike kept shifting in his seat. I turned this way and that, slightly irritated but wishing more and more that Rusty and I could just escape. Rusty noticed my discomfort but he saw the subtle exchange of actions around us in a different light. His gaze shifted from the movie to Spike's actions. His eyes flicked to the area of the stage, the curtains surrounding the screen, then back to the movie again. Something felt different. Something was off. I looked behind me. Big tough guy there, too. Lawanda was flirting with a Rambo type guy in a suit, sitting next to Grandma. Grandma's eyes were glued to the screen. My trouble radar tingled. Rusty noticed the change in me. He gave me a reassuring squeeze.

I was relieved when the action in the movie turned to car chase scenes that didn't involve me. This was something that Rusty could get into. But he didn't. His senses were tuned to something else. So were Spike's. Security expected something. The tension in the air was palpable. Rusty felt it, too, but as a detective he knew to watch for little nuances in the officers. More and more I was barely aware of the movie. I was tuned instead to the men in the room.

"What is it?" Rusty whispered.

"My trouble radar is itching," I whispered back.

Spikes ears swiveled behind him.

"Nobody is going to do anything in a crowded theater."

"I wonder if Abraham Lincoln's wife said the same thing."

"Babe…"

"You feel it too. I can tell."

"Just try and enjoy the movie. You're paranoid. Besides, they'd have to get through me and Spike."

"I'm more afraid of that than anything happening to me."

I scooted closer and felt his arm against me. I was paranoid. That had to be it. Just like all the other times my paranoia paid off, but I tried to get back into the movie and Rusty did, too, just to prove I didn't have any worries.

"Watch the car go over the big rig," I whispered. "That was a great scene to shoot. Everybody got so into it."

Grandma was really into the movie. I was glad she didn't have the distractions I did. She'd be able to tell me about it when the movie was over. Lawanda I wasn't so sure about. She seemed more interested in the social aspects of being at a movie premier. She kept looking around for famous faces, then that security guard assigned to us would catch her attention again. For me the movie was a lost cause. Between dissecting the action, keeping track of security, Lawanda, Grandma and Rusty, I decided I'd be better off going to the movie in Joshua Hills with the other officers. I folded up the arm between my seat and Rusty's and settled in waiting for the big fight scene at the end. I was curious how that turned out. It was my first try at doing a fight scene. Plus we had some unexpected surprises I had to deal with and I was wondering how they fit into the main scheme of things.

I didn't show up again in the movie until the last fight scene. I was glad. I could sit back and let the movie unfold. Rusty seemed to relax, though he was still tuned to the security guards. When the love scene between Brock and Sherri came up he went back to tracing little suggestive lines on my arm again. It stirred up thoughts of what was coming later.

I wasn't sure what to expect from the fight scene. There were ten different fighting groups in the big scene. At the time I was having real trouble holding my punches. I kept slipping into fight mode, I mean *real* fight mode. The faces of the men I was working with turned into people who had hurt me and I reacted to the flashbacks. Internal struggles and external struggles blended to make the fight on the screen much more real looking than I thought possible. Rusty had seen this scene being filmed but it still hit him hard. He saw the fight in my eyes, knew the struggle I was faced with in my heart and he just couldn't look. I analyzed my moves. They were still stuck in my mind, the key words Ramon had used echoing as I saw them come to life before me. First Andrew came at me and Rusty's grip tightened again. When the camera caught my eyes he looked away and swallowed hard. He ran his fingers through my hair. Next was Donnal. As the fight unfolded I ended up in a choke hold before the camera switched to another group. Towards the end of the scene, after the fires started, a figure dropped down from the balcony. This was what I was waiting for. This was unplanned. This woman wanted to get to Sherri and I couldn't let her. In this fight scene I wasn't holding my punches. I was fighting for Sherri. This time it was me who tensed up. At the time I didn't have time think about what was happening to me. Man, this woman was a wildcat! She was trying to steal Sherri's show. She was determined to have her spot in the limelight. She certainly managed to do that. I fought until I'd forced the woman to the back of the set, away from Sherri. Then the woman had gotten too close to the fire. She'd run screaming away in flames and I had chased her down, and thrown my leather jacket over her to put the fire out. As soon as I ran after her the action switched to action in another part of the set. My part was over. I'd found out what I came to find out. I patted Rusty's hand so he'd ease up again. Spike sent a thumbs-up over the back of his seat.

Everybody cheered and clapped at the end of the movie. Rusty and I didn't feel very cheerful. We felt like hightailing it out of there but we still had Grandma and Lawanda along. When the lights came on, we waited for the people around us to clear out, then we followed them out into the foyer again.

"Look, Isabel! It's Whitney Washington!" Lawanda said. She tugged Grandma off to go talk to Whitney.

Rusty and I shrugged at each other and let them go. We had no great desire to mingle with the stars. I was kind of hoping Nickolai had some comments to make, but I knew he was also dealing with people who knew him better and were more important to the large picture than I was. I would have liked Sherri to know I came, too, but wasn't concerned enough to fight the press just to make contact. I'd rather find a quiet place to sit and calm our frazzled nerves. We wandered away from the crowd. Two men in black suits wandered away from the crowd, too. I glanced back at them.

"What is it with Security in this place?" I asked Rusty.

"Just ignore them."

"I can't. It's like they think I'm going to turn on them or something. Why us? There are three hundred people out there they can guard."

"Maybe they know the other three hundred aren't targets. Did you notice there was a group of guards around Sherri, too?"

"I noticed there were security guards posted around the walls and in the crowd."

"Not just in the crowd. Strategically placed around you and Sherri. Just let them do their job. You have to remember you and Sherri were targeted more than once during shooting."

"But that is over and the woman who did it was arrested."

"You never know how these things are going to turn out or what odd things her attorney told the judge. I could find out but it's a little late for that. Just forget the guards."

We stopped in a quiet corridor.

"I'm sorry I made you come. I didn't think about the scenes affecting you like they did. I thought you would just see it as a typical action movie."

"You needed an escort. And I am happy to be yours. I didn't know it would affect me either. Even though the movie was all fictional and all those things were happening to some big, bad version of you. The you I know... babe... I'm sorry."

"It's okay. Hey, I wouldn't love you like I do if you didn't have a heart."

"This is the you I want to see," he said holding me out at arm's length.

"Maybe I can get a job as a Bond girl," I said jokingly.

He wrapped his arms around me and the guards all pretended to be doing something else for a moment.

"How long until Grandma goes home?"

"I don't know, but the longer we stall the bigger dose of California glitz she'll get. Let her embarrass herself asking for autographs a while longer. Maybe we can find a handy cleaning closet and get lost for a while."

"I don't think that's necessary."

"Tourist season is coming up. Are you ready for it?" I asked him.

"No, I'm never ready for it but I know Strict is careful about when he calls you out. He only calls you when he really needs you. Katie and I both miss you when you're gone. It's just not the same. It feels empty at home. Katie looks for you."

"She's going to be walking pretty soon."

"I know. I'm dreading it and can't wait at the same time. How did she learn to climb before she learned to walk?"

I laughed, and we talked and talked until we noticed the commotion out in the foyer was a lot quieter. Rusty looked at his watch and his eyebrows shot up.

"We better get going. I bet your grandma has been looking all over for us."

We walked reluctantly back to the lobby and found Grandma and Lawanda, heads together, scheming.

"So it's settled?" Lawanda said.

"Sounds good to me. Did you call in sick?" Grandma asked.

"No, I called in inconvenienced."

"Can you do that?"

"Sure, I'm the boss. If the boss says she's stuck in LA, she's stuck in LA. At least I gave her more notice than I do if I *am* sick."

"Cassidy, is it okay if I stay down here tonight?" Grandma asked. I wanted to elbow Rusty as I felt his eyes light up at the thought of being home alone for one night.

"How are you going to get home?" I asked.

"We'll have Curtis drop us off at a hotel. We'll figure out a way home. If worse comes to worse we'll take a taxi to the airport and catch a shuttle bus back. We want to take that tour of the star's homes. We aren't all Hollywooded out yet."

"If you're sure...we won't drop you off until we know you can get a room."

"And maybe we'll go back to Rodeo Drive and get sticker shock and maybe a few autographs."

"Are we ready?" Rusty asked.

Grandma pulled a card out of her purse. Rusty took it from her and called the limo. We went outside and waited while Curtis once again got in the line of cars. Grandma was excited.

"I got lots of autographs while you two were gone. Look! I got Trey Houston and Simone Madison. And…let's see…I think that says Alonzo Marcos but it's hard to tell. He squiggles when he writes. I need to print the names at the bottom of the pages so I can remember. Oh and that Mister Danti is so nice. He asked where you were and how we liked the movie. He said you were fun to work with. He said he'd sure remember you if he needed a little sneaky blonde again."

"Oh great. Did you tell him my acting days were over?"

"No! I told him I hoped he'd call. I thought you did a great job."

"Grandma I don't want to be an actress. I'd rather be a trouble magnet. In fact the only reason I got this job is because I *am* a trouble magnet."

When Curtis pulled up and opened the door for us Grandma and Lawanda got into the seat that faced the back of the limo and Rusty and I got into the seat facing the front, just like we had on the way to the theater.

"Can you find a hotel with vacancies?" Grandma asked Curtis.

"No problem," he replied, "Where?"

"We want to tour Hollywood tomorrow, so somewhere not too far away."

"Yes ma'am."

The car pulled out and we rode along from one hotel to another until at last we came to one with a vacancy.

"Go look at the room and make sure it's okay," I told Grandma.

Grandma and Lawanda took the key, went up to the room and quickly came back down.

"It's fine," said Grandma.

"Yeah," said Lawanda, "it's real Hollywood. There's a portrait of John Wayne on the wall."

"And Marilyn Monroe too!" said Grandma.

Rusty smiled a little too smugly.

"If you're sure," I said, still unsure I should just leave my grandmother in Hollywood over night with no certain way home.

"Go on. Enjoy the rest of your evening. You don't need an old granny tagging along with you. We want to see the stars!"

"Okay." I left her with a hug and wondered how she was going to manage a tour in a dancing dress and high heels. Oh well, that was up to her.

Chapter 26

When we got back to the limo Rusty handed Curtis a tip saying, "I don't care what route you take home as long as you take at least a couple of hours to do it, and you turn your music up good and loud."

"Rusty!" I said. I could feel the tops of my ears burning.

Curtis smiled knowingly and said, "Yes sir."

Rusty got in and closed the little window between the front and back of the car.

"Now," he said. "I've got you all to myself. It's just us."

"Rusty...I can't! Look! There's people out there."

"They can't see us. Tinted windows."

"But Curtis will know!"

"Curtis wishes me all the luck in the world."

"But..."

He put a stop to my protests with the sexiest kiss I'd had in my life. It bounced off my toes and made its way back up stopping at some very inconvenient spots on the way. He pushed the button on the sunroof.

"Come here," he said pulling me up.

He stood with his head out the sunroof and pulled me up so I could see the city go by. The limo drove around smoothly and the city lights went slowly by.

"We get to see them, but they can't see us. I can do anything I want down here," he said cupping my breasts. "We could be completely nude down here and nobody would know it." Tantalizing touches. Just the setting, the fact that we could be doing this, watching people go about their business while we went about ours was terribly sexy. He slid the strap of my dress down over my shoulder. He ran his hands over my arm and shoulder coming temptingly close to more interesting places. Go on, I thought, touch it. Please touch it. I could feel stirrings. Pretty soon I wasn't going to care what Curtis thought. The other strap came down and I pulled my arm out letting the dress slip down around my waist. He kissed my neck as fingers encircled my nipples. I leaned into him with a little gasp of pleasure. Oh yeah...more...oh...oh man. He loosened his tie and took it off. He removed his suit coat and cast it aside. His belt and pants slid down around his ankles. I wriggled a little until my dress fell around my ankles, then I pressed myself to him feeling his hardness against my backside. Slow, Cass, you always rush these things. Take it slow. Savor it.

The breeze was pulled down through the sunroof creating interesting feelings as it touched my bare skin. Rusty's fingers touching, touching, driving me to a frenzy. I tried to slow it down but I couldn't without making them stop.

Okay, Cass, slow…slow. He sat down on the seat facing forward and I sat on his lap, him inside me as I undid the buttons on his shirt in between kisses. I tightened my muscles making him groan with anticipation. I pushed his shirt back over his shoulders and ran my hands over him. He felt so good to me. Always. He never failed to stir these feelings in me. Sometimes circumstances didn't cooperate but the stirring in my loins was there pushing me frustratingly. Tonight they were pushing me in wonderful abandon to a place I only dreamed of.

"What if those people could see in?" he asked. "What would they think?"

"We'd get arrested."

"We're not talking reality here. What would they say if they were just in our heads? Guys would watch the car go by and get all hard and flustered. Women would gawk and their nipples would stand out. What if we had Curtis park on a busy street and we saw how many people would gather around the car to watch. We'd be in here getting all excited and they'd be out there hyperventilating. We could start an orgy out there. This is California. Things like this happen all the time, right?"

"You're exaggerating."

"It doesn't matter, just think of all those people out there getting turned on by us. Now take all that hot desire and pull it in."

I didn't need any more desire than I was feeling right then. I was doing my best not to tackle him. Oh, man but it was the most complex pleasure I'd ever felt. And that was saying something. Being tempted by Rusty was a pleasure every day. Holding back was the hard part. I was itching for more. Afraid it would come too quickly. Afraid it wouldn't. Gentle touches…oh! Oh! Lips on my breasts. Hands…oh, those luscious hands straying, straying, teasing. Teasing until my back arched with the intensity of the feelings. I reached for him.

"Not yet, babe, take it slow."

"Rusty!"

He grinned that lopsided grin and backed off to kisses. Again he built up the feelings until I climaxed right there in front of him and his eyes drank it all in. I was his and I was alive here beneath his hands, I was alive and I felt every electric surge of it. I'd heard of hour-long orgasms but I didn't think they were real. It went on and on until I had to stop him. I lay back breathing hard reaching for him, needing just closeness for a bit.

"Oh, my girl," he said quietly into my hair as he held me close. "My precious girl. I need you so bad."

"You've got me. I'm all yours."

He started the touches again when I was rested.

"I want to be inside you," he said.

We tried a few different positions but inside a car wasn't the most convenient place for love making. He stretched out between the two seats and I rode him cowgirl style as he faced the back of the limo, running his hands up and down my body as I pumped up and down. Right about then I realized my head was poking up through the sunroof rhythmically. I burst out laughing and he gasped as the laugh radiated down to where he could feel it inside me. I couldn't stop laughing as I thought about other cars driving down the freeway as this woman's head appeared and disappeared rhythmically and with more and more intensity.

"What's so funny?" he said, sitting up slightly. His eyes got big and I wondered how he could climax in this funny situation, but he grabbed my head and twisted until he was on top of me on the floor of the car. Glass exploded around us.

"Oh god…Cassidy…are you all right?"

I was all right, but reality wasn't catching up with me very fast. Rusty kissed me fiercely.

"Babe, you've got to get dressed. Be careful of the glass."

He was pulling on his pants as he buzzed Curtis.

"You're going to pay for that," Curtis said. "You're lucky we're still on the road. You could have killed somebody."

"That wasn't us. It was the car behind us. We've got to take this off the freeway. I want you to get off the freeway but not on city streets. Away from the public, but findable. Got it? I'm calling the police." He stuck his badge through the broken window. "Stay calm and we'll get through this. And you can turn the music off now. You might want to be able to hear instructions."

He called 911. "This is detective Rusty Michaels patch me through to CHP. I've got a situation going on, on the 14. Stay down, babe, as low as you can." Then into the phone again, "I've got shots fired on the 14 freeway. Look for a black, Desert Star Limo being followed by a white, late model Honda, license plate… Curtis, hit your brake pedal just enough to bring on the lights. License plate XXX-555. We're watching for a way off the freeway. Will keep you posted on our progress."

"Canyon Country?" Curtis asked.

Rusty relayed the exit to CHP but told Curtis to keep going. "Don't get off into the city or the canyons. Watch Sierra Highway. If it is less crowded than the freeway, go for that."

He dug his sidearm out of his coat.

"Cass? You aren't armed, are you?"

"Where was I supposed to keep a gun in that dress?"

"It's okay, just checking. I didn't expect you to be. I just thought it would be handy if we could take out two tires at once."

He was now clad in pants, socks and shoes. It was odd how a cop prioritizes. Might need shoes for running. Pants were necessary for decency. After pants and shoes the gun was most important. I bet the woman in that car would dearly love to be chased down by Rusty clad only in pants and shoes.

We could see red lights way off in the distance.

"Agua Dulce," Curtis said. "We can get on Escondido Canyon Road there."

"Okay. If you hear shots hit the gas, if you don't, keep things slow and steady. Give the police a chance to find us. As long as there is traffic try and keep things as normal as possible."

Rusty took his position in the corner of the broken window. Curtis exited and Rusty relayed our actions to the responding officers. Curtis slowed and Rusty watched, sidearm at the ready, but a shot from the other car glanced off the car roof and Rusty leaned back taking cover. Curtis hit the gas. He turned down Agua Dulce Canyon Road and entered the deep canyon that emptied out at the town of Agua Dulce.

"Keep a good steady pace until you get out of the residential area. We don't want any stray shots hitting homes."

We turned down Escondido Canyon road and picked up speed again. As we left the houses behind Rusty saw CHP following.

"Curtis, slow down slightly, let her get a little closer."

As the woman got closer Rusty took his position again took a few seconds to aim and squeezed off a shot. The left front tire blew and the car swerved but kept going. He aimed again. The second shot hit wide but the third took out the other front tire. We left the car behind in a cloud of dust. Through the dust we could see the red lights of the CHP cars reflecting off the white of the Honda. Officers jumped out of their cars surrounding the woman.

"Find a place to pull over and then turn around," Rusty instructed.

"Are you sure?" Curtis asked.

"They've got her now," Rusty said.

He finished getting dressed as we found our way back to the scene behind us. A tight knot of squad cars surrounded the white car. As we approached the cars, the officers wrestling the woman into a CHP car took in Rusty's rumpled clothes, me in my dress. Rusty flashed his badge so they would know they could talk like fellow cops.

The woman struggled, "Fuck you, you bitch!" she screamed.

I almost laughed but it wasn't funny. If she only knew. Hmm, maybe she did.

"Cass, get back in the car," Rusty said.

I reluctantly went back to the limo knowing I'd just make things worse by staying. Rusty, Curtis and the two officers spent a long time sorting things out and getting the story straight.

"You can get a copy of the police report for insurance purposes tomorrow. If your boss gives you a hard time I'll stand up for you," Rusty was saying as they approached the car. "Let's go home."

Rusty gave Curtis a big tip and Curtis claimed he now had a good tale if a passenger asked for his most interesting chauffeuring job story.

Bertie was asleep on the couch in the den and Katie was asleep in her crib when we got home. I put a blanket over Bertie, noting that her clothes were folded in neat piles on the coffee table and she was down to one layer of clothes.

Rusty and I went to bed.

"Now where were we?" I asked but Rusty took me in his arms.

"We'll try it again some time when we don't have jealous actresses after you. But it was fun while it lasted. I keep thinking how a half second later and you would have been blown away. The shot would have gone right through the window and..."

"Hush, you can't dwell on it. It's past and here we are, ready to try it again."

We went to bed in stunned silence. He woke up from uneasy dreams in the night. He felt for me and I snuggled closer.

Katie woke me up early in the morning.

"It's okay, Bertie," I said. "I'm back. I'll take care of her."

"This couch is so soft. I could sleep here forever," she said.

It was old and lumpy and heading towards uncomfortable but it was still my favorite place in the house. I'd mourn the day when the old brown couch had to go.

"Hi baby! Mommy's home," I chatted as I went through the usual changing and feeding motions that began every morning as a mom. Bertie got up promptly at seven, as if it had been trained into her.

"How was your date, last night?" she asked.

"I think I can safely say it was the best and the worst date I've ever been on in my life," I said.

She looked at me perplexed.

"Don't ask. But you might see if there's anything about it on the news."

"Uh oh."

"How about eggs? You said you never get fresh eggs."

"Sounds good. Can I cook them?"

"Sure, I don't know when Rusty will be up. We got in late last night."

"Where's Isabel and Lawanda?"

"Probably eating breakfast at some café before catching a tour of the stars' homes. Grandma and Lawanda didn't get their fix in at the premier, I guess."

"That's too bad. I like your grandma."

"Me too, though I didn't know it until she showed up on my doorstep," I said thoughtfully. "She's quite a character. I didn't know her very well from when I was a kid. I was off in the hills tracking a lot. I didn't know what I was missing."

"You was missing plenty."

"So I see."

Bertie cooked fried eggs, hash browns and toast and we ate quietly while Rusty slept on. While Rusty got ready for work, Bertie packed. I paid her well for her time at my house and she went back to town freshly bathed and with clean clothes. Rusty took Bertie back to town when he went to work.

Katie and I spent a quiet day at home until Grandma and Lawanda arrived home later in the evening.

"Well," said Grandma. "I guess I should be heading for home again. I've seen about as much of southern California as I can in one trip. I bet Grandpap is tired of baked beans. I was going to stay a little longer but I'm not sure it's safe on the roads here. On the way back there was talk of a shooting on the interstate! Imagine that! People taking pot shots at other drivers on the road. I'm going home where the worst we have to worry about is hitting an elk."

Yeah, I thought, imagine that.

That evening I took Grandma to town and we went back to Zeke's for a Zeke's Zoner and Zinger, since she wouldn't see a pizza pie for a long time.

In the morning she tearfully said goodbye, giving hugs all around, playing with Katie, knowing she might never see her again. Seeing in her a little spark of the trouble gene, hopefully not too much. She knew her adventurous spirit lived on and she went back to Montana content in that.

I waved goodbye with a lump in my throat. Though I was dismayed having her land on my doorstep, I was sad to see her go.

The next evening Rusty called.

"Don't fix dinner," he said.

"Okay, why?"

"We have a date."

"Oh, we do?"

"Yeah. Do you still have that dress?"

"Of course."

"Wear the dress."

"Why?"

"Because, I'm determined to finish that ride."

He showed up at the door with Bertie and a limo waiting at curbside. Oh, man! What a night I was in for! I could feel the tingling already and we hadn't even had dinner.